I0660855

Exploring Indigenous Novels in Grades 5–10

Exploring Indigenous Novels in Grades 5–10

Literature Studies Focusing on Indigenized Worlds

Don K. Philpot

ROWMAN & LITTLEFIELD
Lanham • Boulder • New York • London

Published by Rowman & Littlefield
An imprint of The Rowman & Littlefield Publishing Group, Inc.
4501 Forbes Boulevard, Suite 200, Lanham, Maryland 20706
www.rowman.com

86-90 Paul Street, London EC2A 4NE

Copyright © 2024 by Don K. Philpot

All rights reserved. No part of this book may be reproduced in any form or by any electronic or mechanical means, including information storage and retrieval systems, without written permission from the publisher, except by a reviewer who may quote passages in a review.

British Library Cataloguing in Publication Information Available

Library of Congress Cataloging-in-Publication Data

Names: Philpot, Don K., author.
  Title: Exploring indigenous novels in grades 5-10 : literature studies
    focusing on indigenized worlds / Don K. Philpot.
  Description: Lanham, Maryland : The Rowman & Littlefield Publishing Group,
    Inc., 2024. | Includes bibliographical references and index. | Summary:
    "Exploring Indigenous Novels in Grades 5-10: Literature Studies Focusing
    on Indigenized Worlds offers teachers and students in grades 5-10 a
    unique framework and specialized sets of resources for collaborative
    classroom explorations of indigenized worlds created by the Indigenous
    writers"-- Provided by publisher.
  Identifiers: LCCN 2024029583 (print) | LCCN 2024029584 (ebook) | ISBN
    9781475860511 (cloth) | ISBN 9781475860528 (paperback) | ISBN
    9781475860535 (epub)
  Subjects: LCSH: Canadian fiction--Indian authors--Study and teaching
    (Middle school) | Canadian fiction--Indian authors--Study and teaching
    (Secondary) | Children's stories, Canadian--Study and teaching. | Young
    adult fiction, Canadian--Study and teaching. | American fiction--Indian
    authors--Study and teaching (Middle school) | American fiction--Indian
    authors--Study and teaching (Secondary) | Children's stories,
    American--Study and teaching. | Young adult fiction, American--Study and
    teaching. | Indigenous peoples in literature--Study and teaching (Middle
    school) | Indigenous peoples in literature--Study and teaching
    (Secondary)
  Classification: LCC PR9182.2 .P48 2024 (print) | LCC PR9182.2 (ebook) |
    DDC 813.009/897--dc23/eng/20240729
  LC record available at https://lccn.loc.gov/2024029583
  LC ebook record available at https://lccn.loc.gov/2024029584

Dedicated to my Cree language and Indigenous studies mentors Stella Neff and Emma LaRocque, who shaped and reshaped my understandings about the world in profound ways and inspired me to write.

To Stella Neff, who taught me to understand spoken Cree; to read and write the Cree language in different forms; to appreciate Cree stories and humor; and to interact with Cree and other Indigenous peoples within their worlds and in ways they value.

To Emma LaRocque who introduced me to the field of Indigenous Studies and scholarship; generously shared her personal and scholarly insights with me about Indigenous peoples and their experiences past and present; and helped me to understand and articulate more fully my experiences with Indigenous peoples.

Contents

Prefatory Note About In-Text Citations and References   ix

PART I: EXPLORING INDIGENIZED WORLDS   1

Chapter 1: Indigenized Worlds   3

Chapter 2: Classroom Explorations of Indigenized Worlds   19

PART II: INDIGENIZED WORLDS   49

Chapter 3: Historical Worlds (1847–1852)   51

Chapter 4: Historical Worlds (1759–1864)   69

Chapter 5: Contemporary Worlds (1990–2005)   97

Chapter 6: Contemporary Worlds (1978–2000)   119

Chapter 7: Fantasy Worlds (Past, Present, Future)   161

Index   187

About the Author   195

Prefatory Note About In-Text Citations and References

IN-TEXT CITATIONS

In this book, the middle and high school novels cited in chapters 3–7 are identified conveniently and for enhanced readability using titular acronyms. Acronyms and their corresponding book titles are shown below. Likewise for convenience and enhanced readability, page references in these same chapters are simply identified in parentheses.

TBH—*The Birchbark House*, Louise Erdrich (1999).
TCOTS—*The Curse of the Shaman*, Michael Kusugak (2006).
DBDP—*Danny Blackgoat, Dangerous Passage*, Tim Tingle (2017).
DBNP—*Danny Blackgoat, Navajo Prisoner*, Tim Tingle (2013).
DPRRTF—*Danny Blackgoat, Rugged Road to Freedom*, Tim Tingle (2014).
TGOS—*The Game of Silence*, Louise Erdrich (2005).
LLM—*Lana's Lakota Moons*, Virginia Driving Hawk Sneve (2007).
LV—*Little Voice*, Ruby Slipperjack (2001).
TMT—*The Marrow Thieves*, Cherie Dimaline (2017).
TPY—*The Porcupine Year*, Louise Erdrich (2008).
WG—*Will's Garden*, Lee Maracle (2002).
WIB—*Where I Belong*, Tara White (2014).
TWP—*The Winter People*, Joseph Bruchac (2002).

REFERENCES

Bibliographic details for all novels listed above are included in chapters 3–7. Bibliographic details for recommended resources used for individual question sets in chapters 3–7 are included within the question set entry. Bibliographic details for supplementary sources of information used in chapters 1–3 appear at the end of those chapters.

PART I

Exploring Indigenized Worlds

Chapter 1

Indigenized Worlds

TWO VIGNETTES

A Sixth-Grade Literature Study Focusing on the Fictional World and Personal Experiences of Twelve-Year-Old Omakayas in the Indigenous Novel *The Porcupine Year* (Erdrich 2008)

Mr. Gilman and his sixth-grade students have reached the halfway point in their whole-class exploration of the Indigenous novel *The Porcupine Year* by the award-winning Ojibwe author Louise Erdrich. The third novel in the *Birchbark House* series, *The Porcupine Year* focuses on the personal experiences of a twelve-year-old girl named Omakayas in the year 1852 as she and her family travel north by canoe to Lake of the Woods in northern Minnesota seeking a new place to live.

The fictional world of *The Porcupine Year* is largely inhabited by Indigenous people like Omakayas, her family members, and others who are identified as Ojibwe, speak the Ojibwe language, and live in traditional Ojibwe ways. The world in this novel can be understood as indigenized because of the many features that reflect Indigenous perspectives and experiences and focus on Indigenous lands, practices, and concerns. Mr. Gilman and his students explored several indigenizing fictional world features in the first half of their study including Omakayas's naming feast and an engaging story about the legendary Ojibwe figure Bear Girl.

During their four-week study of the Indigenous novel *The Porcupine Year*, students continue to engage in purposeful reading and writing; seek to learn about Ojibwe people and their cultural practices; articulate new understandings and insights about Ojibwe people; develop their curiosity about Indigenous peoples in the United States and Canada; demonstrate openness, flexibility, and humility while learning about people that are different from themselves; engage in difficult conversations about diverse others; and more.

"The second half of our study," says Mr. Gilman, "will focus for now on Ojibwe spirit bundles and the special spirit bundle Omakayas receives from her grandmother for Old Tallow in chapter 12. "What is a spirit bundle? You all have your resource booklet handy. Consult it to answer my question. Consult it quickly. Share your understandings with your assigned partner. I'll give you two minutes."

Two minutes pass. Mr. Gilman calls on Jackie to start them off. "Jackie, you first. Tell us just one thing you know about a spirit bundle?"

"It's a collection of sacred objects," says Jackie.

"Which objects?" asks Mr. Gilman. "Breanna, name one."

"A feather," says Breanna.

"What else? Francisco?"

"Something carved," says Francisco.

Piece by piece students flesh out their understandings about Ojibwe spirit bundles. Mr. Gilman clarifies their understandings about the concept of sacred then shares his own understandings about Ojibwe spirit bundles with his students summatively on a slide.

"You all know what Old Tallow's spirit bundle consists of," resumes Mr. Gilman. "We will talk about those objects another day and why those specific objects were collected to honor Old Tallow, but first I want us to really appreciate the importance of Old Tallow for Omakayas."

Mr. Gilman distributes two chapters from earlier books in the *Birchbark House* series, chapter 2 from *The Birchbark House* and chapter 10 from *The Game of Silence*. "The titles of both chapters include the name *Old Tallow* so we know they will provide key details about her and her importance for Omakayas. Keep your chapters face down for the time being. I want to summarize them for you," says Mr. Gilman.

"'Chapter 2, Old Tallow,' from *The Birchbark House*," explains Mr. Gilman, "offers details about Old Tallow's isolation, her strangeness to others. She was tall, powerful, lean, and surrounded herself with dogs. She was very skilled at using a gun and loved to hunt. She wore a white man's hat with a wide brim, wore a feather in the brim, and more often than not could be seen smoking a pipe. She had little respect for others but treated Omakayas very kindly."

Mr. Gilman now turns to chapter 10, "Old Tallow's Coat," from *The Game of Silence*. "Three years have passed," says Mr. Gilman. "It is now 1850, wintertime, and bitterly cold, dangerously cold. Omakayas and her grandmother have spent a good part of the day setting rabbit snares in the bush. They are home now, but Old Tallow hasn't returned from hunting yet. Night comes but still Old Tallow hasn't returned. Then she arrives but not on her own. Omakayas's father has transported her home on a crude sled. She looks half-dead then suddenly springs to life and reports her day's adventure."

Important details about Old Tallow are also offered selectively in *The Porcupine Year* in chapters 5 (55), 7 (78), and 8 (81–85). Mr. Gilman will assign his students to heterogenous reading groups for the purpose of reading and summarizing the selected pages in these chapters. "In your group, you will seek to better understand Old Tallow and why she is so special and important for Omakayas," says Mr. Gilman.

"And on Thursday and Friday this week," rejoins Mr. Gilman, "you will apply your knowledge about Old Tallow from all these sources including chapters 12 and 16 from *The Porcupine Year* to complete written responses in your dialog journal for these evocative questions about Old Tallow's spirit bundle." He projects the questions on the front screen.

> **Factual questions**. (a) What prompts Nokomis to make a spirit bundle for Omakayas in chapter 12 honoring Old Tallow? (121). (b) What does Old Tallow's spirit bundle consist of? (122). (c) What thoughts cross Omakayas's mind about Old Tallow while holding her spirit bundle under a starry nighttime sky in chapter 16? (179). (d) What location does Omakayas choose as the sacred resting place for Old Tallow's spirit bundle and spirit? (180). (e) What special name will she give that location? (180).

> Inferencing questions. (a) What is doubly significant for Omakayas about the presence of bear fur in the spirit bundle made for her by her grandmother? (cf. 37). (b) What spiritual beliefs are revealed by Nokomis's purposeful arrangement of hair in the spirit bundle (i.e., wrapping Old Tallow's hair in bear's fur)? (122).

> Speculative questions. (a) Why might the repeated action of offering food and drink to a spirit bundle, which Omakayas does for a year, help to reduce the sadness one feels about losing a loved one? (122). (b) How might Old Tallow's spirit protect Omakayas? (129).

A Ninth-Grade Literature Study Focusing on the Fictional World and Personal Experiences of Sixteen-Year-Old Will in the Indigenous Novel *Will's Garden* (Maracle 2002)

Mrs. Amy Norris was born and raised in Tacoma, Washington, and has taught ninth-grade English in the nearby city of North Bend for fourteen years. Amy developed an interest in Indigenous beadwork when a friend of her mother, a young Cree woman from Edmonton, taught Amy to bead during a visit one summer. Two years ago Amy enrolled in a series of online beading workshops offered by a master beader from northern Manitoba and is now an accomplished beader herself.

Imagine Amy's excitement when a new friend of hers from the beading workshop, a middle school teacher from Chilliwack, British Columbia, introduces her to the Indigenous novel *Will's Garden* by Canadian writer Lee Maracle. Maracle, a member of the Sto: loh Nation, published books mainly for adults—novels, short stories, poems, works of nonfiction—and one novel for adolescents, *Will's Garden*, that focuses on the experiences of a sixteen-year-old Sto: loh boy, Will, as he prepares for and participates in an important community event that honors his coming of age as a Sto: loh man.

Will started beading as a boy alongside his cousin Sarah and now at age sixteen uses his skills as a beader to produce beautiful beaded capes for his upcoming Becoming Man ceremony at the community longhouse. Will's interest in beading, his beading activities in the novel, his identification as Sto: loh, his Becoming Man ceremony, his dreamtime experiences, and his descriptions of many traditional Sto: loh practices all contribute to the indigenization of the fictional world presented in the novel.

Amy learned about the indigenization of fictional worlds in Indigenous novels like *Will's Garden* as a member of a Facebook group that focused on teaching Indigenous novels in middle and secondary grades. She and several members of her group designed a literature study for *Will's Garden* that focused extensively on Will's Becoming Man ceremony and his ceremonial preparations. Amy—Mrs. Norris—launched a study of the novel with her ninth-grade students two weeks ago.

It is now Monday, the third week of the study, and she and her students will focus their attention on Will's beading activities in the first half of the novel as he prepares for his Becoming Man ceremony.

"Throughout the week," says Mrs. Norris, pointing to her projected slide, "you will communicate your new understandings to me and your classmates about four important aspects of traditional Indigenous beadwork as described in the novel and other resources: one, items that are typically decorated with beadwork; two, traditional beading techniques and designs; three, Will's beading relationship with his cousin Sarah; and four, Will's adornment of ceremonial capes with traditional floral designs."

Mrs. Norris projects a YouTube page with a video titled "Beading Slipper Tops" and distributes a viewing guide. "We'll start things off by viewing this video together and discussing key points about traditional Indigenous beading and beadwork," says Mrs. Norris. "We'll complete parts of the viewing guide together and parts of it independently. View the video attentively. Aim to have a full viewing experience."

Mrs. Norris reviews the organization and content of the viewing guide with her students then instructs them to list the beading supplies and tools used by the beader in the video and to record their observations about the beader's workspace, her method of preparing a vamp, and her beading technique. "I will pause the video strategically in places, but only briefly, and will prompt you to write," says Mrs. Norris. "I've included a space at the bottom of the guide for other observations you might record. Add to your notes during our after-viewing discussion, then I'll collect your completed guides."

"That will take us roughly to the halfway point in today's class. For the remaining time, after we have viewed and discussed the video," adds Mrs. Norris, now projecting a Google homepage and search box, "you will answer these two sets of questions in your literature study notebooks. These questions are relevant for chapters 2 and 5. Each of you will contribute one colorful image from your Google searches to our first gallery display in the hallway prompted by our study of *Will's Garden*. Please let me know if you can help me with the display after school on Friday."

Internet research questions I. (a) What can be learned from images of beaded barrettes, bags, and vamps (i.e., moccasin tops) obtained from individual Google searches using the exact phrases "First Nations beaded barrettes," "First Nations beaded bags," and "First Nations beaded vamps"? (b) What recurring design elements are observable in these beaded items?

Internet research questions II. (a) What can be learned about the design of beaded roses and beaded rose barrettes from images obtained in a Google search using the exact phrase "Native American beaded rose"? (b) What is distinctively different about the appearance of wild and domestic roses?

On Wednesday Mrs. Norris and her students turn their attention to the last two aspects of traditional Indigenous beadwork mentioned on Monday: Will's beading relationship with his cousin Sarah and Will's adornment of ceremonial capes with traditional floral designs. "You will provide written responses to these new sets of questions in your assigned group," says Mrs. Norris. "As noted on the handout, the first set is relevant to chapter 2 and the second to chapter 6. I'll give you a minute to review the questions with your group members and seek clarification from me."

Assorted Questions Focusing on Will and Sarah's Special Beading Relationship. (a) At what age did Sarah and Will start beading together? (factual, 18). (b) What circumstances landed Will in the living room that day, sitting with his mother and aunt, cleaning and sorting beads? (summative, 18–20). (c) What amazed Will that day watching Sarah beading? (factual, inferencing, 20). (d) What special beading project was Sarah working on that day? (factual, 20). (e) How did Will and Sarah end up working together that day beading? (factual,

20). (f) What motivated Will to do beadwork with Sarah from that point on? (inferencing, speculative, 20–21).

Factual Questions Focusing on Will's Beaded Capes (56–60). (a) On what part of his newly completed cape has Will stitched roses? (b) How many roses has he stitched on this new cape? (c) What is striking about the appearance of these roses (i.e., their size, color)? (d) How has Will achieved the overall effect of a rose garden like his mother's rose garden outside the house using beaded vines, stems, thorns, and buds? (d) What beaded background ornamentation appears on the cape? (e) How do Sarah and Will's brothers respond to this cape? (f) What complementary beading projects do Will and Sarah agree to undertake next to address the mismatch between the beaded design of Will's newly completed cape and Sarah's newly completed barrette?

CHAPTER OVERVIEW AND TARGET QUESTIONS

This chapter serves as a basic introduction to exploratory studies of Indigenous novels and indigenized worlds in grades 5–10. It provides basic information about my companion book *Indigenous Novels, Indigenized Worlds* and its connection to this book. It also provides details about the organization of content in this book, articulates the many benefits of exploring indigenized worlds with young people, and identifies intended readers. For this chapter, readers will seek to answer the following target questions.

How does the current book complement the companion book *Indigenous Novels, Indigenized Worlds*?
How is content organized in this book?
What key terms are defined in this chapter and why are these terms significant?
What general and core academic benefits are derived from exploratory studies of indigenizing features in grades 5–10?
Who are the intended readers for this book?
What distinctive offerings make this book a valuable resource for readers?

TWO BOOKS ABOUT INDIGENOUS NOVELS AND INDIGENIZED WORLDS

Two Books, a Complementary Focus

This book is the second of two that focus on Indigenous novels and indigenized worlds. The first book, *Indigenous Novels, Indigenized Worlds*, focused exclusively on distinctive features found in Indigenous novels for readers age 10–16 that yield indigenized worlds.

This second book, as illustrated by the opening vignettes, focuses on classroom applications of the indigenizing features reported in the first book. The key question addressed in this second book is What new and transformative understandings about Indigenous peoples in the United States and Canada can young people in grades 5–10 gain from classroom explorations of Indigenous novels and indigenized worlds?

Groups and Categories of Indigenizing Features

As reported in the first book, a close analysis of twenty-four Indigenous novels published in Canada or the United States and written for readers age 10–16 revealed more than 150 indigenizing features. These features were organized into primary (Groups A–D) and secondary groups (Categories 1–12) using a methodology discussed in the second chapter of that book.

The grouping and categorization of indigenizing features presented in the first book are reproduced summarily below. Group A includes 12 features organized in 3 Categories, and Groups B–D include 82, 28, and 37 features organized into 2, 4, and 3 categories respectively. The number of features in each category ranges from 3 (Category 2, "Tribal History") to 40 (Category 7, "Cultural Traditions"). An example for each indigenizing feature is provided in the first book.

Group A (1–3). "Time, Tribal History, Ancestry" (twelve features).
Sample features: seasonal habitation cycles, notable people, ancestral beings.

Group B (4–7). "Cultural Beliefs, Values, Events, Traditions" (eighty-two features).
Sample features: visions, expressing gratitude, naming feasts, traditional houses.

Group C (8–9). "Language Use, Stories, Storytelling, Family Life, Kinship" (twenty-eight features).
Sample features: stories about culture heroes, kinship with local animals.

Group D (10–12). "Destruction and Restoration" (thirty-seven features).
Sample features: forced relocation from homeland, sovereignty, recovery.

BOOK ORGANIZATION AND TERMINOLOGY

Book Organization and Chapter Overviews

The present book, *Exploring Indigenous Novels in Grades 5–10: Literature Studies Focusing on Indigenized Worlds*, is divided into two sections. Part I includes the first two chapters, which provide a foundation for the question sets and other resources included in part II, chapters 3–7, that teachers and students can use in their collaborative explorations of Indigenous novels.

Part I: Exploring Indigenized Worlds

Chapter 1 began with two snapshot views of classroom explorations of Indigenous novels in grades 6 and 9. The chapter now concludes with a brief exposition of the value of collaborative classroom explorations of indigenized worlds with students in grades 5–10; definitions of key terms; and the identification of intended readers for and offerings of this book.

Chapter 2 focuses briefly on common literature study frameworks used in middle and secondary grades then turns its attention to the framework adopted in this book for classroom explorations of Indigenous novels. I note at the start of this chapter that common literature study frameworks, including traditional novel studies, literature circles, thematic units, literature study units, and Socratic circles, are not designed for and cannot easily accommodate an explicit and sustained focus on one Indigenous nation, specific indigenizing features, and the personal fictional world experiences of one Indigenous young person.

The bulk of chapter 2 centers on the literature study framework offered in this book, an exploratory framework for middle and secondary grades that focuses explicitly and intentionally on Indigenous peoples and their individual experiences. A complete list of indigenizing features is provided. Framework resources and tools, the framework's theoretical underpinnings, and biographical details about each Indigenous author whose novel is featured in this book are discussed.

Part II: Indigenized Worlds

The five chapters in part II offer resources for classroom explorations of indigenized worlds in eleven Indigenous novels: five historical novels, four contemporary realistic novels, and two fantasy novels. These eleven novels were among the twenty-four used to develop the comprehensive inventory of indigenizing features reproduced in the chapter.

Chapters 3–7 are similarly structured for easy use. Each chapter begins with an overview, target questions, and basic information about the featured novels in the chapter. This basic information includes bibliographic details about the featured novels, published summaries, and the identification of targeted Indigenous groups and individuals and primary physical settings. Tools for exploring a targeted set of indigenizing features for each novel follow, tools that include a complete inventory of indigenizing features found in the novel and sets of questions focusing on each targeted indigenizing feature.

Chapters 3 and 4 focus on historical Indigenous worlds in *The Porcupine Year* (Erdrich 2008), *The Winter People* (Bruchac 2002), and all three novels in the Danny Blackgoat Series (Tingle 2013, 2014, 2017). Chapter 3 provides bibliographic information about the first two novels in the *Birchbark House* series but focuses chiefly on the third novel in the series *The Porcupine Year*, whose events take place in 1852. Question sets in this chapter explore the indigenizing features of seasonal activity cycles; medicine bags; spirit bundles; purification practices; naming feasts; traditional medicines; stories about legendary individuals; forced relocation from a homeland; and smallpox.

Events in the four historical novels featured in chapter 4 take place in different historical periods and locations. Events in *The Winter People* (Bruchac 2002) take place in 1759 in the northeastern United States; and events in the Danny Blackgoat novels (Tingle 2013, 2014, 2017) take place in 1863–1864 in the southwestern United States. Question sets in chapter 4 explore the indigenizing features, for Bruchac's novel, of stories about culture heroes, notable events, water travel, tracking, forced location from homeland, recovery, and restoration; and for Tingle's novels of prayers, purification, herding, forced removal from a homeland, material deprivation, disdain, and brutality.

Chapters 5 and 6 focus on contemporary Indigenous worlds in *Lana's Lakota Moons* (Sneve 2007), *Where I Belong* (White 2014), *Will's Garden* (Maracle 2001), and *Little Voice* (Slipperjack 2001). Events in these four novels take place in time periods ranging from 1978 to the early 2000s and in different regions of Canada and the United States.

Question sets in chapter 5 explore the indigenizing features for Sneve's novel of notable events, the hoop dance, the Lakota naming ceremony, and closeness to cousins; and for White's novel the indigenizing features of dreams, spirit guides, drumming, diabetes, defense of homes and homeland, and restoration. Question sets in chapter 6 explore the indigenizing features for Maracle's novel of dreamtime, the Sto: loh Becoming Man ceremony, and traditional beadwork; and for Slipperjack's novel of ancestral lands and identity, water travel, traditional foods, and wood carving.

Chapter 7 focuses on fantasy (mythical and dystopian) worlds inhabited by Indigenous peoples in *The Curse of the Shaman (*Kusugak 2006) and *The Marrow Thieves* (Dimaline 2017). Events in these novels take place in the Canadian northlands, one on the northwest shore of Hudson Bay near Rankin Inlet and the other in northern Ontario.

Question sets in chapter 7 explore the indigenizing features for Kusugak's novel of ancestral lands, snow travel, boat building and repair, supernatural powers, large game hunting, and widely circulated stories of contemporary renown; and for Dimaline's novel of material appropriation, forced separation of children from parents, subjugation, and personal stories.

Chapters 3–7 include additional resources that will help middle and secondary grade students read the novel in logical parts and better understand the significance of specific indigenizing features within the novel. All but the Danny Blackgoat novels have been subdivided into parts derived from the logical grouping of chapters. For example, the novel *Little Voice* (Slipperjack 2001) has been subdivided into four parts. As shown in textbox 1.1, part I includes four chapters; part II, three chapters; part III, five chapters; and part IV, one chapter.

Textbox 1.1.
Book Sectioning for Little Voice (Slipperjack 2001)

Part I: First Summers with Grandma, 1978–1979 (1–4)
Part II: First Full Summer with Grandma, 1980 (5–7)
Part III: Longest Visit with Grandma, 1981 (8–12)
Part IV: A Seagull Summer, 1982 (13)

An alternative organizational scheme for the Danny Blackgoat novels appears in chapter 4. This organizational scheme groups chapters sequentially in terms of Danny's experiences across the three novels.

Chapters 3–7 offer two other resources that will help to enhance students' explorations of indigenized worlds. First, indigenizing features requiring clarification (e.g., disdain, brutality, subjugation, prescience, and dreamtime) are explicitly defined; and second, lists of supplementary resources for individual indigenizing features appear in each chapter. These resources include previewed and recommended information books, guides, web pages, and YouTube videos.

Key Terms

Four key terms are used throughout this book: *Indigenous peoples* or *people*, *Indigenous person*, *Indigenous novel*, and *indigenized world*. The term *Indigenous peoples* is used as a collective name for all first peoples of the

United States and Canada and their descendants (see Government of Canada), and the terms *Indigenous people* and *Indigenous person* are used respectively to identify a specific Indigenous group (e.g., Anishinaabe; Sto: loh; Choctaw; Navajo) or an individual member of an Indigenous group.

An Indigenous novel is a fictional narrative published in the form of a novel that is written by an Indigenous person and focuses on one or more fictional individuals who belong to an Indigenous group. A (fictional) world is indigenized when the personal experiences of its prominent inhabitants substantively align with the experiences of Indigenous peoples.

THE VALUE OF STUDYING INDIGENIZED WORLDS

Through the fictional worlds they indigenize for adolescent readers, Indigenous authors like Louise Erdrich, Ruby Slipperjack, Lee Maracle, and Joseph Bruchac provide unique access to the lived experiences of Indigenous peoples past, present, and future and the worlds they inhabit. Through classroom explorations of an indigenized world, say, in *Danny Blackgoat, Navaho Prisoner* (Tingle 2013), *Little Voice* (Slipperjack 2001), *Lana's Lakota Moons* (Sneve 2007), or *The Curse of the Shaman* (Kusugak 2006), adolescent readers will be well positioned to develop a range of general and core academic competencies.

A sixth-grade study of the novel *The Porcupine Year* (Erdrich 2008) and the indigenizing features of forced relocation from homeland, spirit bundles, and stories about legendary individuals; or a ninth-grade study of the novel *Will's Garden* (Maracle 2001) and the indigenizing features of the Sto: loh Becoming Man ceremony, traditional beadwork, and dreamtime enables middle and high school students to develop cultural curiosity and cultural competence. By studying the indigenized worlds in these novels, students will learn about new cultures; value diverse peoples and cultures; identify their personal biases about diverse people and cultures; and challenge their personal beliefs, attitudes, assumptions, and behaviors about diverse others.

Moreover, studies of indigenized worlds position students in middle and secondary grades to develop curricular competencies in Indigenous studies, social studies, and English language arts. Such studies help students think critically and creatively about issues of concern to Indigenous peoples, develop respect for the histories and contemporary lifestyles of Indigenous peoples, understand how physical and human characteristics of places are connected to human identities and cultures, and explain how cultures influence people's thoughts and actions within specific environments.

Studies of indigenized worlds may be situated in English, social studies, or Indigenous studies classrooms. But regardless of their physical or curricular situation, these studies will engage students actively in reading and writing. As shown in textbox 1.2, studies of indigenized worlds engage students in purposeful reading, position them in fictional worlds for sustained periods of

Textbox 1.2.
The Value of Studying Indigenized Worlds

General Academic Value: Cultural Curiosity and Cultural Competence

Literature studies focusing on indigenized worlds in grades 5–10 help students to develop general academic skills of cultural curiosity and competence. In collaborative explorations of individual indigenizing features in Indigenous novels with teachers and classmates, students in grades 5–10

Cultural Curiosity
seek to learn about diverse people and cultures
ask complex questions about diverse people and cultures

Cultural Competence
value diverse people and cultures
articulate their understandings about diverse people and cultures
demonstrate openness, flexibility, and humility when learning about
    diverse people and cultures
develop a set of strategies for learning about diverse people and
    cultures
identify their personal biases about diverse people and cultures
engage in difficult conversations to better understand their attitudes
    towards diverse others
challenge their personal beliefs, attitudes, assumptions, and behav-
    iors regarding diverse others

Core Academic Value: Indigenous Studies and Social Studies

Literature studies focusing on indigenized worlds in grades 5–10 help students to develop core academic skills in Indigenous studies and social studies. In collaborative explorations of individual indigenizing features in Indigenous novels with teachers and classmates, students in grades 5–10

Indigenous Education
seek to learn about Indigenous peoples and cultures
develop informed understandings about matters relating to Indigenous
  peoples
think critically and creatively about issues of concern to Indigenous
  peoples
develop an understanding and respect for the histories and contemporary lifestyles of Indigenous peoples
appreciate the role of Indigenous peoples in the development of
  Canada and the United States
understand the social, economic, and political systems of Indigenous
  peoples in traditional and contemporary contexts
make personal connections to enhance their understanding of and
  respect for Indigenous peoples, cultures, languages, histories,
  rights, and perspectives
apply new understandings about Indigenous peoples and key concepts in Indigenous studies to real-world inquiries about diversity,
  nation-to-nation relationship building, the environment, social
  justice, and cultural identity

Social Studies
understand (a) how the distinctive features of cultures and communities and the similarities and differences between people and places
  are shaped by specific relationships between people and their
  environments, and (b) how the physical and human characteristics
  of places are connected to human identities and cultures
understand (a) how human settlements and movements relate to the
  locations and use of various natural resources, and (b) how culture
  influences the way people think and act within their environment

Core Academic Value: English Language Arts

Literature studies focusing on indigenized worlds in grades 5–10 help
students to develop core academic skills in English language arts.
In collaborative explorations of individual indigenizing features in
Indigenous novels with teachers and classmates, students in grades 5–10

Reading
engage in purposeful reading
read historical, contemporary realistic, and fantasy novels produced
  by Indigenous writers

maintain their focus on and position themselves within the fictional world presented by the novel

attend closely to the experiences of prominent fictional-world individuals

aim to develop comprehensive understandings about prominent fictional world individuals, their personal experiences, and their cultures

develop entry-level knowledge about unfamiliar topics through listening, reading, and viewing

engage in the during-reading actions of reading for understanding, inferencing, formulating, and building coherence

engage in the after-reading actions of summarizing, reconfiguring, and clarifying

engage in the actions of close reading

Writing
seek to enhance their understandings about Indigenous novels through writing

seek insights about fictional worlds through writing

produce informative written responses to questions focusing on specific fictional world features and narrative content

produce cohesive and cogent written responses of varying lengths to assigned questions

provide textual evidence to support a written response

Note: For detailed descriptions and examples of the during- and after-reading actions of reading for understanding, inferencing, formulating, building coherence, summarizing, reconfiguring, and clarifying, readers may consult the first two books in the Reading Actively Series, chapters 4 and 5 (Philpot 2019, 2020).

time, and help them produce cohesive and cogent written responses of varying lengths to thoughtful sets of carefully crafted questions.

INTENDED READERS AND OFFERINGS

This book is primarily intended for teachers in grades 5–10, in-service teachers, pre-service teachers, and teacher educators with specializations in English language arts, social studies, history, or Indigenous studies.

The book has many distinctive offerings that will make it a valuable resource for a broad group of readers, offerings that include

- a sustained focus on novels for middle and high school students written by contemporary Indigenous writers
- a highly readable and diverse set of novels that represent all major novel genres (historical, realistic, fantasy)
- highly engaging novels that feature a broad range of North American Indigenous characters and cultures in different geographic and temporal settings
- highly relevant content for students in grades 5–10
- a highly useable framework for exploring Indigenous novels
- a transdisciplinary approach to reading in middle and secondary grades
- an approach to school reading that emphasizes personal growth and transformative understandings about Indigenous peoples
- information about Indigenous people that many Indigenous and non-Indigenous middle and secondary grade students are not likely to encounter elsewhere or locate easily on their own
- a broad range of resources that will help to enhance students' engagement with one or more of the featured novels
- a teacher- and student-friendly format

REFERENCE LIST

Government of Canada. "Indigenous Peoples and Communities." www.rcaanc-cirnac.gc.ca/eng/1100100013785/1529102490303.

National Child Welfare Workforce Institute. https://ncwwi.org.

National Council for the Social Studies. "College, Career, 7 Civic Life C3 Framework, for Social Studies State Standards." Silver Spring, MD: National Council for the Social Studies, 2013.

Northern Illinois University. "Baccalaureate Student Learning Outcomes, Intercultural Outcomes." www.niu.edu/general-education/about/learning-outcomes.shtml.

Ontario Ministry of Education. "First Nations, Metis, and Inuit Connections: Scope and Sequence of Expectations." 2016.

Pennsylvania Department of Education. "Culturally-Relevant and Sustaining Education (CR-SE) Program Framework Guidelines." 2022.

Philpot, Don K. *Indigenous Novels, Indigenized Worlds: Exploring the Indigenization of Fictional Worlds*. Lanham, MD: Rowman & Littlefield, 2023.

Philpot, Don K. *Reading Actively in Middle Grade Science: Teachers and Students in Action*. Lanham, MD: Rowman & Littlefield, 2020.

U.S. Department of Health and Human Services. "Cultural Competency." www.childwelfare.gov/pubs/acloserlook/culturalcompetency/culturalcompetency2/.

Chapter 2

Classroom Explorations of Indigenized Worlds

CHAPTER OVERVIEW AND TARGET QUESTIONS

This chapter provides details about a literature study framework developed by the author and informed by Indigenous perspectives that enables students in grades 5–10 to explore Indigenous novels and indigenized worlds collaboratively with their teacher and classmates. The details provided in this chapter focus on the framework's theoretical underpinnings, specific tools and resources, and information about each author whose novel is featured in this book.

The chapter also offers a brief exposition on common literature study frameworks used in middle and secondary grades that limit rather than invite sustained exploration of indigenized worlds.

For this chapter, readers will seek to answer the following target questions.

What common literature study frameworks do not readily support sustained explorations of indigenized worlds in grades 5–10?
Which individual indigenizing features have been classified as Groups A–D and Categories 1–12 features?
How is the literature study framework offered in this book informed by various disciplinary perspectives?
What criteria were used to select Indigenous novels for this book?
What types of questions are included in the framework question sets?
What range of resources are provided for the featured novels?
What biographical details are provided for each Indigenous author whose novel is featured in this book?

COMMON LITERATURE STUDY FRAMEWORKS
AND THEIR LIMITATIONS

Six frameworks are commonly used for literature study in middle and secondary grade English (language arts) classrooms in Canada and the United States. These frameworks are traditional novel study, the reading workshop, literature circles, thematic units, commercial literature study units, and Socratic circles. Each framework is described below from the author's perspective in terms of target grades, duration, purpose, learning outcomes, notable elements, and preferred questions.

Use of these frameworks spans a time period of roughly seventy years from 1950 to the present. The traditional novel-study framework was used in the early 1950s and perhaps earlier for middle grade novels like *The Adventures of Tom Sawyer* (Twain 1876) and *Johnny Tremain* (Forbes 1943). A comprehensive description of the reading workshop framework appeared in a book by Atwell (1987). The literature circle framework was described by different names and in varying degrees of detail in books by Harste, Short, and Burke (1988); Peterson and Eeds (1990); and Daniels (1994).

The first published resources for thematic units appeared in 1989–1990; were aligned with whole language principles; were intended for early childhood teachers; and were focused on the topics of animals (bears, skunks), trees (oak trees, other trees), and oceans. The fullest description of thematic, literature-based units for grades 5–8 appears in a book by Rothlein and Meinbach (1991).

Commercial literature study guides for middle grades were made popular by the Scholastic Corporation in the mid-1990s. Among the first literature guides published by Scholastic were those focused on award-winning novels like *Julie of the Wolves* (George 1972) and *Bridge to Terabithia* (Paterson 1977), both Newbery Medal winners. The Socratic circles framework and its forerunner the Socratic seminar were described in an article and book by Lambright (1995; Socratic seminars) and Copeland (2005; Socratic circles).

Traditional Novel Study

Target grades. 6–12

Duration. 3–5 weeks

Purpose. A traditional novel study seeks to help students to develop comprehensive understandings about one novel through assigned questions that focus largely on the text.

Summary. In a traditional novel study, students read an assigned novel independently and complete written responses to assigned questions for one or several chapters that they submit weekly for teacher feedback and evaluation.

Learning outcome focus. Literary elements, vocabulary, point of view, author craft, textual evidence.

Notable elements. Teacher-selected canonical novel. Use of home and school time to complete assigned readings and written responses. Summative assessment by a concluding test.

Preferred questions. Questions typically focus on learning outcomes and include factual, inferencing, comparison, and evaluative questions.

Reading Workshop

Target grades. 6–8

Duration. Variable

Purpose. The reading workshop offers students a supportive workshop environment that enables them to read and respond to self-selected novels.

Summary. In a reading workshop, students engage in a recursive cycle for one or more school terms of reading, thinking, writing, and sharing their thoughts about a self-selected novel.

Learning outcome focus. Self-selected or guided by their teacher.

Notable elements. Student-selected novels from various collections. Weekly teacher-student conferences. Peer conferences. Daily mini-lessons focusing on literary concepts, literature study, and reading skills. Response journals and reading logs. Written response exemplars. Reproducibles. Note: Reading workshops are often embedded in a larger workshop framework focusing on reading and writing.

Preferred questions. Questions tend to focus on readers' present interests and may be prompted by specific interactions with their teacher or classmates.

Literature Circles

Target grades. 4–8

Duration. 3–5 weeks

Purpose. A literature circle seeks to help students to develop new understandings about a novel through daily, small, peer-group discussion largely driven by students.

Summary. In a literature circle, students meet daily with group members to share their personal responses to or discuss some aspect of their chosen book.

Learning outcome focus. Personal meanings.

Notable elements. Input into novel selection. Limited number of eligible novels (typically ten or less). Group-assigned reading tasks. Discussion roles. Reading logs. Response journals. Graphic organizers. Culminating group projects. Summative assessment by student participation, written work submitted by individual students, and a culminating project.

Preferred questions. Discussion questions may be provided by the teacher. Questions posed by students are typically WH–type questions that focus on personal meanings.

Thematic Units

Target grades. K–8

Duration. 4–6 weeks

Purpose. A thematic unit seeks to help students to develop broad and specific disciplinary understandings about the theme explored in a range of literary and informational texts.

Summary. In a thematic unit, students complete sets of activities or assignments related to unit texts (including a novel) using the six language arts and other disciplinary concepts and tools. The six language arts are listening, speaking, reading, writing, viewing, and representing.

Learning outcome focus (for language arts). Literary elements, vocabulary, author craft, point of view, personal meanings.

Notable elements. A set of unit texts that include literary and informational texts—articles, information books, short stories, and one or two novels. Identified learning outcomes for content areas other than language arts (e.g., science, social studies, health). Cross-curricular learning. Assigned reading tasks and directives. Limited questions for individual chapters in the target novel. Discussion. Flexibility. Unit study notebooks. Graphic organizers. Informal writing. Culminating group or individual projects with options for creative expression. Summative assessment by student participation, written work submitted by individual students, and other unit assignments.

Preferred questions (for language arts). Questions focus mainly on a common textual theme and other learning outcomes and may include WH–type, factual, inferencing, intertextual, and evaluative questions.

A Commercial Literature Study Unit

Target grades. 4–8

Duration. 3–5 weeks

Purpose. A commercial literature study seeks to help students to develop new understandings about a novel by completing activities provided by a commercial literature guide.

Summary. In a commercial literature study, students complete daily tasks assigned by the teacher mainly from the study guide.

Learning outcome focus. Literary elements, vocabulary, point of view, author craft, textual evidence, personal meanings.

Notable elements. One class novel. Biographical details about the author. Details about the physical or temporal setting of the novel. Assigned reading tasks and questions. Large and small group discussion. Literature study notebooks. Reproducibles. Culminating group or individual projects with options for creative expression. Summative assessment by written work submitted by individual students and a culminating project.

Preferred question. Questions focus almost exclusively on the first four learning outcomes above and include factual, inferencing, interpretive, comparison, and evaluative (critical) questions.

Socratic Circles

Target grades. 6–12

Duration. 2–4 weeks

Purpose. Socratic circles seek to help students to expand their understandings about a novel through peer dialog.

Summary. In Socratic circles, students read a short passage selected from the class novel by their teacher, prepare for a whole-class dialog about the passage, actively participate in a dialog with classmates either as an inner or outer circle member, and complete a written reflection about their dialogic experience.

Learning outcome focus. Literary elements (especially theme and character development), point of view, author craft, textual evidence. **Notable elements.** One teacher-selected class novel. Use of novel excerpts. Text annotation. Scaffolded support for question development. Inner circle member discussion. Feedback from outer circle members. Written reflection by all students. Summative assessment by student participation and written work submitted by individual students.

Preferred questions. Questions focus on selected learning outcomes and students' own questions and include inferencing, interpretive, and evaluative (critical) questions.

Common Framework Limitations

None of these six literature study frameworks can easily engage middle or secondary grade students in a sustained study of indigenizing fictional world features in one Indigenous novel. The reading workshop and literature circles frameworks are not designed to accommodate teacher-selected novels and strongly prefer student-generated questions over questions provided by the teacher. The Socratic circles framework expressly aims to engage students in the process of question development, question refinement, critical thinking, and meaningful dialog with classmates that in time yields new understandings about a given text.

Nor are thematic units designed for a sustained study of indigenizing features let alone a sustained focus on one novel for three or four weeks, the length of time typically required for an exploratory study of an indigenized world. A notable element in the design of a thematic unit is the number and range of texts selected for the unit. In a thematic study, the exploration of individual texts, including longer texts like a novel, is typically limited to three or four days.

Likewise, time constraints limit the flexibility of literature studies structured and driven by the content of commercial literature guides. While these studies limit their focus to one novel, the number of activities typically offered in a guide that engage students in all six language arts—listening, speaking, reading, writing, and viewing as well as multiple forms of representing (i.e., performing, drawing, and musical responses)—render these studies too full to accommodate even a limited study of indigenized worlds.

The traditional novel study framework, on the other hand, could accommodate a sustained study of indigenized worlds if it aimed to do so—that is, if the novel selected for study were an Indigenous novel; if the learning outcomes focused substantively on indigenizing features; if framework questions were broader in scope and included framing, research, speculative, and other types of questions; and if a more diverse set of literature study practices were included. But the longevity of this framework in its present form makes it doubtful that the framework will allow these changes.

AN EXPLORATORY FRAMEWORK FOR STUDYING INDIGENIZED WORLDS

The exploratory framework for studying indigenized worlds offered in this book overcomes the limitations of common literature study frameworks and offers middle and secondary grade students unique sets of tools and resources that will enable them to explore indigenized worlds collaboratively with their teacher and classmates in a focused and sustained way. The framework is grounded in theoretical perspectives from the fields of Indigenous studies, cultural studies, cultural anthropology, linguistics, and narrative studies.

Key Framework Details

A literature study in grades 5–10 focusing on the indigenization of the fictional world in a selected Indigenous novel will have a unique purpose, focus on a unique set of learning outcomes, include unique elements, and favor types of questions that are not typically posed in common literature study frameworks.

Key Framework Details

Target grades. 5–10

Duration. 3–4 weeks

Purpose. An exploratory framework for studying indigenized worlds seeks to help students to gain new understandings and insights about Indigenous people through sustained engagement with an Indigenous novel.

Summary. In an exploratory framework for studying indigenized worlds, students use framework tools and resources to read, research, discuss, and write about an Indigenous novel selected by their teacher. Framework tools include a full inventory of indigenizing features that appear in the selected novel and sets of questions focusing on 5–17 of these features. Framework resources include lists of recommended books, web pages, and videos that provide additional information about specific indigenizing features. **Learning outcome focus.** Key ideas and details, text analysis, literary elements, point of view, textual evidence, reading range, proficient reading actions (before, during, after reading); selected writing, Indigenous education, and social studies competencies.

Notable elements. One teacher-selected class novel. Framed reading and rereading tasks. Teacher support for understanding and responding to questions focusing on indigenizing features. Close reading actions. Flexible grouping, Large and small group discussion. Assignment flexibility. Summative assessment by written work submitted by individual students.

Type of questions. Questions focus on a specific Indigenous nation, prominent fictional world individuals, and individual indigenizing features. They include factual, inferencing, speculative, comparison, summative, evaluative, research, supplementary resource, background, framing, feature-focused, personal response, word meaning, and literal-figurative meaning questions. (An example for each type of question is provided below.)

Theoretical Groundings

An Indigenous Studies Perspective

Indigenous studies is "an interdisciplinary field of study that centers [places at the epistemological center of scholarly inquiry] the knowledges, priorities, aspirations and lived experiences of Indigenous peoples" (University of Buffalo 2023). Scholars in the field of Indigenous studies focus on topics of concern to Indigenous peoples, seek to explain the impact of non-Indigenous governing systems and ideas on Indigenous peoples, and offer new ways of thinking about and responding to complex problems in the world using the theories and practices of Indigenous peoples.

Understandings about Indigenous peoples, Indigenous writing, and Indigenous knowledge—articulated by Indigenous peoples, scholars and others—are foundational to the literature study framework offered in this book for exploring indigenized worlds.

American writer and scholar Louis Owens (1994) observes that the act of writing for him and many Native American writers is "an attempt to recover identity and authenticity by invoking and incorporating the world found within the oral tradition" (5) and that the novels produced by him and other Native American writers represent on one hand a "process of reconstruction, self-discovery, and cultural recovery" (11) and on the other the "possibility of recovering a centered sense of personal identity and significance" (19).

Canadian writer Kateri Akiwenzie-Damm (2016) writes about the tradition from which Indigenous literature uniquely arises. "First Peoples' literature," she writes, "arises out of the culture, the beliefs, values, aesthetics, humour, spirituality, and experiences of various Indigenous peoples of this land . . . stretching backwards to our creation and forwards into forever" (54). Her own writing arises from this tradition and positions her uniquely as an Indigenous person at the center of a web of ancestors and descendants that is intersected by time (past, present, future) and place (spiritual and physical realms).

Akiwenzie-Damm (2016) recognizes the fundamental and inextricable connection between Indigenous peoples and their ancestral lands, their ancestral environments. In the first part of her chapter about First Peoples' literature she writes, "As Indigenous peoples we belong to this land . . . This land recognizes us and knows us . . . It provides for us . . . It holds the bones of our ancestors . . . It is our connection to the land that makes us who we are, that shapes our thinking, our cultural practices, our spiritual, emotional, physical, and social lives" (53).

For Battiste and Henderson (2000), Indigenous knowledge is located in the environments (i.e., ecosystems) that Indigenous peoples inhabit, belong to, and depend on. Battiste argues that all Indigenous knowledge is structurally similar. All include localized understandings about the interdependence of all things in an ecosystem; unseen powers; what is sacred; what is ethical; the importance of interpersonal and kinship relations; and the way language shapes our real-world perceptions and perceptions of reality.

Individual indigenizing features identified and described in the companion book (Philpot 2023) and the sets of exploratory questions offered in this book reflect the distinctive understandings and experiences of Indigenous peoples in terms of ancestral lands, ancestral identity, cultural recovery, values, spirituality, traditional practices, kinship relations, and more.

A Cultural Studies Perspective

In *Teaching Literature to Adolescents* (2020), Beach, Appleman, Fecho, and Simon include the postcolonial perspective as one of ten critical perspectives middle and secondary grade students can apply as a lens for analyzing texts. Farrell (2008) describes postcolonialism (i.e., a postcolonial sensibility or perspective) as a "critical concept within contemporary cultural studies characterized by attempts to explain the development, conditions, and consequences of the experience of modern colonialism."

The analytic lens of postcolonialism may focus on the colonial subject (the colonizer) or the colonial object (the colonized). Literature studies focusing on colonized Indigenous people in Canada or the United States will aim to understand the specific impacts of colonization, negative or positive, on specific groups of people (e.g., Mohawk people, Ojibwe people). Negative impacts may focus on one's experience of disempowerment, disconnection, poverty, or disease while positive impacts may focus on one's restoration to health or reassertion of a national identity and specific cultural practices.

The literature study framework offered in this book, aligned with a postcolonialism (cultural studies) perspective, engages students in thoughtful exploration of the positive and negative impacts of colonization on Indigenous peoples in the United States and Canada. These impacts are reflected in Group D Categories 10–12 indigenizing features (e.g., forced relocation from homeland, cultural denigration, disease, defense of homes and homeland, recovery, and restoration).

A Cultural Anthropology Perspective

Ethnography, a key mode of inquiry in the field of cultural anthropology, can be succinctly defined as a scientific description of a society's culture by someone who has lived in that society. Cultural anthropologists seek to describe diverse peoples of the world in terms of language, patterns of subsistence, religion, kinship relations, political organization, economic systems, and more using ethnographic data, archaeological findings, folklore, and language study.

Wolcott (1999) describes ethnographic study as a way of seeing and identifies three essential field-based methods that enable ethnographers to produce expansive and informative descriptions of diverse peoples and cultures. The first field-based method, experiencing, positions ethnographers as close observers of events that occur naturally within a society. In this way ethnographers learn about everyday events through their own personal experiences as events unfold in real time.

The second field-based method, inquiring, engages ethnographers in instructive conversations about an observed event with members of a local society that will help the ethnographer to understand the purpose and meaning of the observed event to local participants. The third field-based method, examining, may involve a close examination of cultural descriptions of a given society produced by others but more often involves a close examination of everyday things (i.e., tangibles) that will expand or clarify an ethnographer's understandings about a society.

The literature study framework offered in this book, aligned with an ethnographic (cultural anthropology) perspective, positions students as close observers in a fictional world for sustained periods of time seeking to develop specific, expansive, and transformative understandings about prominent Indigenous individuals and their fictional world experiences. Students will develop these understandings by responding to questions on topics of great interest to ethnographers including cultural events, cultural values, cultural traditions, family life, and storytelling.

A Linguistics Perspective: Systemic-Functional Linguistics

Systemic-functional linguistics is a theory of language that focuses on the function or functioning of language in social contexts. Systemic-functional linguists are keenly interested in the workings of language in various social contexts, how language is used for particular purposes, and the choices language users make in their selection of words and wordings to achieve particular purposes.

Systemic-functional linguistics offers unique sets of resources for analyzing written stories like novels. A central function and primary purpose of novels written for young people age 10–16 is the construal of personal experiences—experiences particular to an individual. The Indigenous novel *The Winter People* (Bruchac 2002), for example, focuses largely on the personal experiences of fourteen-year-old Saxso as he travels south by canoe from his village in present-day Quebec seeking to free his mother and sisters from captivity in the fall of 1759.

Saxso's personal experiences in *The Winter People* (Bruchac 2002) consist of his doings, sensations (i.e., seeing, hearing, smelling), thoughts, emotional responses, and conversations with other Abenaki people. At the start of the novel, Saxso is situated outside the dance hall in his village. He is "standing" by himself; "looking around"; "thinking" that the hissing words he has just heard were not spoken by a native Abenaki speaker; calling ("saying") the name of a Mahican friend; and "seeing" in his head the destruction of the village church (6–9).

Systemic-functional linguistics offers an illuminating set of resources that helps readers to explore an indigenized world like Saxso's and the personal experiences of a prominent fictional world young person like Saxso. Described by Halliday and Matthiessen (2014), these experiential resources include the concepts of processes (doing, sensing, thinking, emoting); participants (individuals involved in a process); and circumstances (of time, place, purpose, conditionality, and more).

Indeed, the terms *fictional world* and *fictional world individual* are understood within the context of systemic-functional linguistics and the experiential metafunction of language as described by Halliday and Matthiessen (2014).

A Narrative Studies Perspective

Merriam-Webster defines *narrative* as a way of presenting or understanding a situation or series of events that reflects and promotes a particular point of view. A definition of narrative from the field of narrative studies and initial toolkit of terms, concepts, and methods for studying narrative fiction (e.g., novels) is provided by Herman (2007). Narrative is defined as "a basic human strategy for coming to terms with fundamental elements of our experience, such as time, process, and change" (3), and the toolkit includes resources for exploring fiction in terms of story, plot, narration, time, space, character, dialogue, focalization, and genre.

Herman (2007) writes that "stories are accounts of what happened to particular people—and of what it was like for them to experience what happened—in particular circumstances with specific consequences" (3). This is the central focus of the literature study framework offered in this book: the particular circumstances, experiences, and understandings of Indigenous peoples in a given context. In a classroom exploration of the fictional world in an Indigenous novel, students will use an analytic toolkit that includes the resources offered by the field of narrative studies.

Framework Tools

Two essential literature study tools—a summative set of indigenizing features for a given novel and sets of customized questions that focus on specific indigenizing features—enable students in grades 5–10 to gain substantive and transformative understandings about Indigenous novels, indigenized worlds, and Indigenous writers. These two sets of exploratory tools are described below. Details about the selection of novels used in this book are also provided.

Feature Summaries for Eleven Indigenous Novels

The complete inventory of indigenizing features reported in the companion book *Indigenous Novels, Indigenized Worlds* (Philpot 2023) is shown in textbox 2.1. More than 150 indigenizing features appear in the inventory, and these features are organized into primary (Groups A–D) and secondary groups (Categories 1–12). Framework tools and resources for eleven Indigenous novels, including a comprehensive feature summary for each novel, are provided in that book.

Textbox 2.1.
Complete Inventory of Indigenizing Features (Philpot 2023)

Group A: Time, History, Ancestry

  1. Time
       seasonal activity cycle
       seasonal habitation cycles
       prescience (foresight)
       dreamtime
  2. Tribal History
       notable people
       notable events
       notable places
  3. Ancestry
       ancestral lands
       ancestral identity
       ancestral beings
       ancestral scents
       ancestral symbols

Group B: Cultural Beliefs, Values, Events, Traditions

4. Religious Beliefs and Practices
   beliefs about the Creator
   cosmic coherence
   spirit helpers, guides, protectors
   spiritual travel
   supernatural powers
   visions
   praying and prayers
   sacred offerings
   sacred songs
   sacred objects (miscellaneous)
   medicine bags
   spirit bundles
   sacred drums and drumming
   honoring the dead
   purification practices
5. Cultural Values
   expressing gratitude
   valuing dreams
   valuing sharing and peaceful relations with neighboring nations
   acting calmly, humbly, and honorably
   respecting others
6. Cultural Events
   toss and catch games
   stick and ball games
   snow snakes
   game of silence
   traditional dancers
   harvest, thunder, and moon dances
   hoop dance
   grass dance
   fancy dance
   round dance
   winter gathering dance
   traditional songs and singing
   special celebratory event feasts
   naming feasts

strawberry festival, maple festival, and corn harvest
spring festival
celebratory dance
Lakota naming ceremony
Choctaw wedding ceremony
Inuit wedding ceremony
Sto: loh Becoming Man Ceremony
Indigenous coming-of-age ceremony
7. Cultural Traditions
traditional knowledge about local wildlife
traditional skills: outdoor fire-making
traditional roles
large game hunting
rabbit hunting
bird hunting
snaring
trapping
fishing
clamming
whaling
herding
tracking
plant and wild rice harvesting
water travel
snow travel
infant travel
stealth
traditional houses
traditional shelters
house & shelter building
boat building and repair
net making
tanning
traditional clothes
traditional clothing accessories
blankets and blanket making
mats and baskets
wood carving
beadwork and quillwork

tattooing and embroidery work
toy making
traditional implements
traditional weapons
traditional materials
traditional foods
traditional drinks
traditional medicines
food preparation
food storage

Group C: Language, Storytelling, Family Life, Kinship

8. Language Use, Stories, and Storytelling
    ancestral language
    names and naming
    storytelling time
    the art of storytelling
    stories about the Creator
    stories about culture heroes
    stories about legendary individuals
    mythical stories
    stories about animal tricksters
    evil being stories
    eagle stories
    personal stories
    family stories
    widely-circulated stories of contemporary renown
    Indigenous writing
9. Family Life and Kinship
    extended family households
    sibling care
    sibling avoidance
    closeness to cousins
    childbirth
    childhood play
    coming of age experiences
    courtship
    arranged marriages

respecting one's in-laws
clan membership
extending kinship to strangers
kinship with local animals

Group D: Destruction & Restoration

10. Divestments, Denigration, Subjugation, Disease
    material appropriation
    forced relocation from homeland
    forced removal from homeland
    forced separation of children from parents
    forced sterilization
    material deprivation
    cultural denigration
    disdain
    ancestral identity concealment
    harassment
    subjugation
    brutality
    smallpox
    diabetes
11. Sovereignty, Defense, Leadership
    sovereignty
    defense of sovereignty
    defense of homes and homelands
    clan mothers
    chiefs
    councils
    elders
    societies
12. Restoration and Recovery
    recovery
    restoration
    cultural pride

Novel Selection Criteria

The criteria used to select twenty-four Indigenous novels for an analysis of indigenizing features in *Indigenous Novels, Indigenized Worlds* (Philpot

2023) bear repeating. Novels were eligible for selection if they met criteria related to authorial identity, the identity and age of prominent fictional world individuals, place of publication, genre, and target readership.

Specifically, texts deemed eligible were (1) written by Indigenous American or Canadian authors, (2) focused on the personal experiences of an Indigenous young person age 10–16; (3) published by a mainstream American or Canadian publishing company; (4) specifically contemporary realistic, historical, or fantasy novels; and (5) primarily for readers age 10–16.

Additional criteria were used in this book to select eleven novels from the larger pool of twenty-four. Novels selected for this book (6) have been recommended by professional reviewers (e.g., *Kirkus Reviews*; *School Library Journal*; *Horn Book*; *ALA Booklist*; *Publishers Weekly*); (7) feature interesting storylines and characters; (8) are indigenized in distinctive ways; and (9) may be purchased new by a school.

The eleven novels featured in this book focus on diverse groups of Indigenous peoples in Canada and the United States, feature diverse geographical locations and landscapes, and are balanced in terms of authorship (male, female, Canadian, American, new writers, experienced writers) and genre (historical, contemporary realistic, fantasy).

Question Sets

Question sets focusing on specific Indigenous nations, prominent fictional young people, and individual indigenizing features are offered in chapters 3–7. These question sets are centrally important for exploratory studies of indigenized worlds. On average, two sets of questions are offered for each novel although three or five sets of questions are offered for several.

Question sets may focus exclusively on factual questions but typically focus on the four most common types of questions: research, background, factual, and inferencing. Question sets may also prompt students to explore an indigenized world with other types of questions including speculative, comparison, summative, evaluative, supplementary resource, framing, feature-focused, personal response, word meaning, and literal-figurative meaning questions. Descriptions and examples of each type of question follow.

Factual questions. Factual questions direct readers to specific sentences in a novel where important ideas are explicitly presented. Words and wordings used in factual questions are drawn from actual sentences in the novel. Factual questions typically begin with the pronouns *who* or *what* or the adverbs *when, where, why,* or *how* but may also begin with the pronouns *which, whom,* or *whose*. To answer a factual question, readers will identify one or more source sentences in a novel and communicate the gist of those sentences accurately in a short written response.

Examples. (a) What action do the soldiers take when the Navajo prisoners do not respond to their order to halt and keep walking? (b) How does the commanding officer respond when the prisoners at the front of the line start running? (c) Which two Navajo prisoners are quickly shot by soldiers? (d) How does the commanding officer respond to the shooting of the two Navajo prisoners? (DBNP, relevant chapter: 2).

Inferencing questions. Inferencing questions direct readers to specific sentences and whole paragraphs within stretches of text in a novel where important ideas are implicitly presented. Inferencing questions frequently begin with the pronoun *what* or adverb *why* and less frequently begin with the adverb *how*. To answer an inferencing question, readers will locate relevant stretches of text in one or several chapters, identify individual words or phrases that prompt them to infer meaning relevant to a given question in a set, and communicate these meanings succinctly and intelligibly in a short written response.

Examples. What qualifies the removal and depletion of fresh water resources on Indigenous ancestral lands as material appropriation? (TMT, relevant chapter: 3). Why does High Eagle provide instruction about the hoops before his performance? (LLM, relevant chapter: 4). How specifically do the song lyrics at the start of chapter 9 reflect Wolverine's experiences later in the chapter when he visits his grandparents for the first time? (TCOTS, relevant chapter: 9).

Speculative questions. Speculative questions invite readers to offer possible explanations about specific objects, events, situations, experiences, communications, and meanings encountered in a novel. Speculative questions may focus on a fictional world object, event, situation, or phenomenon; an individual's actions, motivations, thoughts, feelings, challenges, preferences, or learning; experiential benefits, consequences, or outcomes; a story, speech, or prayer; and personal meanings, causal relationships, consequences, word use, or insights.

Most speculative questions begin with the pronoun *what* or adverb *why* and include the auxiliary verbs *would* or *might*. They may also include the adverb *likely* indicating possibility (*would, might*) or probability (*likely*). To answer a speculative question, readers will use their informed understandings about a novel, their specific understandings about a given thing (e.g., a challenging situation), and the perspective of one or more individuals who figure prominently in the novel to produce a short, plausible, and coherent written response.

Examples. (a) What difficulties would a ten-year-old face caring for loved ones infected with smallpox? (b) Who likely urged young Tallow to burn the possessions of her dying and deceased family members? (c) What difficulties would a ten-year-old face burning the possessions of her parents and other loved ones? (d) Why would Tallow wait so many years before sharing these experiences with her best friend Nokomis? (TPY, relevant chapter: 16).

Comparison questions. Comparison questions focus on the similarities and differences between several fictional-world things (e.g., physical locations, personal experiences, objects, the words of a prayer) and direct readers to specific pages in a novel where key details about the compared things are explicitly or implicitly presented. Comparison questions invariably begin with the pronoun *what* or adverb *how*. To answer a comparison question, readers will locate relevant stretches of text or paragraphs in one or more chapters (or books in a series); identify individual sentences, words, or phrases that provide explicit or implicit details about compared things; and use those details to produce a short written response.

Example. How are the situations and experiences of the school-age members of Miig's family similar and different from the situation and experiences of many residential school survivors? (TMT, relevant chapters: 1–3, 9).

Summative response questions. Summative response questions require readers to provide a concise written account of a fictional world event, individual experience, experiential outcome, set of circumstances, communication, or series of communications that focuses on key details presented explicitly or implicitly in a novel. Summative response question predominantly begin with the pronoun *what* but may also begin with the adverb *why* or *how*. Summative written accounts will include highly relevant story details from one or more locations in the novel, follow the structure of a written summary, and typically not exceed two paragraphs.

Examples. How does Ray's mother improve her spirits and bring hope to her children by sharing ancestral Ojibwe stories and legends around a fire? (LV, relevant chapter: 1). What key points from chapters 17–28 would you include in a summative account of Saxso's recovery of his captured family members? (TWP, relevant chapters: 17–28).

Evaluative questions. Evaluative questions require readers to make informed judgments positive or negative about a fictional world event from the perspective of an identified fictional world individual. Evaluative questions begin with the pronoun *what* or adverb *how* and include a positively or negatively valued word (e.g., successful, unsuccessful) that prompts readers to make a judgment. To answer an evaluative question, readers will locate key details from one or more locations in the novel that support a positive or negative judgment and communicate a judgement with supporting details in a short written response.

Example. How is Saxso's flight from St. Francis by canoe during the attack both successful and unsuccessful? (TWP, relevant chapter: 7).

Research questions. Research questions direct readers away from a novel temporarily to other sources of information that will enhance their understandings about specific ideas explored in a novel. A specific source of information may be identified in a research question (e.g., the title of book or video). Sources of information include books, videos, maps, images, and websites. To answer a research question, readers will synthesize the information obtained about a given idea from their research activities and share their new understandings verbally.

Examples. (a) What modern American village now stands on land previously occupied by Saxso's grandparents and ancestors? (b) Where precisely is this modern American village located? (c) Where in proximity to present-day American cities and other notable American landmarks was the Abenaki village called Village Below the Falls located? (d) What motivated Indigenous people like Saxso's Abenaki ancestors to settle by the falls? (TWP, relevant chapter: 2).

Supplementary resource questions. Like research questions, supplementary resource questions direct readers away from a novel temporarily to other sources of information that will enhance their understandings about specific ideas explored in a novel. Supplementary resources are provided for questions in chapter 6 and include three traditional Ojibwe stories and a summative account of the traditional use of trees by Ojibwe people. To answer the supplementary resource questions in chapter 6, readers will use key ideas from the given supplementary resources to produce short and enlightened written responses.

Examples. What meaning do ancestral trees contribute to traditional stories about the Ojibwe culture hero Nanabozho? (Resource: Three traditional stories containing ancestral trees). What traditional knowledge about the important uses of ancestral trees did Ojibwe men and women impart to Frances Densmore? (Resource: Important uses of ancestral trees).

Background questions. Background questions, worded in the present or past tense, direct readers away from a certain point in a novel to an earlier chapter (or book, as for series novels like TPY or DBDP) for the purpose of retrieving story details that will help readers to answer subsequent questions within a set with greater understanding, clarity, and completeness. Readers will locate specific story details using the book, chapter, or page references provided, take note of these details mentally, keep them in mind, and use them to formulate responses to specific questions in a set.

Example. (a) How did Omakayas obtain the feathers her father kept for her in his medicine bag? (b) How many feathers did Omakayas obtain that day? (c) Why are feathers plucked from a living bird more valuable than feathers dropped by a bird? (TPY, background details from chapter 5 that are highly relevant for chapter 10 questions focusing on medicine bags).

Framing questions. Framing questions prepare readers to think explicitly, substantively, and expansively about a particular subset of questions focusing on the fictional world experiences of one or more individuals, experiential benefits and intersections, shifting references, physical relocation or contexts, conversational triggers, or shared human experiences. Framing questions begin with the pronoun *what* or adverb *how* and include specific words that aim to shape and sharpen one's understandings about prominent fictional world individuals. To answer a framing question, readers will locate relevant details in a chapter and use these details to produce a short written response.

Example. How does the shifting reference to different generations of grandparents, as in chapter 5, enhance the meaning and significance of the memories and perspectives framing this dreamtime experience as well? (WG, relevant chapter: 9).

Feature-focused questions. Special questions focusing on the indigenizing features of seasonal time and traditional foods are uniquely offered in chapter 3. To answer these feature-focused questions, readers will use explicit seasonal references and the information provided about traditional foods to produce short written responses.

Example. What is the focus of each traditional Indigenous food group identified in the section "Traditional Indigenous Foods"? (TPY, food group focus).

Personal response questions. Two personal response questions in chapter 5 invite readers to express their personal thoughts about the relationship between two Lakota cousins in the novel LLM. To answer these personal response questions, readers will use their informed understandings about the novel along with their personal knowledge, beliefs, attitudes, and judgments about human experience to produce personally relevant and insightful short written responses.

Examples. (a) How would you describe Lori and Lana's relationship as sisters? (b) What is significant for you about Lori and Lana's relationship as sisters? (LLM, relevant chapters: 1–12).

Word meaning questions. Word meaning questions require readers to obtain the precise definition of a word or idiom that appears in a forthcoming set of questions. Readers are directed away from the novel temporarily to obtain the full definition of a word or phrase from a preferred dictionary or an online search. Preferred dictionaries include the *American Heritage Dictionary*, *Free Dictionary* by Farlex, and *Collins Dictionary*. Word meaning questions focus mainly on English words (e.g., *eiderdown*, *purpose*) but also focus on naturalized English words and foreign words (e.g., *pemmican*, *portage*, *l'apogée*).

To answer a word meaning question, readers locate the most applicable definition of a given word or phrase in the preferred dictionary, record the definition accurately, seek to understand both the definition and usage of the word in the context of the novel, then keep the definition handy as they respond to forthcoming questions in a set.

Examples. How does the online *Free Dictionary* by Farlex define the idiom "lighten (one's) load"? (WG, relevant chapter: 12). How does the online *Collins Dictionary* define the word *portage*? (LV, relevant chapter: 3).

Literal-figurative meaning questions. Two interrelated literal-figurative meaning questions in chapter 5 require readers to articulate their understandings about the meanings conveyed by repeated elements in a series of dreams (e.g., guns, gunfire, drumming, a white bird).

Dreams convey two types of potential meanings. On one hand, they convey experiential meanings: people's real-world experiences including a person's real-world location, sensory experiences, actions, speech, thoughts, and feelings. Experiential meanings are often called literal meanings. On the other hand, dreams can also convey metaphorical meanings that dreamers may choose to consider. Metaphorical meanings are often called figurative meanings. Literal-figurative meaning questions require readers to consider both types of meanings.

To answer the two literal-figurative meaning questions in chapter 5, readers will carefully consider the two types of meanings—literal (experiential) and figurative (metaphorical)—conveyed by each repeated dream element and communicate these meanings in an informative, illuminating, and comprehensible written response.

Example. (a) What literal (experiential) meanings are conveyed in Carrie's real-time dreams by each repeated element in table 5.3? (b) What figurative (metaphorical) meanings are conveyed by each repeated element? (WIB, relevant chapters: 1–5, 7, 9–11, 13, 14).

Optional Literature Study Practices

Middle and secondary grade teachers will surely enliven and motivate students and enhance the quality of a literature study focusing on indigenized worlds by using a range of organizational, reading, discussion, and writing practices in classroom explorations of an Indigenous novel. Beach et al. (2020) identify and describe a range of practices that will help students to engage constructively for sustained periods of time with a target novel.

For literature study units with students in middle and secondary grades, Beach et al. (2020) recommend the organizational practices of flexible seating and flexible grouping; the discussion practice of backchanneling; and the informal writing practices of free writing, blog writing, and dialog journaling. These practices are easily located in their book. Other literature study practices that will surely enhance classroom explorations of indigenized worlds are described on trustworthy websites for teachers. These practices include reading logs, close reading practices (text annotating, note-making), concentric circle discussions, webbing, quick writing, and summary writing frames.

The core writing genres of opinion and argument writing may also be useful for literature study units focusing on indigenized worlds. These common core writing genres are described at length by Calkins (2020) and others. These writing options along with the aforementioned organizational, close reading, discussion, and informal writing practices are shown summatively in table 2.1.

Engaging students in large group (teacher-led) or small group (student-led) discussions about some aspect of a novel is no easy task. In *The Art of Discussion-Based Teaching* (2008), Henning offers many practical suggestions for teachers in middle and secondary grades that will enhance the

Table 2.1. Optional Practices for Literature Studies in Middle and Secondary Grades

Organizational	Close Reading	Discussion	Informal Writing	Core Genre Writing

flexible seating
flexible
  grouping
reading logs
	annotating
	note-making
		backchanneling
		concentric
		  circles
			free writing
			quick writing
			note-making
			webbing
			dialog
			  journaling
			blog writing
				opinion writing
				argument writing

quality of classroom discussions. His chapters on teacher follow-up moves, creating discussions, building a climate for discussion, and supporting cultural and linguistic diversity are especially relevant and informative for classroom discussions about individual indigenizing features.

Framework Resources

Extratextual resources are provided for each novel in chapters 3–7 that students can read or view to enhance their understandings about individual indigenizing features. These resources were vetted and selected by the author and include highly relevant and informative books, guides, and various online resources (YouTube videos, online encyclopedias, web pages). An example for each type of resource follows.

Book Resource Example
Robertson, R. G. *Rotting Face: Smallpox and the American Indian*. Caldwell, Idaho: Caxton Press, 2001.
Video Resource Example
Suite1491. "Old Style Grass Dance Contest Song 3." YouTube. www.youtube.com/watch?v=-BmH0fxnHfY.
Publication Guide Example
Burnaby Village Museum. "Indigenous History in Burnaby Resource Guide." Burnaby, BC: City of Burnaby, 2019.
Web Page Resource Example
Maureen Lee and Glen Lee. "Thermopsis Rhombifolia (Golden Bean)." Saskatchewan Wildflowers. www.saskwildflower.ca/nat_Thermopsis-rhombifolia.html.
Online Encyclopedia Resource Example
Gadacz, René R. "Sweat Lodge." *Canadian Encyclopedia*. Historica Canada.
Wikipedia Resource Example
Wikipedia. "Turners Falls, Massachusetts." https://en.wikipedia.org/wiki/Turners_Falls,_Massachusetts.

INDIGENOUS AUTHORS

Bruchac, Joseph (Abenaki, United States)—Joseph Bruchac is an Abenaki writer and storyteller. To date he has published over 120 books for children and adults. His books for children include picture books, short stories, traditional stories, biographies, and novels.

Bruchac's novels for younger readers age 10–12 include *Children of the Longhouse* (1996), *Eagle Song* (1997), *Heart of a Chief* (1998), *Skeleton Man* (2001), *The Journal of Jesse Smoke* (2001), *Arrow Over the Door* (2002), *Hidden Roots* (2004), *The Warriors* (2004), *Dark Pond* (2004), *Whisper in the Dark* (2005), *Wabi: A Hero's Tale* (2006), *Return of Skeleton Man* (2006), *Bear Walker* (2007), *Dragon Castle* (2011), and *Rez Dogs* (2022).

Bruchac's novels for older readers age 13–16 include *The Winter People* (2002), *Code Talker* (2005), *The Way* (2007), *March Toward the Thunder* (2009), *Wolf Park* (2011), *Trail of the Dead* (2015), *Rose Eagle* (2014), *Long Run* (2016), *Talking Leaves* (2017), *Killer of Enemies* (2017), *Night Wings* (2018), *Two Roads* (2019), *Found* (2020), *Arrow of Lightning* (2021), and *Peacemaker* (2022).

Bruchac holds a bachelor's degree from Cornell University, a master's degree in literature and creative writing from Syracuse University, and a doctorate in comparative literature from the Union Institute and the University of Ohio. In 1999, Bruchac received the Lifetime Achievement Award from the Native Writers' Circle of the Americas.

Dimaline, Cherie (Metis, Canada)—Cherie Dimaline is a member of the Georgian Bay (Ontario) Métis Nation on Lake Huron. Her published works for adults include novels, collections of short stories, individual short stories, and magazine articles. In 2013 she was founding editor of *Muskrat Magazine*, an online Indigenous arts and culture magazine. In 2014 she was selected as the Emerging Artist of the Year at the Ontario Premier's Awards for Excellence in Arts, and in 2015 she served as writer in residence at Toronto Public Library.

The Marrow Thieves (2017) is Dimaline's first novel for young people. The novel received two national literary awards in Canada: the Governor General's Award for Young People's Literature (2017), and the Burt Award for First Nations, Inuit and Métis Young Adult Literature (2018). Dimaline currently lives in Toronto.

Driving Hawk Sneve, Virginia (Sicangu Lakota, United States)—Virginia Driving Hawk Sneve is a member of the Rosebud Sioux Tribe (Sicangu Lakota Oyate or Burnt Thigh Nation). In her long career as a teacher and writer, Sneve has written more than twenty books, fiction and nonfiction, for children and adults. In 1972 she published two novels for young people: *Jimmy Yellow Hawk*, and *High Elk's Treasure*. Her other novels for young people include *When Thunders Spoke* (1974), *The Chichi Hoohoo Bogeyman* (1993), *The Trickster and the Troll* (1997), and *Lana's Lakota Moon* (2007).

Sneve was born in 1933 and grew up on the Rosebud Indian Reservation in South Dakota. She earned a high school diploma from St. Mary's School for

Indian Girls in Springfield, South Dakota, and undergraduate and graduate degrees from South Dakota State University in 1954 and 1969 respectively. In 1979 she received an honorary doctorate of letters from Dakota Wesleyan University and in 2000 was awarded the National Humanities Medal for her literary efforts by President Clinton.

Erdrich, Louise (Anishinaabe, United States)—Louise Erdrich is a member of the Turtle Mountain Band of Chippewa Indians in North Dakota. Her books for children and adults, including her *Birchbark House* series for children age 8–12, have earned her international acclaim as an American writer. Erdrich published her first novel for adults in 1984 and her first work of fiction for children, a picture book, in 1996.

Erdrich's *Birchbark House* series for children includes *The Birchbark House* (1999), *Game of Silence* (2005), *The Porcupine Year* (2008), *Chickadee* (2012), and *Makoons* (2016). Two novels in the series, *Game of Silence* and *Chickadee*, received the Scott O'Dell Award for Historical Fiction. Erdrich has won numerous awards for her novels, short stories, and poems. Her recent novel for adults *The Night Watchman* (2020) won the Pulitzer Prize for Fiction, and in 2020 Erdrich received a Lifetime Achievement Award from the Native Writers' Circle of the Americas.

Erdrich holds a bachelor's degree in English from Dartmouth College and a master's degree in writing from Johns Hopkins University. Erdrich currently lives in Minneapolis.

Kusugak, Michael (Inuit, Canada)—Michael Kusugak is an Inuk writer of fiction and nonfiction for children. *The Curse of the Shaman* (2006) is Kusugak's only novel and only written work for readers age ten and up. Kusugak has published many books for younger children, most notably *Baseball Bats for Christmas* (1990), *Northern Lights: The Soccer Trails* (1993), *Arctic Stories* (1998), *The Littlest Sled Dog* (2008), *The Most Amazing Bird* (2020), and his first book, *A Promise Is a Promise*, cowritten with Robert Munsch.

Kusugak was born in 1948 on a point of land called Qatiktalik (Cape Fullerton) on the west side of Hudson Bay and spent the first part of his life at Repulse Bay, Nunavut. In 1948, Kusugak's parents and grandparents lived traditionally as Inuit people by hunting and fishing, wearing traditional seal and caribou skin clothes, traveling by dog sled and kayak, and sleeping in igloos and skin tents. All of Kusugak's books, including his only novel *The Curse of the Shaman* (2006), feature Inuit people living in traditional ways that reflect his own childhood experiences.

Kusugak was forced to attend school, his first residential school, in 1954 at Chesterfield Inlet many miles south by airplane from his family's home at Repulse Bay. He went on to attend several other residential schools before graduating from high school in Saskatoon and attending a university. Kusugak finally pursued a writing career in the late 1980s at Robert Munsch's suggestion.

In 2008 Kusugak was the recipient of the Vicky Metcalf Award for Literature for Young People honoring him for his lifetime contribution to Canadian children's literature. Today Kusugak travels widely from his home near Lake Winnipeg in northern Manitoba, sharing his stories with children.

Maracle, Lee (Sto: loh, Canada)—Lee Maracle (1950–2011), a member of the Sto: loh Nation, was born and raised in North Vancouver, British Columbia. Maracle wrote one novel for adolescent readers, *Will's Garden* (2002), five novels for adults, several collections of short stories and poems, and nonfiction works focusing primarily on the lives of Indigenous women.

In 2009 and 2019 Maracle received honorary doctorates from St. Thomas University and the University of Waterloo. For varying periods of time she served as writer-in-residence (University of Toronto First Nations House, University of Guelph), visiting professor and instructor (University of Waterloo, University of Toronto, Western Washington University), and cultural director for the Indigenous Theatre School in Toronto.

In 2018 for her outstanding contributions to Canadian literature and service to the nation, Maracle was named an officer of the Order of Canada.

Slipperjack-Farrell, Ruby (Ojibwe, Canada)—Ruby Slipperjack-Farrell is a member of the Eabametoong First Nation in Ontario. She has written six novels for middle grade readers including *Honor the Sun* (1987), *Silent Words* (1992), *Weesquachak and the Lost Ones* (2000), *Little Voice* (2001), *Dog Tracks* (2008), and *These Are My Words* (2016). The majority of these novels focus on contemporary Anishinaabe people, their language, and culture. Slipperjack-Farrell speaks the Anishinaabe language fluently.

Slipperjack-Farrell was born at Whitewater Lake in Ontario in 1952 and spent the first part of her life on her father's trapline. Between the years 1988 and 2005 Slipperjack-Farrell earned undergraduate and graduate degrees in history and education.

In 2017 Slipperjack-Farrell received the Vicky Metcalf Award for Literature for Young People honoring her for her lifetime contribution to Canadian children's literature. She retired shortly thereafter from her position as professor of education in the Indigenous Learning Department at Lakehead University in Thunder Bay, Ontario, where she currently resides.

Tingle, Tim (Choctaw, United States)—Tim Tingle is a member of the Choctaw Nation of Oklahoma and has written twenty books for young people and a series of self-published novels for adults (the Travis Lee Series). Tingle's novels for younger readers age 10–12 include *House of Purple Cedar* (2014), *When a Ghost Talks, Listen* (2018), and *Stone River Crossing* (2019). He has also produced four collections of short stories or tales for this same age group.

Tingle's first two novels, *House of Purple Cedar* (2014) and *How I Became a Ghost* (2013/2015), received the American Indian Youth Literature Award in the categories of middle school and young adult readers respectively.

Tingle has also written two series of novels for older readers age 12–16. The Danny Blackgoat Series includes *Danny Blackgoat, Navajo Prisoner* (2013), *Danny Blackgoat, Rugged Road to Freedom* (2014), and *Danny Blackgoat, Dangerous Passage* (2017). The No Name Series includes *No Name* (2014), *No More No Name* (2017), *A Name Earned* (2018), *Trust Your Name* (2018), and *Name Your Mountain* (2020).

Tingle holds bachelor's and master's degrees in English and English literature from the University of Texas and University of Oklahoma respectively. Tingle was a featured speaker at the National Museum of the American Indian in 2006–2007 and is a featured storyteller at special storytelling events throughout the United States.

White, Tara (Mohawk, Canada)—Tara White is a member of the Mohawk Nation from Kahnawake, Quebec. She holds a master's degree in business administration and is a certified management accountant. *Where I Belong* (2014) is White's first novel. White published her first picture book for children, *I Like Who I Am*, in 2016. White currently lives in Bowmanville, Ontario.

REFERENCE LIST

Theoretical Perspectives

Akiwenzie-Damm, Kateri. "First Peoples' Literature in Canada." In *At the Crossroads of Culture and Literature*, edited by Chattopadhyay Suchorita and Debashree Dattaray, 53–62. Delhi: Primus Books, 2016.

Battiste, Marie Ann, and James Youngblood Henderson. *Protecting Indigenous Knowledge and Heritage: A Global Challenge*. Saskatoon, SK: Purich Publishing, 2000.

Farrell, Molly. "Postcolonialism." In *The Oxford Encyclopedia of the Modern World*. Oxford: Oxford University Press, 2008. www-oxfordreference-com.proxy-ship .klnpa.org/view/10.1093/acref/9780195176322.001.0001/acref-9780195176322-e -1276.

Halliday, Michael, and Christian Matthiessen. *Halliday's Introduction to Functional Grammar*. Fourth edition. Abingdon, UK: Routledge, 2014.

Herman, David, ed. *The Cambridge Companion to Narrative*. Cambridge: Cambridge University Press, 2007.

Owens, Louis. *Other Destinies: Understanding the American Indian Novel*. Norman: University of Oklahoma Press, 1992.

Philpot, Don K. *Indigenous Novels, Indigenized Worlds: Exploring the Indigenization of Fictional Worlds*. Lanham, MD: Rowman & Littlefield, 2023.

Wolcott, Harry F. *Ethnography: A Way of Seeing*. Lanham, MD: Altamira Press, 2008

Literature Study Resources

Atwell, Nancie. *In the Middle: Writing Reading and Learning with Adolescents*. Portsmouth, NH: Heinemann Educational Books, 1987.

Beach, Richard, Deborah Appleman, Bob Fecho, and Rob Simon. *Teaching Literature to Adolescents*. Fourth edition. New York: Taylor & Francis Group, 2021.

Calkins, Lucy. *Teaching Writing*. Portsmouth, NH: Heinemann Educational Books, 2020.

Copeland, Matt. *Socratic Circles: Fostering Critical and Creative Thinking in Middle and High School*. Portland, ME: Stenhouse Publishers, 2005.

Daniels, Harvey. *Literature Circles: Voice and Choice in the Child-Centered Classroom*. York, ME: Stenhouse Publishers, 1994.

Harste, Jerome Charles, Kathy Gnagey Short, Carolyn L. Burke, and Gloria Kauffman. *Creating Classrooms for Authors: The Reading-Writing Connection*. Portsmouth, NH: Heinemann Educational Books, 1988.

Henning, John E. *The Art of Discussion-Based Teaching: Opening Up Conversation in the Classroom*. New York: Routledge, 2008.

Lambright, Lesley L. "Creating a Dialogue: Socratic Seminars and Educational Reform." *Community College Journal* 65 (1995): 30–34.

Peterson, Ralph, and Maryann Eeds. *Grand Conversations: Literature Groups in Action*. New York: Scholastic, 1990.

Rothlein, Liz, and Anita Meyer Meinbach. *The Literature Connection: Using Children's Books in the Classroom*. Glenview, IL: Scott Foresman, 1991.

Novels for Middle and Secondary Grades

Forbes, Esther. *Johnny Tremain*. Boston: Houghton Mifflin, 1943.

George, Jean Craighead, and John Schoenherr. *Julie of the Wolves*. New York: Harper & Row, 1972.

Paterson, Katherine, and Donna Diamond. *Bridge to Terabithia*. New York: Crowell, 1977.

Twain, Mark. *The Adventures of Tom Sawyer*. Hartford, CT: American Publishing Company, 1876.

PART II

Indigenized Worlds

Chapter 3

Historical Worlds (1847–1852)

CHAPTER OVERVIEW AND TARGET QUESTIONS

This chapter focuses on the fictional world in the historical novel *The Porcupine Year* (Erdrich 2008), the third novel in the *Birchbark House* series. The novel recounts the experiences of a twelve-year-old Ojibwe girl named Omakayas in 1852 as her family travels north by canoe seeking a new home and life for themselves. This novel is suited for an exploratory study of indigenized worlds in grades 5–7. For this chapter, readers will seek to answer the following target questions.

What basic story details for the first three novels in the *Birchbark House* series are conveyed through publisher summaries?

What is similar about these three novels?

What common set of indigenizing features appears in the three novels?

Which specific indigenizing features appear in *The Porcupine Year* (TPY)?

Which indigenizing features are specifically defined and how are they defined?

What specific information is provided about traditional Indigenous foods?

How is TPY subdivided for an exploratory study?

What sets of questions and recommended resources can be used to explore the indigenizing features shown in textbox 3.1?

Which specific questions and recommended resources can teachers and students use in grades 5–7 to gain insights about the Indigenous young person Omakayas, her family, and her community?

51

Textbox 3.1.
Targeted Indigenizing Features in The Porcupine Year (Erdrich 2008)

Group A features: seasonal activity cycle
Group B features: medicine bags, spirit bundles, purification practices, valuing dreams, naming feasts, sweat lodges, sweat lodge
building, traditional medicines, traditional foods
Group C features: stories of culture heroes, stories about legendary
individuals, personal stories, extended family households
Group D features: forced relocation from homeland, divestments,
smallpox

THREE HISTORICAL WORLDS

Selected Series and Novels

The Birchbark House *Series*

The *Birchbark House* series consists of five historical novels published for
readers ages 8–12 over a period of seventeen years from 1999–2016. The
first three books in the series report the personal experiences of a young
Ojibwe girl Omakayas at three distinctive periods in her life. Books 1–3 (*The
Birchbark House*; *The Game of Silence*; and *The Porcupine Year*)—situate
Omakayas at or while relocating from her home village on the Island of the
Golden-Breasted Woodpecker in Wisconsin at ages 8, 10, and 12 respectively.

Bibliographic Information and Individual Summaries

Erdrich, Louise. 1999. *The Birchbark House.* New York: Hyperion. Paperback.
244 pages. Fourteen chapters. Includes an author's note and glossary.
Illustrated. Historical fiction. Middle grade novel. Guided Reading Level
T. Lexile Measure 970L.
     Story details from back cover. Omakayas and her family live on the land
her people call the Island of the Golden-Breasted Woodpecker. Although
the *chimookoman*, white people, encroach more and more on their land, life
continues much as it always has: every summer they build a new birchbark
house; every fall they go to their ricing camp to harvest and feast; they move
to the cedar log house before the first snows arrive; and they celebrate the
end of the long, cold winters at their maple-sugaring camp. In between,
Omakayas fights with her annoying little brother, Pinch; plays with the ador-
able baby, Neewo; and tries to be grown-up like her big sister Angeline. But

the satisfying rhythms of their life are shattered when a visitor comes to their lodge one winter night bringing with him an invisible enemy that will change things forever—but that will eventually lead Omakayas to discover her calling.

Erdrich, Louise. 2005. *The Game of Silence.* New York: HarperCollins. Hardcover. 256 pages. Sixteen chapters. Includes an author's note, glossary, and additional notes. Illustrated. Historical fiction. Middle grade novel. Lexile Measure 900L.

Story details from front flap. Her name is Omakayas, or Little Frog, because her first step was a hop, and she lives on an island in Lake Superior. It is 1850, and the lives of the Ojibwe have returned to a familiar rhythm: they build their birchbark houses in the summer, go to the ricing camps in the fall to harvest and feast, and move to their cozy cedar log cabins near the town of LaPointe before the first snows. The satisfying routines of Omakayas's days are interrupted by a surprise visit from a group of desperate and mysterious people. From them, she learns that all their lives may drastically change. The chimookomanag, or white people, want Omakayas and her people to leave their island in Lake Superior and move farther west. Omakayas realizes that something so valuable, so important that she never knew she had it in the first place, is in danger: her home and her way of life.

Erdrich, Louise. 2008. *The Porcupine Year.* New York: HarperCollins. Hardcover. 193 pages. Sixteen chapters. Includes an author's note, glossary, and additional notes and a map. Illustrated. Historical fiction. Middle grade novel. Lexile Measure 840L.

Story details from front flap. Here follows the story of a most extraordinary year in the life of an Ojibwe family and of a girl named Omakayas, or Little Frog, who lived a year of flight and adventure, pain and joy, in 1852.

When Omakayas is twelve years old, she and her family set off on a harrowing journey. They travel by canoe west from the shores of Lake Superior along the rivers of northern Minnesota in search of a new home. While the family has prepared well, unexpected danger, enemies, and hardships will push them to the brink of survival. Omakayas continues to learn from the land and the spirits around her, and she discovers that no matter where she is, or how she is living, she has the one thing she needs to carry her through.

The Birchbark House: Key Fictional World Details

Specific Indigenous Groups and Individuals
Ojibwe, Omakayas (age 7)

Historical Settings
  1847, Minnesota, Lake Superior Region, Madeline Island

The Game of Silence: Key Fictional World Details

Specific Indigenous Groups and Individuals
  Ojibwe, Omakayas (age 10)
Historical Settings
  1850, Minnesota, Lake Superior Region, Madeline Island

The Porcupine Year: Key Fictional World Details

Specific Indigenous Groups and Individuals
  Ojibwe, Omakayas (age 12)
Historical Settings
  1852, Minnesota, Lake Superior Region

Books 1–3: Common Features

The fictional worlds in Books 1–3 of the *Birchbark House* series are indigenized by a common set of twenty features. As shown in textbox 3.2, these features span the categories of ancestry, religious beliefs and practices, cultural traditions, language use, family life, and disease. The full set of indigenizing features for Book 3, *The Porcupine Year*, is shown in textbox 3.3.

Textbox 3.2.
Common Indigenizing Features in the *Birchbark House* Series (Erdrich 1999–2008)

  Group A features. (3) <u>Ancestry</u>: ancestral identity
  Group B features. (4) <u>Religious Beliefs and Practices</u>: beliefs about the Creator, spirit helpers, guides, protectors, praying and prayers, sacred offerings; (7) <u>Cultural Traditions</u>: large game hunting, fishing, water travel, snow travel, traditional houses, traditional shelters, house and shelter building, traditional clothing accessories, traditional foods, food preparation, food storage
  Group C features. (8) <u>Language Use</u>: ancestral language, names and naming; (9) <u>Family Life</u>: childhood play
  Group D features. (10) <u>Disease</u>: smallpox

Textbox 3.3.
Indigenizing Features Summary for *The Porcupine Year* (Erdrich 2008)

Group A features. (1) <u>Time</u>: dreamtime; (3) <u>Ancestry</u>: ancestral lands, ancestral identity, ancestral beings
Group B features. (4) <u>Religious Beliefs and Practices:</u> beliefs about the Creator, spirit helpers, guides, protectors, praying and prayers, sacred offerings, sacred songs, sacred objects (miscellaneous), medicine bags, spirit bundles, honoring the dead, purification practices; (5) <u>Cultural Values</u>: valuing dreams, acting calmly, humbly, and honorably, respecting others; (6) <u>Cultural Events</u>: traditional songs and singing, naming feasts, Indigenous coming-of-age ceremony; (7) <u>Cultural Traditions</u>: traditional knowledge about local wildlife, traditional skills: outdoor fire-making, traditional roles, large game hunting, rabbit hunting, bird hunting, trapping, fishing, plant and wild rice harvesting, water travel, snow travel, traditional houses, traditional shelters, house and shelter building, traditional clothing accessories, blankets and blanket making, traditional implements, traditional foods, traditional drinks, food preparation, food storage
Group C features. (8) <u>Language Use, Stories, Storytelling</u>: ancestral language, names and naming, storytelling time, stories about culture heroes, stories about legendary individuals, personal stories, family stories; (9) <u>Family Life and Kinship</u>: extended family households, sibling avoidance, childhood play
Group D features. (10) <u>Divestments and Disease</u>: material appropriation, forced relocation from homeland, smallpox; (11) <u>Leadership</u>: elders; (12) <u>Restoration</u>: recovery, restoration

OMAKAYAS'S WORLD IN *THE PORCUPINE YEAR*

Features Summary

The fictional world in the Indigenous novel *The Porcupine Year* (Erdrich 2008) is indigenized by fifty-seven features in the categories of time, ancestry, religious beliefs and practices, cultural values, cultural events, cultural traditions, language use, stories, and storytelling, family life and kinship, divestments and disease, leadership, and restoration. The full set of indigenizing features for this third historical novel in the *Birchbark House* series is shown in textbox 3.3.

Exploratory Question Sets Focus

Four sets of exploratory questions are provided for the novel *The Porcupine Year* (Erdrich 2008). Question sets 1 and 2 focus on Group A and B features respectively: seasonal activity cycle (Category 1); medicine bags, spirit bundles, purification practices (Category 4); valuing dreams (Category 5); naming feasts (Category 6); and sweat lodges, sweat lodge building, traditional medicines, and traditional foods (Category 7).

Question sets 3 and 4 focus on Group C and D features respectively: stories of culture heroes, stories about legendary individuals, personal stories (Category 8); extended family (campsite) households (Category 9); and forced relocation from homeland, divestments, and smallpox (Category 10).

Defined Features

Definitions and additional information for the Categories 4 and 8 features of spirit bundle, medicine bag, and extended family household appear below. These three indigenizing features are explored in questions sets for *The Porcupine Year* (Erdrich 2008).

spirit bundle: a collection of sacred objects used for healing, protection, good fortune, individual or group empowerment, clairvoyance, or spiritual communication. Spirit bundles may be owned by one or more member of a cultural group, and each object within a bundle is typically connected to a cultural event, belief, ritual, story, song, responsibility, or taboo (Hirschfelder and Molin 2001).

medicine bag: a small leather pouch containing objects such as plant leaves, feathers, shells, rock crystals, or carvings used by their owners for healing purposes (Hirschfelder and Molin 2001). A medicine bag may be owned by a respected family member or by a medicine man or woman who conceals the bag in her clothing or suspends it from a cord around her neck or waist.

extended family household: a kinship group consisting of a nuclear family (parents and their children), various relatives (e.g., grandparent, aunt, uncle, and cousin), and adopted children—all living in the same dwelling.

Traditional Indigenous Foods

An impressive number of traditional Ojibwe foods are identified and described in *The Porcupine Year* (Erdrich 2008). As noted in *Indigenous*

Novels, Indigenized Worlds (Philpot 2023), the Category 7 indigenizing feature of traditional foods is conveniently subdivided into six Indigenous food groups.

Group 1: Fresh, Boiled, Fried, Roasted, Dried, Smoked, and Powdered Meat
Group 2: Soup, Broth, and Stew
Group 3: Baking Powder Breads, Puddings, and Dumplings
Group 4: Fruit, Vegetables, Legumes, Rice, Nuts, and Roots
Group 5: Fats and Sweets
Group 6: Other Traditional Foods

Book Sectioning

Part I: Summer (1–7)
Part II: Fall (8–9)
Part III: Winter (10–13)
Part IV: Spring (14–16)

Question Set 1: Group A Features

Seasonal Activity Cycle (Category 1), The Porcupine Year

Seasonal Activity Cycle Questions 1: Seasonal Identification

Chapter relevance questions. 1–7, 8–9, 10–13, 14–16

Explicit seasonal reference questions. (a) What explicit reference is made to the Ojibwe season of summer (*neebin*) in chapter 4? (33). (b) What explicit reference is made to the Ojibwe season of fall (*dagwaging*) in chapter 9? (90). (c) What explicit reference is made to the Ojibwe season of winter (*biboon*) in chapter 13? (141). (d) What explicit reference is made to the Ojibwe season of spring (*zeegwun*) in chapter 14? (154).

Time span support questions. How in addition to the explicit identification of seasons in chapters 4, 9, 13, and 14 does the time span of events in chapters 1–7, 8–9, 10–13, and 14–16 support the seasonal organization of chapters as in Books 1 and 2 in the *Birchbark House* series?

Seasonal Activity Cycle Questions 2: Seasonal Activities

Chapter relevance questions. 1–7, 8–9, 10–13, 14–16

Assorted questions focusing on seasonal activity. (a) What traditional activities do Omakayas and her family members engage in seasonally during the summer

(1–79), fall (80–98), winter (99–144), and spring (145–82)? (summative). (b) What limits some of these traditional activities to one season (e.g., wild rice harvesting, fall) (inferencing)?

Question Set 2: Group B Features

Medicine Bags, Spirit Bundles, and Purification Practices (Category 4), The Porcupine Year

Medicine Bag Questions

Relevant chapter. 10

Contextualizing event. Deydey laments the loss of his medicine bag.

Background questions (51–53). (a) How did Omakayas obtain the feathers her father kept for her in his medicine bag? (b) How many feathers did Omakayas obtain that day? (c) Why are feathers plucked from a living bird more valuable than feathers dropped by a bird?

Factual questions (107). (a) What special items, stored in Deydey's medicine bag, were stolen from him in chapter 9? (b) What made these items so special for Deydey?

Spirit Bundle Questions

Relevant chapters. 12, 16

Contextualizing event. Omakayas uses a newly made spirit bundle to grieve the loss of Old Tallow (chapter 12). Omakayas's love for Old Tallow grows when she learns about Old Tallow's past from her grandmother (chapter 16).

Background question 1 (Book 1, TBH): Tallow's personal recount. What personal information does Tallow share with Omakayas near the end of book 1? (232–37).

Background question 2 (Book 3, TPY): Tallow's death. (a) What is noble—selfless, loving, and generous—about the way Old Tallow dies in chapter 11 in TPY? (111–19). (b) How does Old Tallow's death affect Omakayas? (119, 121).

Factual questions. (a) What prompts Nokomis to make a spirit bundle for Omakayas honoring Old Tallow? (121). (b) What does Old Tallow's spirit bundle consist of? (122). (c) What thoughts cross Omakayas's mind about Old Tallow while holding her spirit bundle under a starry nighttime sky in chapter 16? (179). (d) What location does Omakayas choose as the sacred resting place for Old Tallow's spirit bundle and spirit? (180). (e) What special name will she give that location? (180).

Inferencing questions. (a) What is doubly significant for Omakayas about the presence of bear fur in her spirit bundle made for her by her grandmother? (cf. 37). (b) What spiritual beliefs are revealed by Nokomis's purposeful arrangement of hair in the spirit bundle (i.e., wrapping Old Tallow's hair in bear's fur)? (122).

Speculative questions. (a) Why might the repeated action of offering food and drink to a spirit bundle, which Omakayas does for a year, help to reduce the sadness one feels about losing a loved one? (122). (b) How might Old Tallow's spirit protect Omakayas? (129).

Purification Practices Questions

Relevant chapter. 5

Contextualizing event. Omakayas purifies herself in preparation for an important event in her life.

Internet research question. What traditional purification outcome is typically sought by North American Indigenous peoples?

Factual questions (55–57). (a) Who locates the special stones that will be used for purification purposes in chapter 5? (b) What purifying actions are performed by Old Tallow and Nokomis during the women's turn in the sweat lodge? (c) How are the white-hot stones moved safely to the interior of the sweat lodge? (d) Who keeps the fire going and replaces cool stones with newly heated one during the second purification round in the sweat lodge in chapter 5? (e) What important cultural event follows everyone's purification at the end of chapter 5?

Recommended Resource
Gadacz, René R. "Sweat Lodge." *Canadian Encyclopedia*. Historica Canada.

Traditional Shelters and Purification Practices (Categories 4 and 7), The Porcupine Year

Sweat Lodge Questions

Relevant chapter. 5

Contextualizing event. A sweat lodge is required by Omakayas's family members for an important family event.

Research question. What can be learned about traditional Ojibwe sweat lodges from a trustworthy website?

Recommended Resources
Anishnawbe Mushkiki, Aboriginal Health Access Centre. "Traditional Teaching: Sweat Lodge." https://mushkiki.com/our-programs/sweat-lodge/.

Sweat Lodge Building Questions

Relevant chapter. 5

Contextualizing event. Deydey calls for the building of a sweat lodge to celebrate an important family event.

Factual questions (55). (a) What materials are used by Fishtail, Angeline, Nokomis, and others to construct a traditional Ojibwe sweat lodge? (b) How is the construction of the sweat lodge in chapter 5 accomplished collaboratively?

Traditional Medicines (Categories 7), The Porcupine Year

Traditional Medicine Questions

Relevant chapter. 10

Contextualizing event. Omakayas and her grandmother collect important medicinal plants from the nearby swamp.

Factual questions (103–4). (a) What five medicinal plants does Omakayas help her grandmother to collect from the nearby swamp to replace the ones that were stolen from her in chapter 9? (b) What specific parts of these plants, as noted by Omakayas, are used medicinally by her grandmother? (c) What specific knowledge about the medicinal use of each plant does Omakayas possess? (d) How long does it take for Omakayas and her grandmother to collect all the medicinal plants they will need for the winter months?

Internet research question. What images of the medicinal plants collected by Omakayas and her grandmother are available on Wikipedia?

Valuing Dreams, Naming Feasts, and Traditional Foods (Categories 5–7), The Porcupine Year

Valuing Dreams Questions 1

Relevant chapter. 4

Contextualizing event. A future-oriented summertime conversation and dream center on Omakayas's imperious and ferocious cousin Two Strike Girl.

Factual questions. (a) What past event, recalled by Old Tallow, prompts her to speak instructively about dogs and their ability to dream? (44). (b) According to Old Tallow, how do dreams shape dogs' relationships with people? (44). (c) What dreamed event centering on Omakayas's cousin Two Strike Girl gets cut short by her brother's porcupine? (46–47).

Inferencing questions (47). (a) What pleases Omakayas about the abrupt ending of her dream about Two Strike Girl? (b) How is Omakayas taunted (or mocked) by her dream about Two Strike Girl?

Speculative question. What life-long observations about dogs have likely informed Old Tallow's beliefs about the content and source of dogs' dreams?

Valuing Dreams Questions 2

Relevant chapter. 5

Contextualizing event. Omakayas listens to details from her father's recent dream.

Factual question (56–57). What details from a recent dream does Deydey now share with Omakayas at the doorway of the sweat lodge when he and Omakayas have been purified?

Speculative question. Why does Deydey choose to wait until he and Omakayas have been purified in the sweat lodge before sharing details with her about his dream from the previous night?

Valuing Dreams Questions 3

Relevant chapter. 11

Contextualizing event. Omakayas has a frightening dream during the wiindigoo moon.

Factual questions. (a) Why does Omakayas seek to dream about animals during the wiindigoo moon? (113). (b) What prevents Omakayas from dreaming during the wiindigoo moon? (113–14). (c) What details from her dream about the bear woman does Omakayas recall when she wakens during the night, dizzy and frightened? (114). (d) What specific detail from Omakayas's dream fills her with dread? (114–15). (e) Why does Omakayas seek her bear spirit after her frightening dream about the bear woman? (115–16).

Naming Feast Questions

Relevant chapter. 5

Contextualizing event. Omakayas's parents and other family members hold a special naming feast for her.

Factual questions. (a) What remarkable sight centered on his daughter Omakayas does Deydey behold for himself during his timely emergence from the woods? (53). (b) How is Omakayas injured by her physical encounter with an eagle? (53). (c) Why, for Deydey, does Omakayas's encounter with an eagle warrant a feast? (53). (d) What are Omakayas's first thoughts about receiving a new name? (54). (e) Why does Omakayas feel so strangely buoyant while helping her father to replenish the meat on the drying rack? (54). (f) What special dishes does Omakayas's mother Yellow Kettle prepare for her daughter's naming feast? (55). (g) What new name does Omakayas receive from her father after their purification? (57).

Traditional Food Questions

Relevant chapters. 3–5, 7–10, 16

Food group classification question. What is the focus of each traditional Indigenous food group identified above in the section "Traditional Indigenous Foods"?

Factual question. What Groups 1–6 traditional Ojibwe foods are identified in each chapter or chapter set listed below?

a. Group 1 foods: chapters 4, 8, 10 (40, 80, 103)
b. Group 2 foods: chapters 3 and 4 (29, 48)
c. Group 3 foods: chapter 3 (29)
d. Group 4 foods: chapters 4, 9, 10 (33, 89, 103, 108)
e. Group 5 foods: chapters 4 and 7 (75, 174)
f. Group 6 foods: chapters 5 and 16 (49, 181)

Question Set 3: Group C Features

Stories (Category 8), The Porcupine Year

Stories Of Culture Heroes Questions: Nanabozho

Relevant chapter. 12

Contextualizing event. Nokomis tells Omakayas a story about the Ojibwe culture hero Nanabozho.

Factual questions (120–31). (a) Why is it necessary for Nanabozho to be near the buffalo in order to kill one for a meal? (b) How do the buffalo respond to Nanabozho's request to smell them? (c) How differently does Nanabozho address the buffalo a second time when he seeks to lure one close? (d) What explanation does Nanabozho offer the buffalo for wanting to smell them? (e) What happens to the lured buffalo that allows himself to be smelled? (f) What do Nanabozho's arms each seek to gain by controlling Nanabozho's knife? (g) How does Nanabozho try to pacify his arms calmly? (h) How does Nanabozho use his knife to teach his arms to listen to him? (i) How do his arms respond to this lesson? (j) How does the fallen buffalo regain its freedom? (k) What parting words does the newly freed buffalo share with Nanabozho within smelling distance of him?

Speculative questions. (a) What elements in this story of Nanabozho would Omakayas likely find entertaining? (b) What is instructive about this story? (c) What insights about herself might Omakayas gain from the story?

Stories about Legendary Individuals Questions: Bear Girl

Relevant chapter. 12

Contextualizing event. Nokomis tells Omakayas a legendary story about Bear Girl.

Story structure note. The story of Bear Girl unfolds in four parts.

Part 1 factual questions (122–23). (a) What is distinctive about the appearance of the old couple's third daughter Makoons (Little Bear)? (b) What details about Makoons's family members are shared in this first part of the story?

Part 2 factual questions (123–24). (a) What motivates Makoons's two older sisters to leave their home secretly one day and run off to a faraway village? (b) Why are Makoons's sisters ashamed of her? (c) What sequence of actions do Makoons's sisters take to prevent her from following them to the faraway village? (d) Why do Makoons's sisters suddenly change their mind about Makoons when she joins them on the bank of a turbulent river? (e) What is Makoons's purpose for accompanying her sister to the faraway village?

Part 3 factual questions (124–26). (a) Why does Makoons advise her sisters to exercise caution in their interactions with an old woman and her daughters on the way to the faraway village? (b) What observations make Makoons suspicious about the beautiful silver earrings the old woman gives her sisters to wear? (c) What actions does Makoons take in the old woman's lodge to keep her sisters safe? (d) What makes the old woman so angry that she seizes the moon and sun from the sky and locks them away in her lodge? (e) How do the three sisters manage to locate the faraway village in the dark?

Part 4 factual questions (126–28). (a) How does Makoons agree to help the village as soon as she arrives? (b) What compensation does Makoons seek for helping the village? (c) How does Makoons retrieve the moon and sun from the old woman's lodge? (d) How does the village chief compensate Makoons for her efforts? (e) How specifically does Makoons's new husband mistreat her? (f) What direction does Makoons give her husband to be free of her? (g) How is Makoons transformed by the fire she emerges from? (h) What is Makoons's purpose for returning home to live with her parents?

Speculative questions. (a) What elements in this story about the legendary Bear Girl would Omakayas likely find wondrous? (b) How might Omakayas use Bear Girl's experiences and ways of responding to challenging situations in the story to shape her own development as a young Ojibwe woman?

Personal Stories Questions: Old Tallow

Relevant chapter. 16

Contextualizing event. Nokomis tells Omakayas a personal story about Tallow.

Prefatory note. Nokomis's personal story about Old Tallow unfolds in six parts. Nokomis titles the story "The Girl Who Lived With the Dogs" and stops twice during the story to speak to Omakayas briefly about two important story topics.

Part 1 factual questions: Tallow becomes an orphan (122–23). (a) At what point was young Nokomis forced to stop playing with her childhood best friend young Tallow (i.e., Light Moving in the Leaves)? (b) What forced young Nokomis and Tallow to stop playing with each other? (c) What is similar about the way Omakayas and young Tallow were orphaned during childhood?

Part 2 factual questions: Tallow is sold to a voyageur (171–72). (a) How does the novice voyageur Charette, young Tallow's new owner, use her in his business near a long portage? (b) How does young Tallow fare carrying her first man-size load of supplies on her back through the forest?

Part 3 factual questions: Tallow is treated like a dog by her new owner (172). (a) In what ways does young Tallow's unscrupulous new owner Charette treat her like a dog? (b) How does young Tallow first fare sleeping and eating with Charette's dogs?

Part 4 factual questions: Tallow becomes stronger (171–72). (a) How does young Tallow manage to become stronger despite her habitual mistreatment by Charette? (b) What does Charette do when he discovers young Tallow cracking bones and eating marrow from the bones like a dog? (c) What prevents young Tallow from noticing her increasing strength? (d) In what ways is young Tallow mistreated by Charette during the winter months? (e) What positive effect does ingesting bone marrow have on young Tallow? (f) How does Charette denigrate young Tallow socially?

Part 5 factual questions: Tallow stands tall (175–77). (a) What sudden realization propels young Tallow to stand up to Charette one notable day? (b) How do the dogs help young Tallow to stand defiantly against Charette? (c) What changes in Charette are quickly discernible to young Tallow? (d) What kindness does young Tallow show Charette after he pleads for her help?

Part 6 factual questions: Tallow is freed by the dogs (177–78). (a) What do the dogs tell young Tallow during her long consultation with them that compels her to leave Charette's fate in their hands? (b) What justice do the dogs serve on Charette?

Extended Family Households (Category 9), The Porcupine Year

Extended Family Campsite Household Questions

Relevant chapters. 3, 6, 7, 9

Contextualizing event. Omakayas travels north by canoe with her family.

Factual questions. (a) What nuclear family members, grandparents, in-laws, and other relatives (uncle and cousin) does Omakayas identify as members of her extended family campsite household in chapter 3? (23–24). (b) What circumstances in chapter 6 enlarge Omakayas's extended family campsite household by two? (60–65). (c) What are the names of the two new family members? (79). (d) What circumstances in chapter 9 reduce Omakayas's extended family campsite household by two? (93–98).

Question Set 4: Group D Features

Divestments and Disease (Category 10), The Porcupine Year

Forced Relocation From Homeland and Other Divestment Questions

Relevant section and chapters. Prologue, 7, 10, 11

Contextualizing event. Omakayas and members of her extended household travel north by canoe searching for a new place to live.

Background questions 1 (Book 2, chapter 2, TGOS): The Removal Order. (a) What details about the American government's removal order for Ojibwe people does Omakayas learn about in chapter 2? (20–21). (b) What concerns Omakayas's father about relocating his family members to the lands set aside for them in the west by the American government? (21–22). (c) Why does Fishtail volunteer to travel west on his own and spend a year with the Ojibwe people who have already settled on the new land provided for them by the American government? (22–24).

Background questions 2 (Book 2, chapter 16, TGOS): Fishtail's Report. (a) What does Omakayas note about Fishtail's appearance while standing close to him on the lakeshore? (234). (b) What details does Fishtail include in his report about the quality of food and its effect on people at the new Ojibwe settlement in the west; the American government's position on the removal order; the arrival of an agent of the United States government; and the agent's forthcoming announcement? (234–35). (c) How do the people on the lakeshore, listening to Fishtail, respond to his report? (234–35). (d) How does Omakayas personally respond to Fishtail's report? (235–36).

Background questions 3 (Book 2, chapter 16, TGOS): Forced Relocation from Homeland. (a) What essential items does Omakayas help Nokomis to pack in preparation for their forced departure from the Island of the Golden-Breasted Woodpecker, their ancestral homeland? (236–37). (b) How does Nokomis respond to Omakayas's concern about her permanent separation from the little man who has faithfully helped her since childhood? (238). (c) What other essential items do Omakayas and her family members take with them for their forced relocation and long journey northward by canoe? (239).

Background questions 4 (Book 2, chapter 16, TGOS): Material Losses. (a) What material losses envisioned by Omakayas while listening to Fishtail's dispiriting report will her family members and other Ojibwe people experience by their forced relocation from the Island of the Golden-Breasted Woodpecker? (234–35). (b) What possessions and pets are Omakayas and her family members forced to leave behind in preparation for their forced departure from their ancestral lands? (239–40).

Factual questions. (a) What information about the forced relocation of young Omakayas, her family members, and other Ojibwe people from their ancestral homeland in 1852 is reported in the prologue? (xi). (b) What danger, anticipated by Deydey in Book 2 (TGOS 21–22), becomes terribly real for Omakayas and members of her family during their relocation northward from their homeland in chapter 7? (74–79). (c) What unexpected hardships recorded in chapters 10 and 11 would likely have been averted had Omakayas and her family members not been forced to relocate from their homeland? (99–119).

Smallpox Questions

Relevant chapter. 16

Contextualizing event. Omakayas learns from her grandmother how Tallow's life completely changed course because of smallpox.

Internet and book research questions. (a) What can be learned about the infectious disease known as smallpox from trustworthy websites like Wikipedia or book sources? (b) What symptoms are exhibited by people infected with smallpox? (c) How is smallpox most often transmitted from person to person? (d) How does an infected person appear when covered with ordinary smallpox bumps? (e) What is distinctive about a person's appearance when infected with hemorrhagic smallpox? (f) What impact did smallpox have on North American Indigenous peoples? (g) Which North American smallpox epidemic most severely impacted the Indigenous people of the Great Lakes, and most notably Ojibwe people?

Background questions (Book 1, TBH). (a) What details about Omakayas's own infection with smallpox appears in the introductory and final chapter in Book 1? (1–2, 232–37). (b) What event reported in chapter 10 changed the course of the winter for residents of the Island of the Golden-Breasted Woodpecker? (142). (c) What action did island residents take after the winter gathering dance to protect themselves from the deadly sickness that killed a voyageur? (142–43). (d) How does the spread of smallpox on the island following the winter gathering dance affect Omakayas's family members? (143–55). (e) How does Omakayas respond to the death of her baby brother? (156–59).

Factual question (171). How did smallpox change the course of Tallow's life at age ten?

Speculative questions (171). (a) What difficulties would a ten-year-old face caring for loved ones infected with smallpox? (b) Who likely urged young Tallow to burn the possessions of her dying and deceased family members? (c) What difficulties would a ten year-old face burning the possessions of her parents and other loved ones? (d) Why would Tallow wait so many years before sharing these experiences with her best friend Nokomis?

Recommended Resources
Robertson, R. G. *Rotting Face: Smallpox and the American Indian*. Caldwell, ID: Caxton Press, 2001.
Wikipedia. "History of Smallpox." https://en.wikipedia.org/w/index.php?title=History_of_smallpox&oldid=1160219825.
Wikipedia. "Native American Disease and Epidemics." https://en.wikipedia.org/w/index.php?title=Native_American_disease_and_epidemics&oldid=1159342885.
Wikipedia. "Smallpox." https://en.wikipedia.org/w/index.php?title=Smallpox&oldid=1162337468.

REFERENCE LIST

Hirschfelder, Arlene, and Paulette Molin. *Encyclopedia of Native American Religions.* New York: Checkmark Books, 2001.

Chapter 4

Historical Worlds (1759–1864)

CHAPTER OVERVIEW AND TARGET QUESTIONS

This chapter focuses on fictional worlds in four historical novels: *The Winter People* (Bruchac 2002), and three novels in the Danny Blackgoat Series (Tingle 2013, 2014, 2017). The first novel recounts the experiences of a fourteen-year-old Abenaki boy named Saxso as he travels by canoe in 1759 seeking to rescue his mother and sisters from their white captors. The three Danny Blackgoat Series novels recount the experiences of a sixteen-year-old Navajo boy Danny Blackgoat as he struggles to live as an inmate in several internment camps for Navajo people during the years 1863–1864.

All four novels are suited for exploratory studies of indigenized worlds in grades 7–10. For this chapter, readers will seek to answer the following target questions.

What basic story details for each novel are conveyed through publisher summaries?

Which indigenizing features are specifically defined and how are they defined?

Which specific indigenizing features appear in each novel?

How is each novel subdivided for an exploratory study?

What sets of questions and recommended resources can be used to explore the indigenizing features shown in textbox 4.1?

Which specific questions and recommended resources can teachers and students use in grades 7–10 to gain insights about two Indigenous young people, Saxso and Danny Blackgoat, their families, and their communities?

Textbox 4.1.
Targeted Indigenizing Features in *The Winter People* (Bruchac 2002) and the Danny Blackgoat Series (Tingle 2013, 2014, 2017)

Group A features: notable events, ancestral lands
Group B features: wood carving, water travel, tracking, stealth, prayers, praying, purification, herding
Group C features: stories about culture heroes
Group D features: forced location from homeland, defense of homeland, recovery, restoration, forced removal from homeland, material deprivation, disdain, brutality

FOUR HISTORICAL WORLDS

Selected Series and Novels

The Danny Blackgoat Series

The Danny Blackgoat Series consists of three historical novels published for readers ages 12–16 over a period of four years from 2013–2017. The three books focus on Danny Blackgoat's personal experiences at age sixteen as a Navajo prisoner and escapee at the midway point in the American Civil War.

In Book 1 *Danny Blackgoat, Navaho Prisoner* (Tingle 2013), Danny is arrested near his home in Canyon De Chelly, New Mexico, and transported by foot to a Civil War prison in Texas. In Books 2–3, *Danny Blackgoat, Rugged Road to Freedom* (Tingle 2014) and *Danny Blackgoat, Dangerous Passage* (Tingle 2017), Danny—first as an escapee and then as a recaptured prisoner—seeks to unify his family and resume his life as a herder in his ancestral homeland.

Bibliographic Information and Individual Summaries

Tingle, Tim. 2013. *Danny Blackgoat, Navajo Prisoner.* 7th Generation. Paperback. 151 pages. Seventeen chapters. Includes an author's note. Not illustrated. Historical fiction. Grades 7–10 novel. Not leveled.

Story details from publisher's website. Danny Blackgoat is a teenager in Navajo country when United States soldiers burn down his home, kill his sheep, and capture his family. They are forced, along with other captured Navajo, to march on the Navajo Long Walk of 1864. During the journey, Danny is labeled a troublemaker and given the name Fire Eye. Refusing to accept captivity, he is sent to Fort Davis, Texas, a Civil War prisoner outpost.

There he battles bullying fellow prisoners, rattlesnakes, and abusive soldiers until he meets Jim Davis. Davis teaches Danny how to hold his anger and starts him on the road to literacy. In a stunning climax, Davis—who builds coffins for the dead—aids Danny in a daring and dangerous escape. Set in troubled times, Danny Blackgoat, Navajo Prisoner is the story of one boy's hunger to be free and to be Navajo.

Tingle, Tim. 2014. *Danny Blackgoat, Rugged Road to Freedom.* 7th Generation. Paperback. 163 pages. Twenty-one chapters. Not illustrated. Historical fiction. Grades 7–10 novel. Not leveled.

Story details from publisher's website. This second volume of the trilogy continues the dramatic story of Danny Blackgoat, a Navajo teenager who, after being labeled a troublemaker on the Long Walk of 1864, is separated from his family. After a daring escape from prison in the first volume, in this second volume Danny must face many dangerous obstacles in his effort to rescue his family and find freedom. Whether it's soldiers and bandits chasing him or the dangers of the harsh desert climate, Danny ricochets from one bad situation to the next but his bravery doesn't falter and he never loses faith.

Tingle, Tim. 2017. *Danny Blackgoat, Dangerous Passage.* 7th Generation. Paperback. 162 pages. Twenty-two chapters. Includes an afterword and recommended resources. Not illustrated. Historical fiction. Grades 7–10 novel. Not leveled.

Story details from publisher's website. Suspected horse thief Danny Blackgoat narrowly escapes capture by the authorities as he makes the dangerous journey to reunite with his family being held in prison. Along his route, Danny helps old friends, continues to dodge capture, and falls in love. As he nears his destination, he knows he must be very diligent to avoid danger, but when Danny is told his beloved friend Jim Davis is charged with the horse theft, Danny surrenders. Now the fate of both men lies in the balance between the hangman's noose and an unlikely turn of events.

Bruchac, Joseph. 2002. *The Winter People.* New York: Dial Books. Hardcover. 168 pages. Twenty-nine chapters. Includes an author's note. Not illustrated. Historical fiction. Grades 7–10 novel. Guided Reading Level X. Lexile Measure 800L.

Story details from front flap. Saxso is fourteen when the British attack his village. It's 1759, and war is raging in the northeast between the British and the French with the Abenaki people—Saxso's people—by their side. Without enough warriors to defend their homes, Saxso's village is burned to the ground. Many people are killed, but some, including Saxso's mother and two sisters, are taken hostage. Now it's up to Saxso, on his own, to track the raiders and bring his family back home . . . before it's too late.

The Winter People: Key Fictional World Details

Specific Indigenous Groups and Individuals
   Abenaki, Saxso (age 14)
Historical Settings
   1759, British Territories (Now Vermont and southern Quebec), St. Francis
to Crown Point (see front matter map)

Danny Blackgoat Series: Key Fictional World Details

Specific Indigenous Groups and Individuals
   Navajo, Danny Blackgoat (age 16)
Historical Settings
   1863–1864, Canyon de Chelly (New Mexico); Route from Canyon de
Chelly through Fort Sumner (New Mexico) to Fort Davis (Texas)

DEFINED FEATURES

Definitions for six indigenizing features explored in questions sets for *The Winter People* (Bruchac 2002) and Danny Blackgoat Series (Tingle 2013, 2014, 2017) appear below. Definitions are provided for the Category 7 feature of stealth; the Category 10 features of disdain, brutality, subjugation, and material deprivation; and the Category 12 feature of recovery. The term *material deprivation* has been specifically delimited for classroom explorations of indigenized worlds in grades 5–10.

   stealth: the act of moving, proceeding, or acting in a covert way.

   disdain: the treatment of others with contempt. Disdained individuals are regarded as inferior, worthless, or despicable and are often treated abusively.

   brutality: the harsh, inhumane, cruel, or destructive treatment of others; (physically violent) actions directed at others that cause severe distress, pain, suffering, or death (i.e., murder).

   subjugation: a state of forced submission to control by others (*subjugate*, to bring under control especially by military force; to make subordinate to the will of others).

   material deprivation: The word *material* is delimited to four basic material (i.e., physical or bodily) needs: food, water, shelter, and medical attention. When people are intentionally denied access to one or more of these four basic material needs by others, they may be rightfully described as experiencing material deprivation.

recovery: the act or state of getting back or regaining; the regaining of something lost or taken away.

SAXSO'S WORLD IN *THE WINTER PEOPLE*

Features Summary

The fictional world in the Indigenous novel *The Winter People* (Bruchac 2002) is indigenized by forty-five features in the categories of time, tribal history, ancestry, religious beliefs and practices, cultural values, cultural events, cultural traditions, language use and stories, kinship, divestment, subjugation, and disease, defense and leadership, recovery and restoration. The full set of indigenizing features for this stand-alone historical novel is shown in textbox 4.2.

Textbox 4.2.
Indigenizing Features Summary for *The Winter People* (Bruchac 2002)

Group A features: (1) Time: prescience (foresight); (2) Tribal History: notable events; (3) Ancestry: ancestral lands, ancestral identity, ancestral beings, ancestral symbols

Group B features: (4) Religious Beliefs and Practices: beliefs about the Creator, spirit helpers, guides, protectors, spiritual travel, sacred drums and drumming; (5) Cultural Values: expressing gratitude; (6) Cultural Events: traditional songs and singing, celebratory dance; (7) Cultural Traditions: tracking, water travel, stealth, traditional houses, traditional shelters, boat building and repair, traditional clothes, traditional clothing accessories, wood carving, tattooing and embroidery work, traditional materials, traditional foods, traditional drinks, traditional medicines, food preparation

Group C features: (8) Language Use and Stories: ancestral language, names and naming, stories about the Creator, stories about culture heroes, mythical stories, stories about animal tricksters; (9) Kinship: extending kinship to strangers, kinship with local animals

Group D features: (10) Divestments, Subjugation, Disease: material appropriation, forced relocation from homeland, subjugation, brutality, smallpox; (11) Defense and Leadership: defense of homes and homeland, elders; (12) Recovery and Restoration: recovery, restoration

Exploratory Question Sets Focus

Five sets of exploratory questions are provided for the novel *The Winter People* (Bruchac 2002). Question set 1 focuses exclusively on the Group C feature of stories about culture heroes (Category 8). Question sets 2 and 4 focus on Group A–B features including notable events (Category 2); ancestral lands (Category 3); and wood carving, water travel, tracking, and stealth (Category 7). Question sets 3 and 5 focus on four Group D features including forced location from homeland, defense of homeland (Category 10); recovery, and restoration (Category 12).

Book Sectioning

Part I: The Attack (1–13)
Part II: Recovering Loved Ones (14–29)

Question Set 1: Group C Features

Stories about Culture Heroes (Category 8), The Winter People

Stories about Culture Heroes Questions: Gluskabe

Relevant chapter. 2

Contextualizing event. Saxso recalls a familiar story about the culture hero Gluskabe.

Internet research question. What information about Abenaki culture hero Gluskabe (also Glooskap, Glooscap, and other variations) can be found on a trustworthy website?

Factual question (10). What mythical details about the formation of a waterfall and hills in Abenaki ancestral homeland come to mind for Saxso while ruminating about the village where he and his family currently live?

Recommended Resource
Native Languages of the Americas. "Native American Legends: Glooskap (Glooscap)." www.native-languages.org/glooskap.htm.

Question Set 2: Group A–B Features

Ancestral Lands, Notable Events, and Wood Carving (Categories 2–3, 7),
The Winter People

Ancestral Lands Questions: Village Below the Falls

Relevant chapter. 2

Contextualizing event. Saxso recalls the location of an important ancestral village.

Internet research questions. (a) What modern American village now stands on land previously occupied by Saxso's grandparents and ancestors? (b) Where precisely is this modern American village located? (c) Where in proximity to present-day American cities and other notable American landmarks was the Abenaki village called Village Below the Falls located? (d) What motivated Indigenous people like Saxso's Abenaki ancestors to settle by the falls?

Factual questions (10–12). (a) How did Saxso's Abenaki ancestors obtain food at Village Below the Falls? (b) What descriptive words does Saxso use in his recollection of Village Below the Falls?

Recommended Resource
Wikipedia. "Turners Falls, Massachusetts." https://en.wikipedia.org/wiki
/Turners_Falls,_Massachusetts.

Notable Events Questions: The Turners Falls Massacre

Relevant chapter. 2

Contextualizing event. Saxso recalls details about the slaughter of loved ones by Americans that were shared with him by his great-grandfather.

Background question (12). According to Saxso's great-grandfather, what differences did Abenaki people observe in their trade relations with Indigenous, French, and American traders?

Internet research questions. (a) What information about the Turners Fall Massacre can be found on Wikipedia and other trustworthy websites? (b) What details about the massacre are recorded on the stone monument at the massacre's geographic site?

Factual questions (12–13). (a) What details about the slaughter of Abenaki people at Village Below the Falls did Saxso's great-grandfather share with him?

(b) What conclusions did his great-grandfather draw about the Americans who slaughtered his people?

Inferencing question (13). What impelled Saxso's great-grandfather to weep after sharing his personal account of the slaughter at Village Below the Falls?

Recommended Resource
Wikipedia. "Turners Falls, Massachusetts." https://en.wikipedia.org/wiki/Turners_Falls,_Massachusetts.

Wood Carving Questions

Relevant chapter. 2

Contextualizing event. Saxso recalls the wooden figure carved by his great-grandfather during his account of the Massacre at Village Below the Falls.

Inferencing question (13). What personal and cultural meaning(s) did Saxso's great-grandfather likely ascribe to the small figure of the Abenaki winter monster, Kiwakwe, that he carved out of wood in Saxso's presence?

Question Set 3: Group D Features

Forced Relocation and Defense of Homeland (Category 10), The Winter People

Forced Relocation from Homeland Questions

Relevant chapter. 2

Contextualizing event. Memories of a private conversation with an English captive named Mrs. Susannah Johnson cause Saxso to think about the forced relocation of his ancestors from their old hunting grounds by Turners Falls.

Inferencing questions (10–16). (a) How did the Turners Falls Massacre and other deadly encounters with American forces compel Saxso's Abenaki ancestors to relocate from their ancestral homeland by Turners Falls? (b) Why did Saxso's ancestors retreat north?

Defense of Homeland Questions

Relevant chapters. 1–6

Contextualizing event. A handful of men vow to defend their home village of St. Francis from an attack by long knives (i.e., American soldiers).

Background questions. (a) What alarming message about his home village of St. Francis does Saxso receive outside the Council Hall near the end of chapter 1? (8–9). (b) Why does this message and a similar one recalled by Saxso in chapter 3 make Saxso frantic? (9, 20–24). (c) What impels the majority of the people attending the dance in chapter 4 to believe the warnings about their village? (30).

Factual questions. (a) Which villagers vow to defend their village with muskets? (31). (b) What makes a successful defense of St. Francis unlikely? (36). (c) Where do armed village men position themselves for a defense? (41).

Brutality and Subjugation (Category 10), The Winter People

Brutality Questions 1

Relevant chapters. 2, 7, 8, 10, 11

Contextualizing event. Saxso recalls his great-grandfather's account of the brutal massacre of Abenaki people at Turners Falls (chapter 2). Saxso survives a brutal attack on his home village of St. Francis by a British army officer and his men (chapters 7–8, 10–11).

Internet research question. What can be learned about the military experience of British Army Officer Major Robert Rogers and his company of soldiers, known as Rogers's Rangers, from trustworthy websites like Wikipedia?

Author's note questions (160–66). (a) What details about the early morning raid on the village of St. Francis in October 1759 can be learned from Rogers's own account? (b) How does the Abenaki account of this raid differ from Rogers's account?

Factual question (54). What act of brutality committed by Rogers and his men during their attack on St. Francis makes the young man named Tomas cry?

Inferencing questions. (a) In what ways was the slaughter of Abenaki people at Village Below the Falls, as reported to Saxso by his great-grandfather, an act of brutality? (13). (b) What severe distress experienced by Saxso's family members and other Abenaki residents of St. Francis during Rogers's early morning attack in chapter 7 is surely reflected by Saxso's personal observations and experiences reported in the chapter? (44–50). (c) In what ways is the destruction of St. Francis by Rogers and his men in chapter 8—including the looting of the church, the fiery destruction of the church and people's houses, the slaughter of village dogs and farm animals, and the theft of food supplies—an act of brutality? (52–53, 64, 68).

Brutality Questions 2

Relevant chapters. 19, 20

Contextualizing event. Saxso meets a small Abenaki war party led by Chief Gill on the shores of Lake Memphremagog.

Factual question. What devastating news about the people captured and taken away by Rogers and his men does Saxso receive from Chief Gill? (112, 114–15).

Subjugation Questions

Relevant chapter. 12

Contextualizing event. Through the recounts of those who survived the attack, Saxso is able to confirm that his mother and sisters have been captured and taken away by Rogers and his company.

Background questions. (a) What does Saxso surely infer from hearing the sound of anxious voices calling out for loved ones in the village square? (53). (b) From whom does Saxso first learn that some of the villagers were captured and taken away by the White Devil (i.e., Rogers)? (56). (c) From whom does Saxso learn that his mother and sisters were among the villagers who were captured during the attack? (59). (d) Which eye witness, who was not captured during the attack on the village, confirmed the capture of Saxso's mother and two sisters by Rogers and his company? (73).

Factual questions (73–74). What details about the capture of his mother and sisters during the attack does Saxso learn from Dauphine Sausiboite in chapter 12? (b) Why does Saxso blame himself for the capture of his loved ones by the attackers? (Also see chapter 3 [17] and 5 [39])

Question Set 4: Group B Features

Water Travel, Tracking, and Stealth (Category 7), The Winter People

Water Travel Questions 1

Relevant chapters. 7–8

Contextualizing event. Saxso escapes to the other side of the river by canoe during the attack on his village.

Research question. What can be learned about traditional Abenaki canoes from trustworthy websites?

Factual questions. (a) What ancestral beings does Saxso call on for help as he crosses the river by canoe in chapter 7? (46). (b) How precisely are these beings known to help Abenaki people? (46). (c) What prompts Saxso to seek help from these beings? (46). (d) What help does Saxso seek from these beings? (46–47). (e) What difference does Saxso perceive in his movement through the water after communicating with these beings? (47). (f) What spiritual meaning does the Worrier derive from the sighting of a loon overhead during his and Saxso's return to St. Francis by canoe in chapter 8? (51).

Evaluative question (47–48). How is Saxso's flight from St. Francis by canoe during the attack both successful and unsuccessful?

Recommended Resource
Hood Museum of Art. "Northeast Woodlands: Tools & Technology." www.naaer .hoodmuseum.dartmouth.edu/northeast-woodlands/tools-technology/work-4.

Water Travel Questions 2

Relevant chapter. 13

Contextualizing event. Saxso has no coherent recollection of events when he returns to his village wounded.

Factual question (78). What distinctive set of experiences related to water travel strikes Saxso as analogous to the confusion he experiences in chapter 13 as a result of his wound?

Water Travel Questions 3

Relevant chapters. 14, 15, 17

Contextualizing event. Saxso sets out by canoe to free his mother and sisters from captivity on a route divined for him by the Worrier.

Factual questions. (a) What details does Saxso observe in chapter 14 about the new canoe found upside down by the river? (84–85). (b) What does Saxso learn from the Worrier about the ownership of the new canoe? (85). (c) How does the Worrier use dried moose bones in chapter 15 to determine the route Saxso must follow by canoe to recover his mother and sisters? (88–90). (d) What mythical knowledge obtained from his mother about rivers and water travel does Saxso recall in chapter 17? (96). (e) How does Saxso prepare to travel by water when first seated in his canoe? (99). (f) What effect does the old paddling song, sung by Saxso at the outset, have on his movement through the water? (99). (g) Why does Saxso refrain from looking down at the river while traveling swiftly along in his canoe? (99–100).

Inferencing question (100). Why does Saxso refrain from looking back at St. Francis at the end of chapter 17?

Water Travel Questions 4

Relevant chapters. 18–19, 21

Contextualizing event. Saxso continues to travel south by canoe until he reaches the Black River.

Internet research questions. (a) What is a portage? (b) Why is one or numerous portages necessary during shorter or longer journeys by water?

Factual questions. (a) How does Saxso feed himself while traveling by canoe? (102). (b) How does Saxso store his canoe at night during his travels by canoe? (103). (c) What knowledge of Indigenous plant and animal life can Saxso draw on to feed himself while traveling by canoe? (107–8). (d) For how many days does Saxso travel on his own before he meets a small Abenaki war party led by Chief Gill? (109). (e) How much longer does it take Saxso to reach the endpoint of his water travels south by canoe? (118). (f) What does Saxso do with his canoe at the endpoint in his travels by canoe? (118).

Speculative question (109). Why is the portage from St. Francis River to Lake Memphremagog relatively easy for Saxso?

Water Travel Questions 5

Relevant chapter. 28

Contextualizing event. Saxso and his loved ones return to St. Francis together.

Internet and video research question. What can be learned about traditional Abenaki dugout canoes from trustworthy websites and videos?

Factual questions. (a) What details about the submerged dugout canoe retrieved from the Winooski River by Saxso, his mother, and his sisters does Saxso personally recall in chapter 28? (151). (b) What is easy about traveling downstream aboard a dugout canoe? (151–52). (c) What stops Saxso and his family members from completing their journey home aboard the dugout canoe? (153). (d) At what point did Saxso and his family members resume their journey home by water? (155).

Speculative questions (155). (a) What dangers might Saxso have encountered during his travels home by canoe with his mother and sisters? (b) How would

Saxso explain his family's good fortune traveling home safely by canoe over the course of a month?

Recommended Resources

Brick Store Museum. "Canoe Conservation." https://brickstoremuseum.org/ education/archaeology/smar/canoe-conservation-a-step-by-step-process/.

Pemi Baker TV. *"Re-Discovered: Abenaki Canoe Dredged from Squam Lake."* YouTube. www.youtube.com/watch?v=44VuPJ-Suyo.

Tracking Questions

Relevant chapters. 18, 21

Contextualizing event. Saxso uses his tracking knowledge and skills at various times to follow the movements of his mother and sisters as captives.

Research question. What can be learned about tracking animals from trustworthy websites?

Factual questions. (a) What tracking knowledge and skills does Saxso use while traveling south by canoe in chapter 19? (109). (b) What tracking knowledge and skills does he use again in chapter 21 while traveling swiftly by foot through the forest? (118–19). (c) Whom does Saxso identify as his tracking teacher? (119). (d) What information about the movements of Rogers's men and particular Abenaki captives does Saxso obtain in chapter 22 using his tracking knowledge and skills? (123).

Inferencing question. How are Saxso's travels by land and water made safer by his tracking knowledge and skills?

Recommended Resources

Princeton University. "Guide to Animal Tracking." https://outdooraction .princeton.edu/nature/guide-animal-tracking.

Tkaczyk, F. "Tracking Animals: Understanding the Basics." Alderleaf Wilderness College. www.wildernesscollege.com/tracking-animals-2.html.

Stealth Questions

Relevant chapters. 21–25

Contextualizing event. Saxso catches up to Rogers's men in familiar territory (chapters 21–22), follows them for a way (chapters 23–25), then prepares to ambush them at a strategic location along the trail (chapter 26).

Factual questions. (a) Why does Saxso intentionally zigzag downhill in chapter 21? (118). (b) How does Saxso's mother communicate secretly with him in chapter 21? (119). (c) What lessons from his uncle's story about an ambush near Fort Carillion guide Saxso in his cautious approach to Rogers's men in chapter 22? (121–22). (d) What precisely does Saxso's stealthy advance toward the party of Rogers's men in chapter 22 entail? (121, 123, 126). (e) What information does Saxso obtain about Rogers's men and their captives by his stealthy movements through a stand of trees? (123). (f) According to Saxso, from whom did he inherit the ability to move quietly through the forest? (127–28). (g) Where does Saxso newly conceal himself in chapter 24? (133). (h) How does Saxso communicate secretly with his mother in chapter 25, and (i) what is the content of this communication? (137–38).

Question Set 5: Group D Features

Recovery and Restoration (Category 12), The Winter People

Recovery Questions

Relevant chapters. 17–28

Contextualizing event. Saxso embarks from St. Francis alone by canoe determined to recover his family members from captivity.

Summative response question (96–156). What key points from chapters 17–28 would you include in a summative account of Saxso's recovery of his captured family members?

Inferencing question (156). How does Saxso's close embrace of his uncle at the end of chapter 28 relate to Saxso's successful recovery of his family members?

Restoration Questions

Relevant chapter. 29

Contextualizing event. Saxso has significant communications with an old friend and a community elder.

Factual question (157–58). What physical restoration of the village of St. Francis does Saxso report in chapter 29?

Inferencing question (159). How surely have the personal lives of Saxso and others been restored with the restoration of village buildings?

DANNY'S BLACKGOAT'S WORLD IN THE DANNY BLACKGOAT SERIES

Features Summary

The fictional worlds in the three Danny Blackgoat novels (Tingle 2013, 2014, 2017) are indigenized by twenty-seven features in the categories of time, tribal history, ancestry, religious beliefs and practices, cultural values, cultural traditions, language use, family life and kinship, divestments, denigration, and recovery. The full set of indigenizing features for this series of historical novels is shown in table 4.1.

Table 4.1. Indigenizing Features in the *Danny Blackgoat* Series (Tingle 2013, 2014, 2017)

Group A: Time, History, Ancestry			
1. Time	DBNP	DBRRTF	DBDP
prescience (foresight)	✓		
2. Tribal History	DBNP	DBRRTF	DBDP
notable events	✓		✓
notable places	✓	✓	✓
3. Ancestry	DBNP	DBRRTF	DBDP
ancestral lands	✓		✓
ancestral identity	✓	✓	✓
ancestral symbols		✓	
Group B: Cultural Beliefs, Values, Traditions			
4. Religious Beliefs and Practices	DBNP	DBRRTF	DBDP
spiritual travel	✓		
visions	✓		✓
praying and prayers	✓	✓	✓
sacred offerings	✓	✓	✓
purification practices		✓	
5. Cultural values	DBNP	DBRRTF	DBDP
valuing dreams	✓		
6. Cultural Traditions	DBNP	DBRRTF	DBDP
traditional roles		✓	
herding	✓		✓
tracking		✓	
stealth			✓
traditional houses			✓

Group C: Language, Storytelling, Family Life, Kinship			
7. Language Use	DBNP	DBRRTF	DBDP
ancestral language	✓	✓	✓
8. Family Life and Kinship	DBNP	DBRRTF	DBDP
arranged marriages			✓
kinship with local animals		✓	

Group D: Destruction and Restoration			
9. Divestments, Denigration	DBNP	DBRRTF	DBDP
material appropriation	✓		
forced removal from homeland	✓		
material deprivation	✓		
cultural denigration	✓		✓
disdain	✓		
brutality	✓	✓	
10. Recovery	DBNP	DBRRTF	DBDP
recovery			✓

Exploratory Question Sets Focus

Two sets of exploratory questions are provided for the three historical novels in the Danny Blackgoat Series (Tingle 2013, 2014, 2017). Question set 1 focuses on Group A–B features for all three novels: prayers, praying, and purification (Category 4); and herding (Category 7). Question set 2 focuses exclusively on Group D features in the first novel, *Danny Blackgoat, Navajo Prisoner* (Tingle 2013): forced removal from homeland, material deprivation, disdain, and brutality (Category 10).

Sequence of Key Personal Events: Books 1–3

Key Personal Events: Book 1, Danny Blackgoat, Navajo Prisoner

Chapter(s)	Key Event
1	Is captured by soldiers at his home in Canyon De Chelly
2–4	Makes the long walk from Canyon De Chelly to Fort Sumner
	3 Makes a brief escape
	4 Is slung over a horse and tied there as a warning to others; maintains this position for the long journey to Fort Sumner
5	Arrives at Fort Sumner slung over a horse
	Is transported by wagon to Fort Davis
6	Arrives at Fort Davis

	Is placed in the prison barracks with confederate prisoners
	Is befriended by the wagon driver Rick
7–16	Lives day to day imprisoned at Fort Davis

7 Is made to work in the cotton fields during the day; has his first altercation with a mean-spirited prisoner named Dime; is targeted for revenge by Dime; has a supportive exchange with another prisoner named Jim Davis

8 Revives and makes a friend of Jim Davis

11 Is bitten by a rattlesnake placed in his bed by Dime; survives the snake bite because of a quick action taken by his friend Jim Davis

12 Recovers from the snake bite and receives news about his family members from Rick's wife Susan

13 Is permitted to stay at the carpenter's shop

16 Starts his escape from Fort Davis by hiding in a coffin; is buried alive in the coffin in the Fort Davis graveyard

17 Is freed from the coffin by Jim Davis and Rick
Begins his long journey home to Canyon de Chelly as an escaped prisoner with a horse and provisions

Key Personal Events: Book 2, Danny Blackgoat, Rugged Road to Freedom

Chapter(s)	Key Event
1–2	Stops to drink water ten miles from Fort Davis and comes dangerously close to being shot by the daughter of a ranching family named Grady; has a friendly encounter with the family and shares a meal with them
3–8	Is met and transported a distance by Rick before being taken captive by a small band of slavers; is freed from the slave traders close to the Grady ranch when Mr. Grady and his ranch hands kill all but one slaver named Manny; avoids being shot by the surviving slaver when Rick comes to his rescue
9–13	Returns secretly to the vicinity of Fort Sumner with Rick to free his family members who are camped and poorly guarded outside the fort with hundreds of other Navajo prisoners

10 Is visited by his father in a nearby canyon and learns about his other family members imprisoned at Fort Sumner

11 Is aided by his grandfather in a timely escape from the confines of the water wagon

12   Warns his grandfather and others of an imminent raid on the Fort Sumner camps by a small group of slavers led by Manny

13   Leads his family members to safety in the nearby canyon; is purified of death by his grandfather and other family members and reunited with his father

14–21   Leaves the canyon and his family members in order to help the various people who helped him as an inmate and escaped prisoner

15   Ministers to Mr. Grady whom he finds close to death near his ranch

16   Helps to bury two of Mr. Grady's ranch hands who were killed by the slavers

17   Tracks the slavers and their captives, Mrs. Grady and Sarah, to a secret fort in the canyon

18   Gains entry to the fort and shares a rescue plan with Grady's ranch hands, who are also held captive

19   Is caught by Manny in the slavers' fort

20   Collects Mrs. Grady and Sarah as the prisoners make their escape from the slavers' fort

21   Volunteers to live with the Grady family for a while to help them to rebuild their ranch

Key Personal Events: Book 3, Danny Blackgoat, Dangerous Passage

Chapter(s)	Key Event
1–2	Spends the night at a safe distance from the slavers' fort

1   Has a nightmare about his recent imprisonment at and escape from Fort Davis; climbs the tallest hill nearby to say a prayer and sprinkle corn pollen

2   Has an unexpected encounter with Jim Davis at his prayer site on the hilltop

3–9   Returns to the Grady ranch briefly with the Grady family, the surviving ranch hands, and Rick before speeding off with Rick to Fort Sumner on horseback

6   Has a nightmare about his favorite sheep Crowfoot

7   Hides awkwardly under the wagon during its inspection by a troupe of twenty soldiers; is startled by Rick's announcement of his (Danny's) betrothal to Rick's daughter Jane

8 Requests permission to marry Rick's daughter Jane—from Rick's wife Susan—as Rick leaves him near the canyon and heads for Fort Sumner alone

9 Hides in the unused coffin returned by wagon to Fort Sumner by two soldiers

10–22 Arrives at Fort Sumner with firm plans to help his imprisoned family members and Jim Davis

10 Is given temporary refuge by Jim Davis in the carpenter's shop; updates Jim Davis on recent events beyond Fort Sumner

12 Informs Jim Davis that he is needed by his family members and must leave the carpenter's shop; has a brief visit with Jane who comes to the shop on her own

14 Hides in one Navajo camp outside the fort and has his wounds treated by his grandfather

15 Hides among the rocks on the hillside beyond the fort to avoid capture by the soldiers following his bloody trail

18 Learns from Rick that Jim Davis will be hanged in a hour

19 Returns to Fort Sumner with Rick and turns himself in

20 Confesses to Major Henson that he—and not Jim Davis—stole Fire Eye from Fort Sumner during his escape

21 Resolves not to run or cause trouble at the execution site; prays and waits for Rick's next move

22 Shares the story of his capture and escape with General Bucknell; is permitted by General Bucknell to work in the carpenter's shop with Jim Davis; prays with Sarah on the hillside the next morning

Question Set 1: Group B Features

Herding (Category 7), Danny Blackgoat, Navajo Prisoner

Herding Questions 1: Navajo sheep herding (1860 to present)

Book, video, and Internet research questions. (a) What material value does sheep herding have for Navajo people? (b) What spiritual value does sheep herding have for Navajo people? (c) What is unique about the species of sheep raised by Navajo people? (d) What responsibilities do Navajo sheep herders have? (e) What special sheep herding skills do young Navajo people need to develop during childhood and adolescence?

<u>Inferencing questions</u>. (a) What sheep herding responsibilities would a young Navajo man of sixteen (Danny Blackgoat's age) have in the early 1860s? (b) What special sheep herding skills and sensitivities would a young Navajo man have developed by age sixteen?

<u>Recommended Resources</u>

Birchfield, D. L. *Navajo*. Milwaukee, WI: Gareth Stevens Publishing, 2004.

Bird, F. A., and Kelsey Dayle John. *Navajo*. Minneapolis, MN: Checkerboard Library, 2022.

Bowman, Donna Janell. *The Navajo: The Past and Present of the Diné*. North Mankato, MN: Capstone Press, 2016

Craats, Rennay. *The Navajo*. New York: Smartbook Media, 2018.

Cunningham, Kevin, and Peter Benoit. *The Navajo*. New York: Children's Press, 2011.

Dwyer, Helen, and D. L. Birchfield. *Navajo History and Culture*. New York: Gareth Stevens Publishing, 2012.

Kyle, Amarie. *Navajo*. New York: PowerKids Press, 2016.

McIntosh, Kenneth. *Navajo*. Philadelphia: Mason Crest, 2004.

Orr, Tamra. *The Navajo*. Kennett Square, PA: Purple Toad Publishing.

Reed, Jack, dir. *Navajo: The Herding Life*. Salt River Project Videotape Production, 2016.

Thomson, Peggy, and Paul Conklin. *Katie Henio Navajo Sheepherder*. New York: Cobblehill Books/Dutton, 1995.

Herding Questions 1: Danny Blackgoat's sheep and sheep herding routines

<u>Relevant chapter</u>. 1

<u>Contextualizing event</u>. At sunrise, Danny leads his small herd of sheep to good grazing land at the end of the Canyon de Chelly.

<u>Factual questions (1–2)</u>. (a) At what time of the day does Danny routinely take his sheep to graze? (b) Where are the Blackgoat sheep kept? (c) How does Danny greet his sheep as he releases them from the corral? (d) What name did Danny give his favorite sheep? (e) What is distinctive about Danny's favorite sheep? (e) Where does Danny take his sheep to graze today? (f) What impels Danny to graze his sheep hurriedly today?

<u>Inferencing question (2)</u>. What knowledge has Danny surely acquired about stormy weather in Canyon de Chelly and its impact on sheep?

<u>Speculative questions (1–2)</u>. (a) Why might Danny think of his sheep more as pets than livestock? (b) What circumstances might have impelled Danny to name his favorite sheep Crowfoot?

Prayers and Praying (Category 4), Books 1–3

Prayer and Praying Questions 1: Book 1, *Danny Blackgoat, Navajo Prisoner*

Relevant chapter. 1

Contextualizing event. High up on the canyon wall, Danny looks out on his world and recites a prayer taught to him by his grandfather.

Internet research questions (3). (a) What does corn pollen look like? (b) How do Navajo people obtain corn pollen? (c) What is the spiritual significance of corn pollen for Navajo people?

Factual questions (3–4). (a) Where does Danny situate himself to pray? (b) In which direction does Danny face when reciting his prayer? (c) Who taught Danny this prayer? (d) What action does Danny perform first before reciting his prayer? (e) How many full sentences appear in Danny's prayer? (f) What word begins the prayer? (g) What groups of words are repeated in the prayer? (h) Which groups of words are repeated most often in the prayer? (i) What directional words (prepositions) appear in the prayer? (j) What does Danny see in each direction looking out on his world? (k) What full sentence ends the prayer?

Inferencing questions (3–4). (a) How does Danny sprinkle corn pollen on the dawn? (b) Why does Danny address his prayer to the rising sun and first rays of morning light? (c) What distinguishes a house made of dawn from other kinds of houses? (d) What makes everything (beyond and within) so notably beautiful to Danny?

Speculative questions (3–4). (a) Why does the prayer open with the longest sentence and close with the shortest sentence? (b) What is reassuring about the use of the future tense in the closing sentence of the prayer? (c) What circumstances might have inspired or compelled Danny's grandfather to compose this prayer in the past?

Personal experience questions. (a) How does corn pollen feel in the palm of your hand? (b) How does corn pollen feel on your fingertips? (c) What sensations accompany the action of sprinkling corn pollen in the air? (d) What sensations accompany the action of watching a sunrise outdoors?

Prayer and Praying Questions 2: Book 1, *Danny Blackgoat, Navajo Prisoner*

Relevant chapter. 16

Contextualizing event. Danny seeks strength through prayer while buried underground.

Factual questions (135–40). *First day underground.* (a) Who does Danny think about first when he is alone in the Fort Davis graveyard buried underground? (b) Who does Danny think about next? (c) What memory of his favorite sheep comes to life for Danny at that moment? (d) Whose sudden presence soon comforts Danny? (e) What series of comforting effects does this presence have on Danny? *Second day underground.* (f) What worries Danny when he awakens the next day still buried underground? (g) What comforting effect do Navajo songs bring Danny? (h) What fearful sequence of thoughts takes hold of Danny when for the first time he touches the chest of the dead man lying in the coffin with him? (i) What contrasting thoughts about Jim Davis and his grandfather are prompted by the strong smell of leather in the coffin? (j) What Navajo prayer does Danny recite at this point?

Speculative question (140). What compels Danny to recite his grandfather's prayer fully?

Prayer and Praying Questions 3: Books 1–2, *Danny Blackgoat, Navajo Prisoner* and *Danny Blackgoat, Rugged Road to Freedom*

Relevant chapter (Book 2). 9

Contextualizing event (Book 2). Danny spends the night alone in a canyon close to Fort Sumner after escaping from Fort Davis with the help of friends.

Factual question (Book 2: 67–68). Where does Danny position himself to pray on his first morning in the canyon close to the Navajo campsites at Fort Sumner?

Comparison questions (Books 1–2; see page references previously provided). (a) What is similar and different about the site of Danny's sunrise prayer here in Book 2 near Fort Sumner and the sites of his sunrise prayers in Book 1? (b) What is similar and different about the wording of the sunrise prayers at these three sites? (c) What is similar and different about Danny's demeanor before and after reciting his grandfather's sunrise prayer at these three sites?

Prayer and Praying Questions 4: Book 2, *Danny Blackgoat, Rugged Road to Freedom*

Relevant chapter. 13

Contextualizing event. Danny recites his grandfather's sunrise prayer surrounded by family members after his cleansing from death.

Factual question (95–96). How does Danny respond to his grandfather's invitation to bless the morning?

Inferencing question (94–96). What physical sensations does Danny experience before reciting the sunrise prayer?

Speculative questions (96). What prompts Danny to walk quietly away from family members to recite his grandfather's sunrise prayer? (b) Why does this recitation of his grandfather's prayer, like the earlier recitation in chapter 9, repeat the phrase about nothing changing?

Prayer and Praying Questions 5: Book 3, *Danny Blackgoat, Dangerous Passage*

Relevant chapters. 1, 8, 12, 21, 22

Contextualizing event. Danny prays numerous times on his return to Fort Sumner.

Factual questions (7, 57, 85, 146–48, 154, 157). (a) Where is Danny positioned each time he prays near or at Fort Sumner? (b) Who stands close to or with Danny while he prays at various times? (c) What is distinctive about Danny's prayers in chapters 12 and 21? (d) What memory of praying enters Danny's thoughts when he learns that he and Jim Davis will both be hanged for horse stealing?

Inferencing questions. (a) Why does it make sense for Danny to pray more often now than before his return to Fort Sumner in Book 3? (b) Why, in chapter 21, does General Bucknell assume that Danny offers a silent prayer while sharing his experiences of being in a coffin? (c) Why, from the end of Book 1 through to the end of Book 3, does Danny continue to pray and recite his grandfather's sunrise prayer word for word without altering it?

Purification Practices (Category 4), Book 2, *Danny Blackgoat, Rugged Road to Freedom*

Relevant chapters. 12, 13

Contextualizing event. Danny leads his family members to safety up a steep hill to a special location high on the mesa overlooking Fort Sumner.

Video research question. *Navajo Traditional Teachings YouTube Channel*: "Traditional Navajo View on Death and Grieving." According to Navajo historian Wally Brown, what events in Navajo history caused Danny's ancestors to fear dead people and to move away from dead bodies as quickly as possible?

Factual question 1 (87). What is special about the location high on a hill on the other side of the arroyo—high up on the mesa—beyond the Navajo campsites where Danny is directed by his father to lead his family members?

Factual questions II (93–96). (a) What did Danny learn about death (i.e., dead people) growing up? (b) What sequence of actions does Danny's grandfather engage in to cleanse (i.e., purify) Danny from death? (c) What happens to Danny during the cleansing ceremony when Danny slumps over and rests his chin on his chest? (d) At what point does the cleansing ceremony end?

Inferencing questions (94–99). (a) What has made Danny unclean (i.e., impure) and needing to be cleansed (i.e., purified) in a formal Navajo ceremony? (b) Why is it necessary for someone like Danny's grandfather to take a leading role in cleansing Danny from death? (c) What compels Danny's grandfather to perform a purification ceremony so quickly for Danny? (d) What makes the sound of his grandfather's rattle sound so sweet to Danny? (e) Why is nothing more said about Danny's unclean encounter with a dead person after he faces the morning sun and recites his grandfather's prayer fully?

Question Set 2: Group D Features

Forced Removal from Homeland (Category 10), Book 1, Danny Blackgoat, Navajo Prisoner

Forced Removal Questions 1: The Long Walk

Relevant chapters. 1–4

Contextualizing event. Members of the Navajo Nation like sixteen-year-old Danny Blackgoat and his family members were forcefully removed from their homeland in Canyon de Chelly in the spring of 1864.

Book and Internet research questions. (a) What circumstances prompted Major General James H. Carleton to order the invasion of Canyon de Chelly by American soldiers in the winter of 1863–1864? (b) How did the leader of this invasion, American frontiersman and American army colonel Kit Carson, secure the surrender of Navajo people in Canyon de Chelly and elsewhere? (c) Why were Navajo prisoners like the Blackgoat family forced to travel by foot a distance of roughly three hundred miles from Canyon de Chelly to Fort Sumner in the spring of 1864? (d) What were Navajo people told about the reason for their forced removal from their homeland? (e) How many forced removals from their homeland did Navajo people experience during the years 1864–1868? (f) For how many days did Navajo prisoners typically walk before arriving at Fort Sumner?

Recommended Resources
Bial, Raymond. *The Long Walk: The Story of Navajo Captivity.* New York: Benchmark Books, 2003.

Bruchac, Joseph, and Shonto Begay. *Navajo Long Walk: The Tragic Story of a Proud People's Forced March from Their Homeland.* Washington, DC: National Geographic Society, 2002.

Cheek, Lawrence W. *The Navajo Long Walk.* Tucson, AZ: Rio Nuevo. https://archive.org/details/navajolongwalk0000chee, 2003.

Denetdale, Jennifer. *The Long Walk: The Forced Navajo Exile.* New York: Chelsea House, 2008.

Forced Removal Questions 2: Danny Blackgoat's Forced Removal from Canyon de Chelly

Relevant chapters. 1–4

Contextualizing event. Sixteen-year-old Danny Blackgoat along with his parents and sister, numerous relatives, neighboring families, and other members of the Navajo Nation are captured by one hundred soldiers on horseback and forcibly removed from their homeland in Canyon de Chelly to Fort Sumner hundreds of miles away.

Factual questions (4–15). (a) How many soldiers does Danny spot approaching his family's house, while looking down from a nearby hilltop? (b) Where do soldiers catch Danny when he returns home with his flock of sheep? (c) How do the soldiers use their rope on Danny? (d) What circumstances propel Danny to struggle against the soldiers' ropes and try to free himself? (e) How do the soldiers prevent Danny, his parents, and sister from escaping that night? By the morning, (f) how many new Navajo prisoners have appeared near the burned remains of the Blackgoat house? (g) What common elements appear in the personal reports shared by the new Navajo prisoners when they speak freely to each other about their capture? (h) What provisions are offered by soldiers to Danny and the other Navajo prisoners during their captivity before and during their forced removal to Fort Sumner? (i) How are Danny and other Navajo prisoners fed soup in chapter 3 (20)?

Speculative questions. (a) How do the Navajo prisoners support each other during their long walk to Fort Sumner? (b) Why do so few Navajo prisoners try to escape? (c) Why, in chapter 3, do Danny's father and grandfather respond so calmly to Danny when he shares his escape plans with them? (19–20).

Material Deprivation (Category 10), Book 1, Danny Blackgoat, Navajo Prisoner

Material Deprivation Questions 1: Food, Water, and Shelter

Relevant chapters. 1–3

Contextualizing event. Danny Blackgoat and roughly four hundred Navajo men, women, and children are forcibly moved from Canyon de Chelly to Fort Sumner by foot with their hands bound.

Factual questions. (a) How often are the Navajo prisoners deprived of their basic material needs of food and water during their long walk to Fort Sumner? (b) What protection from poisonous desert wildlife like scorpions and snakes are the Navajo prisoners given during their long walk to Fort Sumner?

Speculative questions. (a) How might the soldiers justify depriving the Navajo prisoners of their basic material needs of food, water, and shelter during the long walk to Fort Sumner? (b) How are the Navajo prisoners likely impacted each time they are deprived of food and water by soldiers during their long walk to Fort Sumner?

Material Deprivation Questions 2: Medical Attention

Relevant chapter. 4

Contextualizing event. Danny Blackgoat and roughly four hundred Navajo men, women, and children are forcibly moved from Canyon de Chelly to Fort Sumner by foot with their hands bound.

Factual questions. (a) How often is Danny Blackgoat in need of basic medical attention but deprived of it during the last part of the long walk to Fort Sumner? (b) What circumstances create a need for Danny to receive basic medical attention? (c) How is Danny impacted each time he is deprived of basic medical attention by soldiers?

Speculative question. How might the soldiers justify depriving Danny of basic medical attention at any point during his long walk to Fort Sumner?

Disdain (Category 10), Book 1, Danny Blackgoat, Navajo Prisoner

Disdain Questions 1: The Long Walk to Fort Sumner

Relevant chapters. 1–4

Contextualizing event. Danny Blackgoat and hundreds of Navajo men, women, and children are forcibly removed from their homeland in Canyon de Chelly by soldiers and transported as prisoners to Fort Sumner three hundred miles away.

Inferencing questions. How is the soldiers' disdain of their Indigenous (Navajo) prisoners in chapters 1–4 made manifest by (i) the manner in which Danny's favorite sheep Crowfoot is killed by a soldier (6–7); (ii) one soldier's suggested method of teaching their prisoners proper line formation and the action of spitting (9); (iii) the commanding officer's praise of a soldier's marksmanship and his order to leave the bodies of the two Navajo prisoners on the road (15); (iv) the waterman's treatment of an older Navajo woman (17); and (v) another soldier's comment about making saddles out of young Navajo men like Danny Blackgoat (30)?

Disdain Questions 2: Fort Sumner, Fort Davis

Relevant chapters. 5, 6, 11

Contextualizing event. Danny Blackgoat is transported from Fort Sumner to Fort Davis aboard a supply wagon.

Inferencing questions. How is the disdain for Indigenous (Navajo) prisoners like Danny Blackgoat of non-Indigenous civilians, soldiers, and inmates at Forts Sumner and Davis made manifest in chapters 5, 6, and 11 by (i) the jailer's suggested method of handling troublesome Indigenous (Navajo) prisoners, his comment about buzzards, and his action of spitting on the ground (33–34); (ii) a soldier's action of yanking Danny to the ground by the hair (45); and (iii) an inmate's comment about Danny being better off dead than alive (81)?

Brutality (Category 10), Book 1, Danny Blackgoat, Navajo Prisoner

Brutality Questions 1: Brutal treatment of Mr. Begay and his daughter

Relevant chapter. 2

Contextualizing event. The Navajo prisoners start to run at the sound of gunshots.

Factual questions (14–15). (a) What action do the soldiers take when the Navajo prisoners do not respond to their order to halt and keep walking? (b) How does the commanding officer respond when the prisoners at the front of the line start running? (c) Which two Navajo prisoners are quickly shot by soldiers? (d) How does the commanding officer respond to the shooting of the two Navajo prisoners?

Inferencing questions (13–15). (a) What compels the Navajo prisoners to keep walking after being ordered to stop at the appointed location for lunch? (b) What compels the Navajo prisoners to walk more quickly then run? (c) What qualifies the soldiers' treatment of Mr. Begay and his daughter as brutal?

Brutality Questions 2: Brutal treatment of Danny Blackgoat, The Long Walk to Fort Sumner

Relevant chapters. 3, 4

Contextualizing event. Danny briefly escapes from the soldiers but is quickly recaptured and brutally punished.

Factual questions (24–27). (a) How does the soldier in chapter 3 use his rifle to recapture Danny at the bottom of the canyon? (24). (b) How does the captain in chapter 4 respond to Danny's attempted escape when Danny wakes the next morning surrounded by soldiers? (26). (c) How precisely is Danny made to "ride a horse" for the remaining distance to Fort Sumner?

Speculative questions (24, 27). (a) What compels the soldier in chapter 3 to strike Danny with his rifle? (24). (b) What compels the captain in chapter 4 (i) to remove Danny's shirt himself and tie it around his neck, (ii) to do so roughly, and then (iii) to strike Danny with the butt of his rifle? (27). (c) What qualifies the soldiers' treatment of Danny as brutal?

Brutality Questions 3: Brutal treatment of Danny Blackgoat, Fort Davis

Relevant chapters. 8, 11

Contextualizing event. Danny is delivered to Fort Davis and imprisoned there.

Factual questions. (a) How precisely does Dime use his hoe to fight Danny in chapter 8 (59, 61)? (b) How does Dime's use of the hoe affect Danny during the fight (61)? (c) How does Dime's placement of a rattlesnake in Danny's bed affect Danny?

Speculative questions. (a) What impels Dime in chapter 8 (i) to use his hoe as a weapon to fight Danny and in chapter 11 (ii) to place a rattlesnake in Danny's bed? (b) What qualifies Dime's treatment of Danny as brutal?

Chapter 5

Contemporary Worlds (1990–2005)

CHAPTER OVERVIEW AND TARGET QUESTIONS

This chapter focuses on fictional worlds in two contemporary realistic novels, *Lana's Lakota Moons* (Sneve 2007) and *Where I Belong* (White 2014). The first novel recounts the experiences of a twelve-year-old Lakota girl named Lori as she moves through the last twelve months of her twin sister's life in South Dakota. The second novel recounts the experiences of a fifteen-year-old Mohawk girl named Carrie as she reclaims her Indigenous identity and returns to her ancestral homeland and birth family in Kahnawake, Quebec.

The two novels are suited for exploratory studies of indigenized worlds in grades 5–7 and 7–10 respectively. For this chapter, readers will seek to answer the following target questions.

What basic story details for each novel are conveyed through the publisher summaries?

Which indigenizing features are specifically defined and how are they defined?

Which specific indigenizing features appear in each novel?

How is each novel subdivided for an exploratory study?

What sets of questions and recommended resources can be used to explore the indigenizing features shown in textbox 5.1?

Which specific questions and recommended resources can teachers and students use in grades 5–7 and 7–10 to gain insights about two Indigenous young people, Lori and Carrie, their families, and their communities?

Textbox 5.1.
Targeted Indigenizing Features in *Lana's Lakota Moons* (Sneve 2007) and *Where I Belong* (White 2014)

Group A features: notable events, ancestral lands, identity, symbols
Group B features: traditional dancers, a celebratory dance, the hoop dance, the Lakota naming ceremony, valuing dreams, spirit guides, sacred drums, drumming
Group C features: closeness to cousins
Group D features: diabetes, defense of homes and homeland, restoration

TWO CONTEMPORARY WORLDS

Selected Novels: Bibliographic Information and Individual Summaries

Driving Hawk Sneve, Virginia. 2007. *Lana's Lakota Moons*. Lincoln: University of Nebraska Press. Paperback. 116 pages. Twelve chapters. Not illustrated. Contemporary realistic fiction. Grades 7–10 novel. Not leveled.
    Story details from front flap. Lori is a quiet, contemplative bookworm. Lana is an outspoken adventuress. Different as they are, they are first cousins, sisters in the Lakota way. And when both befriend a Hmong girl new to their school, the discovery of a culture so strange to them and so rich with possibilities brings them together as never before in an experience of life and loss. As the girls learn of the moons of the Lakota calendar, they also learn that the circle of life is never broken even when death comes to one of them.

White, Tara. 2014. *Where I Belong*. Vancouver: Tradewind Books. Paperback. 109 pages. Fifteen chapters. Not illustrated. Contemporary realistic fiction. Grades 7–10 novel. Not leveled.
    Story details from back cover. This moving tale of self-discovery takes place during the Oka Crisis in the summer of 1990. Adopted as an infant, Carrie has always felt somehow out of place. Recurring dreams haunt her, warning her that someone close to her will be badly hurt. When she discovers that her birth family is Mohawk living in Quebec, she makes the long journey and finally achieves the sense of home and belonging that have always eluded her.

Lana's Lakota Moons: Key Fictional World Details

Specific Indigenous Groups and Individuals
    Lakota, Lori (age 12)

Contemporary Settings
  Early 2000s, South Dakota

Where I Belong: **Key Fictional World Details**

Specific Indigenous Groups and Individuals
  Mohawk, Carrie (age 15)
Contemporary Settings
  1990, McDonalds Corners (Ontario), Kahnawake (Quebec)

LANA'S WORLD IN *LANA'S LAKOTA MOONS*

Features Summary

The fictional world in the Indigenous novel *Lana's Lakota Moons* (Sneve 2007) is indigenized by thirty-three features in the categories of time, tribal history, ancestry, religious beliefs and practices, cultural values, cultural events, cultural traditions, language use and stories, family life and kinship, divestments, leadership, and recovery and restoration. The full set of indigenizing features for this first contemporary realistic novel is shown in textbox 5.2.

Textbox 5.2.
Indigenizing Features Summary for *Lana's Lakota Moons* (Sneve 2007)

Group A features: (1) Time: prescience (foresight); (2) Tribal History: notable events; (3) Ancestry: ancestral lands, ancestral identity, ancestral symbols

Group B features: (4) Religious Beliefs and Practices: cosmic coherence, sacred songs, sacred drums and drumming, honoring the dead; (5) Cultural Values: valuing sharing and peaceful relations with neighboring nations; (6) Cultural Events: jingle dancers, hoop dance, grass dance, Lakota naming ceremony; (7) Cultural Traditions: traditional roles, large game hunting, tracking, traditional shelters, traditional weapons, traditional foods

Group C features: (8) Language Use and Stories: ancestral language, names and naming, stories about culture heroes, mythical stories; (9) Family Life and Kinship: sibling care, closeness to cousins, courtship, extending kinship to strangers

Group D features: (10) Divestments: forced relocation from homeland; (11) Leadership: societies; (12) Recovery and Restoration: recovery, restoration, cultural pride

---

Exploratory Question Sets Focus

Three sets of exploratory questions are provided for the contemporary realistic novel *Lana's Lakota Moons* (Sneve 2007). Question sets 1–2 focus on Group A–B features: notable events (Category 2); ancestral lands, ancestral identity, ancestral symbols (Category 3); and traditional dancers, a celebratory dance, the hoop dance, and the Lakota naming ceremony (Category 6). Question set 3 focuses exclusively on one Group C feature: closeness to cousins (Category 9).

Book Sectioning

Part I: Winter (1–3)
Part II: Spring (4–5)
Part III: Fall–Winter (6–11)
Part IV: A New Year (12)

Question Set 1: Group A Features

Notable Events (Category 2), Lana's Lakota Moons

Notable Event Questions: The Battle of Greasy Grass

Relevant chapter. 8

Contextualizing event. At the annual Buffalo Roundup in Custer State Park, Lana's younger brother Chuckie seeks details about hunting buffalo in traditional Lakota ways.

Book research questions. (a) When did the Battle of Greasy Grass take place? (b) Where did the battle take place? (c) What precipitated the battle? (d) What role did the Lakota Sioux play in the battle? (e) What did the Sioux people expect to gain from winning the battle? (f) What is significant about this battle for contemporary Sioux peoples?

Factual questions (84–85). (a) What details does Grandpa High Elk include in his recount of the last buffalo hunt engaged in by their ancestors? (b) What details about the Battle of Greasy Grass does Lori learn from her grandfather?

Inferencing question (79–88). What is personally significant for Lori about the Battle of Greasy Grass?

Recommended Resources

Brown, Dee Alexander. *Showdown at Little Big Horn*. Lincoln: University of Nebraska Press, 2004.

Burnham, Philip. *Song of Dewey Beard: Last Survivor of the Little Bighorn*. Lincoln, NE: Bison Books, 2018.

Donovan, Jim. *A Terrible Glory: Custer and the Little Bighorn—The Last Great Battle of the American West.* New York: Back Bay Books, 2009.

Duffield, Katy. *The Battle of Little Bighorn: Legendary Battle of the Great Sioux War.* Lake Elmo, MN: Focus Readers, 2017.

McLaughlin, Castle. *A Lakota War Book from the Little Bighorn: The Pictographic "Autobiography of Half Moon."* Cambridge, MA: Peabody Museum Press and Houghton Library, 2013.

Walker, Paul Robert. *Remember Little Bighorn: Indians Soldiers and Scouts Tell Their Stories.* Washington, DC: National Geographic, 2015.

Ancestral Lands, Identity, and Symbols (Category 3), Lana's Lakota Moons

Ancestral Land Questions

Relevant chapter. 7

Contextualizing event. On the way to Mount Rushmore, Lana responds to her friend Shoua's question about the naming of the Black Hills.

Book research questions. (a) Where are the Black Hills located? (b) What features of the Black Hills make them physically distinctive? (c) What role do the Black Hills play in traditional Lakota cosmology? (d) What events motivated the American government to take control of and claim ownership of the Black Hills? (e) What impact did the 1980 Supreme Court ruling in United States v. Sioux Nation of Indians have on the ownership of the Black Hills?

Factual question (67). How does Lana respond to her friend's question about the naming of the Black Hills?

Recommended Resources

Horsted, Paul, and Camille Riner. *The Black Hills: Yesterday & Today.* Third edition. Custer, SD: Golden Valley Press, 2015.

Kettlewell, Dick. *Black Hills Impressions.* Helena, MT: Farcountry Press, 2004.

Ostler, Jeffrey. *The Lakotas and the Black Hills: The Struggle for Sacred Ground.* New York: Penguin Books, 2011.

McClintock, John S., and Edward L. Senn. *Pioneer Days in the Black Hills: Accurate History and Facts Related by One of the Early Day Pioneers.* Norman: University of Oklahoma Press, 2000.

Ancestral Identity Questions 1

Relevant chapter. 4

Contextualizing event. Following the performance of the hoop dance in the school gym, Lana, Lori, and some of their classmates are ready to respond to the guest dancer's question about their ancestral identities.

Factual questions (36–37). (a) What question does the guest hoop dancer High Eagle pose that prompts students to share their ancestral identities with him? (b) Which students respond to his question? (c) How does Lana manage to respond to his question first? (d) What ancestral identities do students share with High Eagle?

Inferencing questions (36–37). (a) What is notable about Lana's response to High Eagle's question? (b) What is High Eagle's purpose for inviting students to share their ancestral identities with him after his performance of the hoop dance? (c) What is striking about the brief exchange between Andy Brown Wolf and his friend when he identifies himself as Cheyenne?

Ancestral Identity Questions 2

Relevant chapters. 1–12

Contextualizing event. Lori's ancestral identity is ever present in her speech and thoughts as she moves forward in her life, season by season, moon by moon.

Factual questions. (a) What words or phrases in Lori's speech or thoughts throughout the novel include the identifier *Lakota* (e.g., "Lakota names," "Lakota moons," "Lakota family," "the Lakota way")? (b) What details about these things help readers to understand the distinctive meanings of these Lakota things? (c) Which chapters do not include the word *Lakota* as an identifier? (d) What is the prominent word or phrase that includes the identifier *Lakota*?

Inferencing question. Why are Lakota things ever present to Lori?

Ancestral Symbol Questions

Relevant chapter. 3

Contextualizing event. One day after school, Lori and Lana learn to make star quilts, patterned after the Morning Star, with help from Grandma High Elk, a masterful quilter.

Factual questions (29–30). (a) What figurative meaning does the Morning Star hold for Lakota people according to Grandma High Elk? (b) How does Grandma

High Elk account for the popularity of the star, inspired by the Morning Star, among Lakota quilters?

Question Set 2: Group B Features

Traditional Dancers and Dances (Category 6), Lana's Lakota Moons

Traditional Dancer Questions

Relevant chapter. 9

Contextualizing event. Lana, Lori, their family members, Shoua, and Shoua's parents all attend the first night of the powwow at the Buffalo Roundup.

Video research questions. (a) What can be learned about the traditional grass dance performed at annual powwow events by Indigenous men? (b) What can be learned about the traditional jingle dance performed at annual powwow events by Indigenous women? (c) What can be learned about the inaugural entry of traditional Indigenous dancers at an annual powwow event?

Factual questions (92–95). (a) What does Lori observe about the arrival of dancers on the first night of the powwow? (b) What do the Grass Dancers do to capture Lori's attention? (c) What does Lori observe about the drumming that accompanies the entry of dancers? (d) What catches Lana's attention about the movement and sounds of a group of young women and little girls who enter the arena in satiny dresses? (e) What special name is given to this group of dancers? (f) Why is the name appropriate?

Recommended Resources
Peigan Powwow. "Shakopee Powwow 2021 Grand Entry Saturday Afternoon." YouTube. www.youtube.com/watch?v=01ItaWxopDQ.
Peigan Powwow. "Thunderchild Powwow 2021 Jingle Dress Special 18+ Dancers." YouTube. www.youtube.com/watch?v=abXDsGEQIHc.
Suite1491. "Old Style Grass Dance Contest Song 3." YouTube. www.youtube .com/watch?v=-BmH0fxnHfY.

Celebratory Dance Questions

Relevant chapter. 9

Contextualizing event. Between individual competitive dancing events, Lana, Lori, and Shoua move to the dance floor and participate in a celebratory inter-tribal dance.

Factual questions (93–94). (a) What have Lana, Lori, and Shoua brought with them to the powwow that will make the intertribal dance even more memorable for them? (b) What makes the intertribal dance challenging for Lana and Lori's fathers? (c) How does the intertribal dance differently affect Lana and Lori?

Hoop Dance Questions

Relevant chapter. 4

Contextualizing event. Lana, Lori, and their classmates learn about the hoop dance from an experienced Lakota hoop dancer and dance with hoops for the first time.

Video research question. What can be learned about the traditional hoop dance performed by Indigenous men and women in their home surroundings or at special celebratory events?

Factual questions focusing on the hoops, provided by High Elk (35–37). (a) What four values are represented by High Elk's hoops? (b) Which value does High Eagle identify as the most important value for young people like Lana and Lori? (c) What color are the hoops? (d) What groups of people are represented by the multicolored hoops?

Factual questions focusing on the hoop dancing experience (36–37). (a) What hoop dancing movements do Lana, Lori, and their classmates observe during High Eagle's performance? (b) How do the hoops appear to observers like Lana and Lori at the peak point in the dance when High Eagle is moving at his greatest speed? (c) How does Lori fare in her first experience dancing with the hoops? (d) How does Lana fare in her first experience dancing with the hoops?

Speculative questions (35–37). (a) Why does High Eagle instruct students about the hoops before performing the hoop dance? (b) Why might the values identified by High Eagle be values that appeal to many Indigenous and non-Indigenous peoples? (c) Why might the order of these values, as identified by High Eagle, be particularly significant for Lakota peoples? (d) What specific mixtures might be represented by the multicolored hoops? (e) What purpose is served by the drumbeat in the hoop dance? (f) What is the significance of the arrangement of the hoops at the peak point in the hoop dance? (g) What insights about the hoop dance and dancing does Lori gain personally as a result of High Eagle's visit to her school?

Recommended Resources
Grains in Small Places. "Crazy Horse Cultural Performance: Lakota Hoop Dance." YouTube. www.youtube.com/watch?v=EMgJdeqrc50.
HeardMuseum. "2021 Hoop Dance Winner." YouTube. www.youtube.com/watch?v=J08yaDoPfnw.

Lakota Naming Ceremony (Category 6), Lana's Lakota Moons

Pre-Ceremony Detail Questions 1

Relevant chapter. 3

Contextualizing event. Lori and Lana learn that a special naming ceremony will be held for them in the summertime.

Inferencing questions (27). (a) Why is a Lakota naming ceremony announced several months in advance? (b) What makes a star quilt a meaningful and memorable item to give away at a traditional Lakota naming ceremony?

Pre-Ceremony Detail Questions 2

Relevant chapter. 7

Contextualizing event. Lori, Lana, their mothers, and Shoua make a special trip to the fabric store to buy cloth and ribbon for the special Lakota naming ceremony outfits.

Internet research questions. (a) What do twenty-first-century Lakota ribbon dresses look like? (b) What did nineteenth-century Lakota ribbon dresses look like?

Factual question (72–73). How does Lori's mother reply to her question about ribbon dresses?

Comparison question. What are the differences and similarities between ribbon dresses made by Lakota women one hundred years ago and those made by Lakota women now?

Pre-Ceremony Detail Questions 3

Relevant chapter. 7

Factual questions (25–27). (a) Which family members decide that the time has come for Lori and Lana to have Lakota names? (b) Who announces this decision to the two girls? (c) What Lakota names have Grandma and Grandpa High Elk decided to give Lori and Lana? (d) What do the names mean in English? (e) What significance do these Lakota names have for Grandma and Grandpa High Elk? (f) What information does Lori and Lana receive from Grandma High Elk about traditional Lakota naming practices? (g) What is the larger community significance of Lakota naming ceremonies? (h) How do Lori, Lana, their family members, and others prepare for the upcoming Lakota naming ceremony? (i)

How does Grandma High Elk respond to Lori's question about the reason for giving away quilts at a Lakota naming ceremony? (j) Why does Lori take greater care stitching a quilt that will be given away at her Lakota naming ceremony in several months' time?

Contextualizing event. Lori and Lana get information and special instructions from their grandmother about their upcoming naming ceremony.

Factual questions (73). (a) What information about the upcoming naming ceremony does Lori and Lana's grandmother share with them? (b) What special instructions about the ceremony (dos and don'ts) do Lori and Lana receive from their grandmother?

Pre-Ceremony Detail Questions 4

Relevant chapter. 7

Contextualizing event. Special celebratory foods and beverages are prepared the day before the ceremony.

Factual questions (73). (a) What special foods and beverages will be served at the naming ceremony? (b) Where are these meal preparations made? (c) Who prepares the foods and beverage for the ceremony?

Inferencing question (73). Why does it make good sense for food preparations to be made by family members at Grandma High Elk's house?

Ceremony Day Detail Questions

Relevant chapter. 7

Contextualizing event. Lori, Lana, and their best friend Shoua receive new names in a special Lakota naming ceremony held at the community hall.

Factual questions (74–75). (a) What processional activities open the naming ceremony? (b) What blessings are requested at the start of the ceremony by the presiding holy men, Mr. Iron Shell and Father Jim? According to the Lakota holy man Mr. Iron Shell, (c) what is the main purpose of a Lakota naming ceremony? (d) What is special about the appointed seats for Lana and Lori? (e) Why is Shoua given an appointed seat as well? (f) What special ceremonial item is fastened to each girl's hair? (g) What special prayer, shared by Mr. Iron Shell while standing at the buffalo skull altar, accompanies the ceremonial adornment of each girl's head? (h) What celebratory activities immediately follow the ceremony?

Internet research questions (74). (a) What does an eagle plume medicine wheel look like? (b) What significance does this object bring to the naming ceremony? (c) What significance does the buffalo skull altar bring to the naming ceremony?

Inferencing question (75). Why is a public statement of gratitude from a holy man an appropriate way to end a naming ceremony?

Question Set 3: Group C Features

Closeness to Cousins (Category 9), Lana's Lakota Moons

Closeness to Cousins Questions 1: Kinship relations

Chapter relevance. 1

Factual questions (7). (a) What kinship relation makes Lori and Lana first cousins in one sense (Western paradigm) and sisters in another sense (Lakota paradigm)? (b) How much older is Lori than Lana? (c) What special responsibility does the eldest child in a Lakota family have?

Closeness to Cousins Questions 2: Parts I–II

Chapter relevance. 1–5

Factual questions (3–50). (a) How often are Lori and Lana together after school, in the evenings, on weekends, on holidays? (b) Where do Lori and Lana typically spend time together? (c) What other family members are typically present when Lori and Lana are together? (d) What activities do Lori and Lana engage in when they are together? (e) How do Lori and Lana get along when they are together?

Closeness to Cousins Questions 3: Parts III–IV

Chapter relevance. 6–12

Factual questions (53–116). (a) How often are Lori and Lana together after school, in the evening, on weekends, on holidays? (c) Where do Lori and Lana typically spend time together? (d) What other family members are typically present when Lori and Lana are together? (e) What activities do Lori and Lana engage in when they are together? (f) How do Lori and Lana get along when they are together?

Closeness to Cousins Questions 4: Relationship assessment

Chapter relevance. 1–12

Personal response questions. Based on your responses to Parts I–IV questions, (a) how would you describe Lori and Lana's relationship as sisters? (b) What is significant for you about Lori and Lana's (Lakota) relationship as sisters?

CARRIE'S WORLD IN *WHERE I BELONG*

Features Summary

The fictional world in the Indigenous novel *Where I Belong* (White 2014) is indigenized by twenty-five features in the categories of time, ancestry, religious beliefs and practices, cultural values, cultural traditions, language use and stories, family life, denigration and disease, defense, and restoration. The full set of indigenizing features for this second contemporary realistic novel is shown in textbox 5.3.

Exploratory Question Sets Focus

Textbox 5.3.
Indigenizing Features Summary for *Where I Belong* (White 2014)

Group A features: (3) Ancestry: ancestral lands, ancestral identity, ancestral symbols
Group B features: (4) Religious Beliefs and Practices: beliefs about the Creator, spirit helpers, guides, protectors, praying and prayers, sacred offerings, sacred objects (miscellaneous), sacred drums and drumming, purification practices; (5) Cultural Values: valuing dreams; (7) Cultural Traditions: traditional clothing accessories, beadwork and quillwork, tattooing and embroidery work, toy making, traditional foods, traditional drinks, traditional medicines
Group C features: (9) Family Life: extended family households
Group D features: (10) Divestments, Subjugation, Disease: harassment, diabetes; (11) Defense: defense of homes and homeland; (12) Restoration: restoration, cultural pride

Two sets of exploratory questions are provided for the novel *Where I Belong* (White 2014). Question set 1 focuses on the Group B features of valuing dreams (Category 6); spirit guides, sacred drums, and drumming (Category

4). Two types of dreams are explored in this first set: dreams experienced by Carrie for the first time (real-time dreams) and dreams recorded by Carrie in a special journal (recorded dreams). Question set 2 focuses on three Group D features: diabetes (Category 10), defense of homes and homeland (Category 11), and restoration (Category 12).

Defined Features

In exploratory studies of Indigenous novels and indigenized worlds, the Category 1, 4, and 5 features of prescience, dreamtime, visions, and (valuing) dreams are distinctively defined. Definitions for these four indigenizing features follow. For the contemporary novel *Where I Belong* (White 2014), question set 1 focuses on the feature of dreams (valuing dreams). Three types of dreams are explored: dreams unfolding in present story time (real-time dreams); dreams recorded in a special journal (recorded dreams); and dreams that forewarn (presaging dreams).

prescience: the ability or an instance of foreseeing; foresight; one's knowledge of an action or event before it occurs

dreamtime: a detached state from one's physical surroundings explicitly identified by individuals as a dreamtime experience in which significant life events unfold in a perceived world that is partly real and partly imaginary and is not equivalent to a hypnotic, cataleptic, ecstatic, or anaesthetized state

vision: a mystical experience induced by isolation, fasting, and prayer in which individuals perceive things that are not present to the eye

dream (n.): a succession of images, thoughts, or emotions passing through the mind during sleep

Book Sectioning

Part I: Partly Belonging, Chapters 1–5
Part II: Newly Belonging, Chapters 6–10
Part III: Defending One's Homeland, Chapters 11–15

Question Set 1: Group B Features

Valuing Dreams (Category 5), Where I Belong

Carrie's Real-Time Dream Questions: Dreamed Individuals

Chapter relevance questions. (a) Which chapters begin with a real-time dream? (b) Which chapters include two real-time dreams? (c) Which chapters include no real-time dreams? (d) How many real-time dreams appear in the novel altogether?

Summative response questions. (a) How frequently does Carrie appear in her real-time dreams? (b) How frequently do unnamed individuals simply identified as men (man, guy), women (woman), or children (baby) appear in Carrie's real-time dreams (see table 5.1 row 1)? (c) How frequently do family members (identified by a first name or kinship term) appear in Carrie's real-time dreams (see table 5.1 row 2)? (d) What is striking about the number of unnamed individuals that appear in Carrie's real-time dreams?

Carrie's Real-Time Dream Questions: Repeated Dream Elements

Chapter relevance. All chapters shown in table 5.1

Literal-figurative meaning questions. (a) What literal (experiential) meanings are conveyed in Carrie's real-time dreams by each repeated element in table 5.1? (b) What figurative (metaphorical) meanings are conveyed by each repeated element?

Summative response question. What is striking about one, several, or all of the repeated dream elements?

Carrie's Recorded Dream Questions

Relevant chapter. 3

Contextualizing event. Carrie records another dream in her special journal.

Table 5.1. Repeated Real-Time Dream Elements in *Where I Belong* (White 2014)

Element	Chapter
unnamed people	1–5, 7, 9–11, 13, 14
named people	8, 9, 12
bandannas	3, 8, 9, 10, 13
piled tires	3, 8, 10, 11, 13
guns	3, 8, 9, 11, 13, 15
gunfire	3, 8, 9, 13, 15
drumming	3–5, 7–9, 11–13, 15
death	5, 7–9, 13, 15
white bird	8, 9, 11, 13–15

Factual questions (25–28). (a) What repeated elements in Carrie's real-time dreams also appear in her recorded dreams? (b) Which recorded dreams are similar in content to the real-time dream that appears at the start of chapter 3? (c) What is the date range for the recorded dreams Carrie reviews in her journal in chapter 3?

Speculative question. What benefits does Carrie likely derive from recording her dreams in a journal?

Carrie's Presaging Dream Questions

Relevant chapters. 12–14

Contextualizing event. Carrie makes some startling discoveries about her dreams.

Factual questions (77–97). (a) Which real-time dreams strike Carrie retrospectively as dreams forewarning her about future events? (b) What dreamed individuals or things suddenly appear to Carrie in present time?

Carrie's Response to Dreamed Events Questions

Relevant chapters. 1, 3, 5, 7, 9, 14

Contextualizing event. Carrie crosses paths with a guy who looks remarkably similar to a guy from her dream (chapter 1). Carrie recalls a notable dream about her late neighbor then speaks to her parents about a recurring dream about an unknown woman (chapter 3). Carrie is frightened by a sequence of real-time dreams (chapters 1, 3, 5, 7, 9, 14) and gains troubling and valuable insights about her recent dreams (chapter 11).

Factual questions. (a) What scares Carrie about her recent dreams? (13, 25). (b) Whom does Carrie identify in chapter 1 as the guy who appeared to her in a recent dream? (19). (c) What was startling for Carrie about a dream she had about her neighbor? (26). (d) How does Carrie respond to her father's remark about a recurring dream involving a woman with dark hair? (30). (e) What question, prompted by her recent dream in chapter 5, makes Carrie's heart pound with fear? (42). (f) Why do the hairs on Carrie's arm prickle when she learns that her late grandfather was a sky walker? (68). (g) What troubling insights about her recent dreams does Carrie gain in chapter 11 first from comments made by her father and grandmother about the blockade and then by her travels to town? (80–81).

Inferencing questions. (a) What elements in Carrie's dream in chapter 7 make her scream (fearfully) in her sleep? (51). (b) What elements in Carrie's dreams in chapters 9 and 14 cause Carrie to wake up (fearfully) in a cold sweat? (62,

98). (c) Why does Carrie credit her dreams with saving her grandmother's life in chapter 14? (102).

Ancestral Gift Questions: The Gift of Dreams and Dreaming

Relevant chapter. 13

Contextualizing event. Carrie speaks to her grandmother about the ancestral value of dreams.

Factual questions (95). (a) What does Carrie learn from her grandmother in chapter 13 about the ancestral gift of dreams and dreaming? (b) What other family members, in addition to Carrie, received the gift of dreaming from their Mohawk ancestors?

Spirit Guides, Sacred Drums, and Drumming (Category 4), Where I Belong

Spirit Guide Questions

Relevant chapters. 13–15

Contextualizing event. Carrie clarifies her understandings about the white bird that appears to her while sleeping or awake (chapters 13–15).

Internet research questions. (a) What does a white eagle look like? (b) What makes survival especially challenging for albino wildlife? (c) What spiritual significance is ascribed by some Indigenous peoples to albino eagles, owls, bison, bears, and other animals?

Factual questions. (a) What does Carrie learn from her grandmother about the identity and purpose of the white bird that has appeared to Carrie repeatedly in dreams? (95–96). (b) How does Carrie's new understandings about the white bird impact her last two dreams? (98, 103). (c) How does Carrie's spirit guide appear to her when she is fully awake and called to action in chapters 13–15? (96, 97, 101, 109).

Sacred Drums and Drumming Questions

Relevant chapters. 13, 15

Contextualizing event. Carrie learns about traditional Mohawk drumming from her grandmother (chapter 13) and receives a special gift from her sister Jessica (chapter 15).

Factual questions. (a) What prompts Carrie's grandmother to share her knowledge with Carrie about traditional Mohawk drumming? (95). (b) What specifically does Carrie learn about traditional Mohawk drumming from her grandmother? (95). (c) What is personally meaningful for Carrie about the Mohawk men drumming by the roadblock? (96).

Summative response question (109). Why is the gift of a drum such a meaningful gift for Carrie to receive from her sister at the end of the novel?

Question Set 2: Group D Features

Disease, Defense of Homes and Homeland (Categories 10–11),
Where I Belong

Diabetes Questions

Relevant chapters. 14, 15

Contextualizing event. Carrie springs into action to help her grandmother regain consciousness and be well again (chapters 14–15).

Internet research questions. (a) What basic information about diabetes can be learned from trustworthy websites? (b) How specifically does diabetes affect Indigenous peoples in the United States and Canada? (c) What daily management routine is recommended for people with diabetes? (d) What is diabetic shock?

Factual questions. (a) What observed facts about her grandmother lead Carrie to conclude that her grandmother's collapse and present state of unconsciousness in chapter 14 have been caused by diabetes and not a heart attack? (99). (b) What individual action does Carrie take to help her grandmother in the kitchen? (99). (c) What united action do Carrie and her sister Jessica subsequently take to get help for their grandmother? (100–101). (d) What action does Carrie's mother Dr. Katherine Stowe take to help Carrie's grandmother? (102). (e) What medical emergency, according to Dr. Stowe, has caused Carrie's grandmother's collapse and state of unconsciousness? (102). (f) How does Carrie's grandmother respond to the treatment she receives from Dr. Stowe? (103).

Recommended Resources
Canadian Diabetes Association. "Indigenous Communities and Diabetes." www.diabetes.ca/resources/tools---resources/indigenous-communities-and -diabetes.
Fletcher, Jenna, and Kelly Wood, MD. "What to Know About Diabetic Shock." *Medical News Today.* www.medicalnewstoday.com/articles/is-plant-based -oral-insulin-within-reach-for-diabetes-treatment#Clinical-trials-of-plant -based-insulin-upcoming.

U.S. Department of Health and Human Services, Centers for Disease Control and Prevention. "Diabetes Basics." www.cdc.gov/diabetes/basics/index.html.
U.S. Department of Health and Human Services, Centers for Disease Control and Prevention. "Native Americans with Diabetes." www.cdc.gov/vitalsigns/aian-diabetes/index.html.
World Health Organization. "Diabetes." www.who.int/news-room/fact-sheets/detail/diabetes.

Defense of Homes and Homeland Questions 1

Relevant chapter. 11

Contextualizing event. Carrie learns about the various roadblocks erected by the residents of two Mohawk communities for the purpose of defending their homes and homeland.

Internet research questions. (a) Where are the Mohawk communities of Kanehsatake and Kahnawake located? (b) Where is the village of Oka located? (c) Where is the Mercier Bridge located? (d) What details about the Oka Crisis and blockade erected on Mercier Bridge by Mohawk people in 1990 can be learned from a documentary film and video report produced by the National Film Board of Canada and the Aboriginal Peoples Television Network in Canada? (e) What is the Mohawk War Society? (f) What role did Kahnawake Warriors play in the Oka Crisis?

Background question (65). What information does Tommy share with Carrie in chapter 9 that helps her to understand her father's comment about trouble brewing?

Factual questions. (a) What troubling news do Carrie's grandmother and father learn about the nearby Mohawk community of Kanehsatake from a television report midway through chapter 11? (79). (b) According to Carrie's father, what do the Oka townspeople fail to understand about (the planned expansion of) the Oka golf course? (80). (c) What troubling new developments in the ongoing conflict between Kanehsatake and Oka residents are reported to Carrie by her father at the end of chapter 11? (81). (d) What does Carrie observe about the distinctive appearance of the warriors protecting her grandmother's house and other houses in the community of Kahnawake? (81).

Recommended Resources
Aboriginal Peoples Television Network. "In the Pines: An Oral History of the 1990 Mohawk Resistance at Kanehsatake." YouTube. www.youtube.com/watch?v=fFiR-4zREfQ.
National Film Board of Canada. "Rocks at Whiskey Trench." YouTube. www.youtube.com/watch?v=V3cYG2vORYc.

Defense of Homes and Homeland Questions 2

Relevant chapter. 12

Contextualizing event. Carrie travels to the roadblock with Tommy.

Factual questions. (a) In the opinion of Carrie's grandmother, what do the residents of Kanehsatake and Kahnawake, and more broadly the Mohawk Nation, stand to achieve by retaining blockades near their communities? (83). (b) What compels Carrie's aunt to advise the family to ration their food supplies? (86). (c) What observations does Carrie make at the roadblock that make her worry about Tommy's safety? (87–88). (d) What observations about the situation at the roadblock does Tommy render in words? (87).

Inferencing question (97). What is suggestive about the way Carrie dresses during her visit to the roadblock with Tommy?

Defense of Homes and Homeland Questions 3

Relevant chapters. 13–15

Contextualizing event. Carrie learns firsthand as an Indigenous woman and member of the Mohawk Nation about the inherent dangers and disappointments involved in the defense of one's home and homeland.

Internet research questions. (a) Where is the city of Dorval, Quebec located? (b) Where is the off-island Montreal suburb of Chateauguay located?

Factual questions. (a) How was Carrie's Aunt Becky hurt by a mob while trying to drive through a roadblock near Kahnawake? (91). (b) How was Carrie's father hurt by a mob while buying groceries in Dorval? (91–92). (c) What alarming new developments at the roadblock does Carrie observe at the end of chapter 13? (96–97). (d) What news about the conflict at the roadblocks does Carrie's mother share with Carrie's father by phone at the start of chapter 15? (103). (e) What action does Carrie take in chapter 15 to keep her sister Jessica safe at the roadblock? (104–5).

Inferencing question (104). What new developments at the roadblock in chapter 15 does Tommy want Carrie to capture on film?

Summative response question (108). In the end, how long was the Mercier Bridge closed to traffic during the Oka Crisis?

Restoration (Category 12), Where I Belong

Restored Ancestral Identity

Relevant section and chapters. Introduction, 2–6, 9

Contextualizing event. Carrie's ancestral identity as Mohawk (i.e., Kanien'keha:ka) and more broadly as Indigenous is restored to her through a sequence of events involving the police, Tommy, a social worker, her birth father, and her Mohawk grandmother.

Factual questions. (a) What distinctive physical features possessed by Carrie have always made her feel different (from the people in her home community of McDonalds Corners)? (11). (b) Why does Carrie have such a strong reaction to the group of boys who storm out of the bus with hockey gear in chapter 2? (18). (c) How does Carrie respond to Tommy's question about her Indigenous identity? (19). (d) What strange effect does Tommy have on Carrie while standing so close to her in the arena? (20). (e) What details about Carrie's birth family are known to her adopted parents? (30). (f) What information about Mohawk people does Carrie obtain from her school library in chapter 4, and (g) why does this information make her shudder? (37). (h) What details about Carrie's past, shared with her in chapter 6, help her to understand why the police addressed her as Jessica at the bus depot in chapter 5? (46–50). (i) What information about her ancestral identity as Mohawk does Carrie learn from her grandmother in chapter 9? (69).

Inferencing question (52). How long does it take Carrie to explicitly identify herself as Mohawk once she learns about her birth family?

Restored Family Members 1

Relevant chapters. 6–8

Contextualizing event. Carrie's original family members are restored to her.

Factual questions. (a) How old were Carrie and her twin sister Jessica when their birth father Harold Williams learned about their existence? (50). (b) What explanation does Harold offer Carrie for not knowing anything about his two daughters until five years ago? (54). (c) What details about her birth mother and birth does Carrie obtain from Harold in chapter 7? (53–54). (d) What information about her twin sister Jessica does Carrie learn from Harold and the social worker Beth Davies? (54–55). (e) How does Carrie respond to Harold's comment about her being a family member and not just a visitor? (59). (f) What extended family members turn out to greet Carrie on her first visit to Kahnawake? (59).

Inferencing question (54). Why does the thought of never meeting her birth mother make Carrie want to throw up?

Restored Family Members 2

Relevant chapter. 15

Story context. Carrie's relationship with her twin sister is restored.

Factual questions (106–9). (a) What hard experiences and dreams about her life does Jessica share with Carrie when they are safely back at their aunt's house in Kahnawake? (106–7). (b) What explanation does Jessica offer Carrie for resenting her when she first arrived in Kahnawake? (107). (c) How does Jessica show Carrie that their relationship as sisters has been restored? (107, 109).

Chapter 6

Contemporary Worlds (1978–2000)

CHAPTER OVERVIEW AND TARGET QUESTIONS

This chapter focuses on fictional worlds in two contemporary realistic novels, *Will's Garden* (Maracle 2002) and *Little Voice* (Slipperjack 2001). The first novel recounts the experiences of a sixteen-year-old Sto: loh boy named Will as he prepares for and participates in a special community event that honors him as a full member of the Sto: loh Nation. The second novel recounts the experiences of an Ojibwe girl Ray from age 10 to 14 as she spends increasing amounts of time with her grandmother in their ancestral homeland.

The two novels are suited for exploratory studies of indigenized worlds in grades 8–10 and 5–8 respectively. For this chapter, readers will seek to answer the following target questions.

What basic story details for each novel are conveyed through the publisher summaries?

Which indigenizing feature is specifically defined, how is it defined, and how does its meaning relate to similar terms?

Which specific indigenizing features appear in each novel?

How is each novel subdivided for an exploratory study?

What sets of questions and recommended resources can be used to explore the indigenizing features shown in textbox 6.1?

What supplementary resources are uniquely provided for in an exploratory study of indigenizing features in the second novel?

Which specific questions and recommended resources can teachers and students use in grades 8–10 and 5–8 to gain insights about two Indigenous young people, Will and Ray, their families, and their communities?

Textbox 6.1.
Targeted Indigenizing Features in *Will's Garden* (Maracle 2002) and
Little Voice (Slipperjack 2001)

Group A features: dreamtime ancestral lands and identity
Group B features: the Sto: loh Becoming Man Ceremony, pre-
ceremony details, traditional wood carving, traditional beadwork,
sacred songs, sacred offerings, praying and prayers, purification
practices, expressing gratitude, water travel, traditional foods

TWO CONTEMPORARY WORLDS

Selected Novels: Bibliographic Information and Individual Summaries

Maracle, Lee. 2002. *Will's Garden*. Penticton, BC: Theytus. Paperback. 194 pages. Eighteen chapters. Not illustrated. Contemporary realistic fiction. Secondary grade novel. Not leveled.

Story details from back cover. As Will is preparing for his Coming of Age Ceremony, the whole family teams together, working day and night to prepare. Meanwhile life goes on at school in relationships and with friends. When a gang of jocks tries to overpower the weaker nerds at school, Will steps up and confronts the real issues of power struggles, racism, homophobia, bullying, and name calling.

As ceremony time draws nearer, Will becomes infatuated with the idea of love and longer-term relationships. A sudden and serious illness gives him time to reflect on what he's learned about becoming a man and the women in this life and to consider his future as a Sto: loh caretaker of the land in the modern world.

Slipperjack, Ruby. 2001. *Little Voice*. Regina, SK: Coteau Books. Paperback. 246 pages. Thirteen chapters. Illustrated. Contemporary realistic fiction. Grades 6–10 novel. Not leveled.

Story details from back cover. Kids make fun of her green eyes. And she's got a boy's name. Ray just doesn't fit in. Life's been tough for Ray since her father died in a logging accident. Kids at school make fun of her. She misses her dad very much, and she thinks her mother is too busy to need her. Things get so bad, she almost stops talking. Then Ray gets the chance she's always wanted: to spend the summer with her grandma, an elder and healer in a northern Ontario community. Helping Grandma—canoeing, camping, fishing, berry picking—Ray begins to learn a new way of life. Grandma's wisdom, love, and humor help Ray to understand herself better. Ray discovers that learning in two different ways—from her grandma's traditional teachings and from school—can prepare her for a very special life and help her to find her own voice.

Will's Garden: Key Fictional World Details

Specific Indigenous Groups and Individuals
  Sto: loh, Will (age 15)
Contemporary Settings
  Early 2000s, Cheam Nation, British Columbia

Little Voice: Key Fictional World Details

Specific Indigenous Groups and Individuals
  Ojibwe, Ray (age 10–14)
Contemporary Settings
  1978–1982, northern Ontario

WILL'S WORLD IN *WILL'S GARDEN*

Features Summary

The fictional world in the Indigenous novel *Will's Garden* (Maracle 2002) is indigenized by forty-two features in the categories of time, tribal history, ancestry, religious beliefs and practices, cultural values, cultural events, cultural traditions, language use, stories, and storytelling, family life and kinship, divestments and denigration, and leadership. The full set of indigenizing features for this third contemporary realistic novel is shown in textbox 6.2.

Exploratory Question Sets Focus

Two sets of exploratory questions are provided for the novel *Will's Garden* (Maracle 2002). Question set 1 focuses exclusively on the Group A feature of dreamtime (Category 1). Question set 2 focuses exclusively on Group B features: the Sto: loh Becoming Man Ceremony and pre-ceremony details (Category 6); and traditional wood carving and beadwork (Category 7).

  Embedded in the second set of questions focusing on the Sto: loh Becoming Man Ceremony and pre-ceremony details are the indigenizing features of sacred songs, sacred offerings, praying and prayers, and purification practices (Category 4); and expressing gratitude (Category 5).

Textbox 6.2.
Indigenizing Features Summary for *Will's Garden* (Maracle 2002)

Group A features: (1) Time: dreamtime; (2) Tribal History: notable events; (3) Ancestry: ancestral lands, ancestral identity, ancestral beings, ancestral symbols
Group B features: (4) Religious Beliefs and Practices: beliefs about the Creator, praying and prayers, sacred offerings, sacred objects (miscellaneous), sacred drums and drumming, purification practices; (5) Cultural Values: expressing gratitude; (6) Cultural Events: stationary games, grass dance, fancy dance, traditional songs and singing, Sto: loh Becoming Man Ceremony; (7) Cultural Traditions: fishing, clamming, traditional shelters, traditional clothes, traditional clothing accessories, mats and baskets, wood carving, beadwork and quillwork, traditional materials, traditional foods, food preparation
Group C features: (8) Language Use, Stories, and Storytelling: the art of storytelling, mythical stories, stories about animal tricksters, eagle stories, personal stories, family stories, Indigenous writing; (9) Family Life and Kinship: courtship, arranged marriages, clan membership
Group D features: (10) Divestments and Denigration: forced separation of children from parents, cultural denigration; (11) Leadership: chiefs, elders

Defined Feature and Related Terms

Question sets for *Will's Garden* (Maracle 2002) respectively focus in part on the Category 1 and Category 5 indigenizing features of dreamtime and expressing gratitude. The term *dreamtime* and comparable terms for expressing gratitude (i.e., to acknowledge; an acknowledgement) are defined below.

dreamtime: a detached state from one's physical surroundings explicitly identified by individuals as a dreamtime experience in which significant life events unfold in a perceived world that is partly real and partly imaginary and is not equivalent to a hypnotic, cataleptic, ecstatic, or anaesthetized state

acknowledge: to express appreciation or gratitude (to someone, for something)

acknowledgement: the act of expressing appreciation or gratitude

Book sectioning

Part I: Still a Boy (1–3)
Part II: Approaching Adulthood (4–8)
Part III: Becoming a Man (9–14)
Part IV: Life as an Adult (15–18)

Question Set 1: Group A Features

Dreamtime (Category 1), Will's Garden

Will's Dreamtime Questions 1

Relevant chapter. 1

Contextualizing event. Lying in bed one night in the dark, Will experiences dreamtime before thanking Gramma Moon for her presence and drifting off to sleep.

Internet research questions. (a) Where is Cheam Mountain (i.e., Cheam Peak) located in British Columbia? (b) What is distinctive about the appearance of Cheam Mountain? (c) What is the significance of Cheam Mountain for Sto: loh people in British Columbia? (d) What is distinctive about the appearance of Canadian cedar and sequoia trees? (e) What does a sequoia sapling look like?

Dreamtime experience segments. Will's dreamtime experience in chapter 1 includes four distinctive dreamtime segments:

Dreamtime segment 1: Images from long ago
Dreamtime segment 2: One ancestral being warning another
Dreamtime segment 3: Looking down from Cheam Mountain
Dreamtime segment 4: A conversation about Cheam Mountain

A dreamtime framing question: Segments 1–4 (5). What does Will observe about the nighttime sky and moon in the first paragraph of the chapter that opens his mind to dreamtime experiences?

Factual questions for Dreamtime Segment 1: Images from long ago. (a) What images from long ago appear to Will in the first paragraph of chapter 1? (5). (b) What dreamtime details in paragraphs 1 and 2 resolve for Will about women from long ago and one young woman in particular who might be his future wife? (5–6).

Assorted questions for Dreamtime Segment 2: One ancestral being warning another (6–7). (a) What ancestral beings appear to Will in dreamtime halfway through chapter 1? (factual). (b) What cryptic dreamtime warning is issued by one being to the other on top of Cheam Mountain? (factual). (c) What is disruptive for Will about one being's dreamtime transformation into an old woman? (inferencing).

Factual questions for Dreamtime Segment 3: Looking down from Cheam Mountain (7). (a) What ancestral trees appear to Will when he is alone on Cheam Mountain in dreamtime, looking down? (b) What realization awes Will about sequoia trees?

Assorted questions for Dreamtime Segment 4 (8–9). (a) What details from a conversation between his mother, grandmother, and aunt about the state of Cheam Mountain resolve for Will near the end of chapter 1? (factual). (b) How might this dreamtime conversation about Cheam Mountain define the direction of Will's life journey? (speculative).

Recommended Resource
Wikipedia. "Cheam Peak." https://en.wikipedia.org/w/index.php?title=Cheam _Peak&oldid=1122386813.

Will's Dreamtime Questions 2

Relevant chapter. 4

Contextualizing event. Lying in bed one morning, Will experiences dreamtime before his mother hollers at him to get up.

Internet research questions. What is the Pacific National Exhibition (PNE)?

Dreamtime experience segments. Will's dreamtime experience in chapter 4 includes five distinctive dreamtime segments:

Dreamtime segment 1: Climbing a hill
Dreamtime segment 2: Shopping in Vancouver, British Columbia
Dreamtime segment 3: Riding a roller coaster at the PNE
Dreamtime segment 4: Digging clams on the muddy seashore
Dreamtime segment 5: An unidentified gathering

Factual questions for Dreamtime Segment 1: Climbing a hill (34). (a) Which cousin and family pet accompany Will climbing a hill in this dreamtime segment? (b) What time of year is it? (c) What activities does Will engage in while climbing a hill?

Factual questions for Dreamtime Segment 2: Shopping in Vancouver (34). (a) What treat does Will receive from his cousin Sarah in this dreamtime segment? (b) What details about his hands resolve for Will in this segment?

Factual questions for Dreamtime Segment 3: Riding a roller coaster at the PNE (34–35). (a) What distinctive sensory experiences resolve for Will in this dreamtime segment? (b) What gender-specific advice about riding roller coasters does Will receive from his brother Tony?

Factual questions for Dreamtime Segment 4: Digging clams on the muddy seashore (35). (a) What aspect about his surroundings first resolves for Will in this dreamtime segment? (b) Who can be seen digging for clams? (c) What personal knowledge about the ocean and ocean life resolves for Will in this segment?

Factual questions for Dreamtime Segment 5: An unidentified gathering (35–36). (a) What people appear to Will in this last dreamtime segment? (b) What does Will observe about the evening light in this segment? (c) What is notable for Will about the appearance of the bones used by the gamblers seated across from him? (d) What is notable for Will about the way the singers sound? (e) What is notable for Will about the girl sitting across from him? (f) What is notable for Will about the women sitting beside the girl?

A dreamtime speculative question. How might specific elements in these five dreamtime segments give Will insight about forthcoming events in his Becoming Man Ceremony?

Will's Dreamtime Questions 3

Relevant chapter. 5

Contextualizing event. Will experiences dreamtime one night in bed while planning his Becoming Man speech.

Word meaning and Internet research question. (a) What does the French word *apogée* mean in English? (b) What does the French word *l'apogée* mean in English? (c) How might the French name *L'apogée*, when used as a generic name for older experienced men, be translated in English? (d) What is distinctive about the appearance of a Clydesdale horse? (e) What is a cowcatcher? (f) What does an old-time cowcatcher look like? (g) What is a plowshare? (h) What is similar about a cowcatcher and a plowshare? (i) Which Indigenous nation speaks the Halkomelem language?

Dreamtime experience segments. Will's dreamtime experience in chapter 5 includes four interconnected dreamtime segments.

Dreamtime segment 1: A view of old-time road building and builders
Dreamtime segment 2: Hauling supplies through a canyon
Dreamtime segment 3: A road-builder's conversation about the coming winter

Dreamtime segment 4: Building a road with a homemade cowcatcher

Factual questions for Dreamtime Segment 1: A view of old-time road building and builders (48). (a) What images about old-time road building in the mountains appear to Will in this first dreamtime segment in chapter 5? (b) What details about the identities of old-time road builders first resolve for Will? (c) Which relative of Will comes into view shortly before the dreamtime landscape sharpens for Will?

Assorted questions for Dreamtime Segment 2: Hauling supplies through a canyon (49–50). (a) What first comes into view as the landscape sharpens for Will in the second dreamtime segment? (factual). (b) Why does the appearance of a Clydesdale horse usually command a person's attention? (inferencing). (c) What important observations does Will make about the following elements in this dreamtime segment? (factual).

- the number of road-builders present
- the languages spoken by the road-builders
- the weather
- the terrain
- the road-builders' activities
- the movement of the supply cart uphill
- the key role played by rope and trees
- the road-builders' relief

Assorted questions for Dreamtime Segment 3: A road-builder's conversation about the coming winter (50–51). (a) What elements in the second and third dreamtime segments likely bring Will's great grandfather sharply into focus at the start of the third segment? (speculative, factual). (b) What is notable for Will about the moonlight in the third segment? (factual). (c) How many generations of men in Will's family figure in this segment? (factual). (d) What personal meaning might Will derive from his great grandfather's limited contributions to the road-building crew's conversation in this third segment? (speculative). (e) What propels the foreman Jimmy to shift the conversational focus away from money matters to his personal respect for the road-builders seated with him? (factual). (f) What words spoken by Jimmy compel Will's great grandfather to accept his foreman's respect? (inferencing).

A dreamtime framing question: Segment 4 (52–54). How does the shifting reference to different generations of grandparents in the fourth segment (i.e., references to Grandpa = Will's father's grandfather; references to Great Grandpa = Will's great grandfather) enhance the meaning and significance of the memories and perspectives framing this dreamtime experience?

Assorted questions for Dreamtime Segment 4: Building a road with a homemade cowcatcher (52–55). (a) What problem does Jimmy articulate to Will's great grandfather and the other old-time road-builders shortly before sunrise one morning? (factual). (b) How do Will's great grandfather and his foreman agree to help each other? (factual). (c) How does the road-building crew manage to solve the problem articulated by their foreman? (factual). (d) What spiritual lesson might Will's grandmother (i.e., Gramma) have wanted Will and her other grandchildren to learn from her comment about the Sto: loh Sunrise Ceremony? (speculative).

Will's Dreamtime Questions 4

Relevant chapter. 6

Contextualizing event. Will experiences dreamtime while beading a cape.

Video and map research questions. (a) What can be learned about the Hells Gate river passage in interior British Columbia? (b) What is distinctive about the appearance of the Hells Gate river passage? (c) Where is the community of Spussum, British Columbia, located? (d) Where is the city of Revelstoke, British Columbia, located?

Dreamtime experience segments. Will's dreamtime experience in chapter 6 includes four interconnected dreamtime segments:

Dreamtime segment 1: Great Grandpa writes his first letter.
Dreamtime segment 2: Great Grandma leaves for Hells Gate.
Dreamtime segment 3: Great Grandma joins the road-building crew at Hells Gate.
Dreamtime segment 4: Great Grandma gives birth to a boy in Revelstoke.

Assorted questions for Dreamtime Segment 1: Great Grandpa writes his first letter (57–58). (a) Why would the building of the first road at a location like Hells Gate be understandably slow moving? (inferencing). (b) What is notable for Will about the appearance of the paper that first comes into view for him at the start of this dreamtime segment? (factual). (c) What is notable for Will about the way his great grandfather prays over the paper before writing on it? (factual). (d) What personal sentiments does his great grandfather express in his first letter to his wife? (factual). (e) What name does his great grandfather use to end the letter? (factual).

Factual questions for Dreamtime Segment 2: Great Grandma leaves for Hells Gate (58). (a) What surprises Will's great grandmother about receiving a letter from her husband? (b) How does his great grandmother disguise herself before packing her bags, saddling her horse, and setting off for her husband's worksite at Hells Gate? (c) What task does his great grandfather undertake to get the road-building crew back on schedule?

Assorted questions for Dreamtime Segment 3: Great Grandma joins the road-building crew at Hells Gate (58–59). (a) What likely motivates Will's great grandmother to join her husband's road-building crew at Hells Gate when she arrives there with her brother? (speculative, inferencing). (b) What road-building tasks performed by Will's great grandmother resolve for him in this third dreamtime segment? (factual). (c) How is she able to perform these tasks for many hours a day? (speculative). (d) What motivates his great grandfather to keep his wife's identity hidden from the foreman? (speculative, inferencing). (e) How do his great grandparents manage to keep his great grandmother's identity as a woman a secret? (factual).

Assorted questions for Dreamtime Segment 4: Great Grandma gives birth to a boy in Revelstoke (59). (a) What was significant for Will's great grandparents about the birth of a healthy baby boy conceived on the same road they helped to build? (speculative, inferencing). (b) What is significant for Will about the birth of his grandfather under such circumstances as revealed to him in dreamtime? (factual).

Recommended Resource
Smithsonian Channel. "The Best Way to See Canada's 'Hells Gate' River Passage." www.youtube.com/watch?v=cj0Gq1Jb86w.

Will's Dreamtime Questions 5

Relevant chapter. 9

Contextualizing event. Will experiences dreamtime again while beading a cape.

Internet research questions. (a) Where is the historic town of Barkerville, British Columbia, located? (b) What can be learned about this historic town from the official Barkerville Historic Town & Park website?

Dreamtime experience segments. Will's dreamtime experience in chapter 9 includes three interconnected dreamtime segments:

Dreamtime segment 1: Old-time packing through the mountains
Dreamtime segment 2: Packing to survive in the olden days
Dreamtime segment 3: Struggling to live on old-time lands

A dreamtime framing question: Segments 1–3. How does the shifting reference to different generations of grandparents, as in chapter 5, enhance the meaning and significance of the memories and perspectives framing this dreamtime experience as well?

Assorted questions for Dreamtime Segment 1: Old-time packing through the mountains (86–87). (a) How might Will's recounting of a recent battle at school with the jocks initiate this specific dreamtime experience? (inferencing). (b) What is notable and likely alarming for Will about the appearance and activity of his great grandmother as she comes into view in this first dreamtime segment? (factual, speculative). (c) How does Will's dreamtime viewing position shift when his great grandfather comes into view? (inferencing). (d) What best explains his great grandfather's grimacing look? (factual). (e) What fatal accident on the mountainside does Will witness in dreamtime? (factual). (f) Why does Will's great grandfather seem to be glad that his wife is not tethered to a horse? (inferencing). (g) How has his great grandfather instructed his wife to fall if she slips on the mountainside trail? (factual).

Factual questions for Dreamtime Segment 2: Packing to survive in the olden days (87–88). (a) What shifting images resolve for Will in the second dreamtime segment that help him to answer the question raised at the end of the first dreamtime segment? (b) What details about the hardships experienced by past generations of Sto: loh people—transmitted orally from two generations of grandfathers to a father and to a son (Will, the last born son in the family)—are spoken to Will in the second dreamtime segment? (c) What accounts for an old grandfather's strong commitment to traditional Sto: loh prayer?

Assorted questions for Dreamtime Segment 3: Growing silence (88–89). (a) What accounts for Lapogee's growing silence at the end of the third dreamtime segment? (inferencing). (b) Why might Sto: loh men like Will's grandfather seek silence in old age? (speculative). (c) How might one's definition of love change over a lifetime? (speculative).

Will's Dreamtime Questions 6

Relevant chapter. 11

Contextualizing event. Will experiences dreamtime while lying in a tent one night.

Dreamtime experience focus. Will's great grandfather appears to him alone in his bedroom and offers his advice about handling changes in his life.

Internet research and background questions (109). (a) What is a hopyard? (b) What is the significance of hopyards in Will's family history?

Dreamtime framing questions (105–11). (a) What personal observations about changes in traditional Sto: loh courtship practices does George share with his brothers Will and Tony? (b) What surprising change in his father's life more than three decades ago at age twenty-eight does Will learn about from George? (c) What is significant for Will about his relocation from a tent in his backyard (before dreamtime) to his bedroom and bed (during dreamtime)?

Assorted dreamtime questions (111). (a) What notable changes in the Sto: loh landscape are identified for Will by his great grandfather in dreamtime? (factual). (b) What specific advice about handling changes in life does Will receive from his great grandfather? (summative).

Will's Dreamtime Questions 7

Relevant chapter. 15

Contextualizing event. Will has a morning dreamtime experience following a grueling late-evening shift of foundation digging at the site of his community's new daycare center.

Dreamtime experience summary. Animals, canyon walls, relatives, seeds, and flowers all appear to Will in rapid dreamtime succession.

Dreamtime framing questions (150). (a) Who experiences pain during birth? (b) What is painful about birth? (c) What painful sounds are associated with birth?

Assorted dreamtime questions (150). (a) What animals appear to Will at the start of the dreamtime experience in this chapter? (factual). (b) What seasonal activity (spring or spring-to-fall activity) is each species of animal engaged in? (factual). (c) Why are domestic animals and specific family members notably absent from this dreamtime experience? (d) How does Will's form of being shift in this dreamtime experience? (factual). (e) What bodily sensations are likely produced for Will by the unfolding and cumulative dreamtime actions of building, hauling, dodging, jumping, changing (into, back into), bursting, blooming, digging, picking, and pushing? (inferencing). (f) What accounts for Will's self-perceived fragility at the end of this dreamtime experience? (factual, inferencing, summative).

Will's Dreamtime Questions 8

Relevant chapter. 16

Contextualizing event. Will experiences dreamtime in the school cafeteria.

Internet, video, and word meaning research questions. (a) What does a hop trellis look like? (b) What can be learned about hop trellising and harvesting from trustworthy sources? (c) What is a binder (i.e., chest binder)?

Dreamtime experience segments. Will's dreamtime experience in chapter 16 includes five dreamtime segments:

Dreamtime segment 1: Courting

Dreamtime segment 2: Preparing for work
Dreamtime segment 3: Working for the parish priest
Dreamtime segment 4: Working at the hopyard
Dreamtime segment 5: Knowing

Dreamtime framing question: Segments 1–5 (150). Why does Wit's centering talk about his cousin Lei-Lani propel Will into a dreamtime experience that focuses on courtship, four generations of Sto: loh women, hard work, and survival? (see 98–102, 114–17, 125–28).

Factual questions for Dreamtime Segment 1: Courting (167). (a) What family members appear to Will in this first dreamtime segment? (b) In what order do these family members come into view? (c) What is notable for Will about the positioning and physical proximity of the women in this segment, his mother and grandmother? (d) How does the appearance of the women change as they listen to the plaintive courtship music coming through the window? (e) What does Will learn about his father as a Sto: loh man and future husband from the observations and comments exchanged by his grandmother and mother?

Assorted questions for Dreamtime Segment 2: Preparing for work (167). (a) What family member appears to Will in this segment? (factual). (b) Which generation of grandmother is this family member? (factual). (c) What is notable for Will about his grandmother's appearance, location, and childhood activities? (factual). (d) What is notable for Will about his grandmother's resilience as a young girl? (inferencing).

Assorted questions for Dreamtime Segment 3: Working for the parish priest (168). (a) What family member appears to Will first in this segment? (factual). (b) Which generation of grandmother is this family member? (factual). (c) What cleaning tasks would a parish priest likely hire a woman like Will's grandmother to perform? (speculative). (d) How old is Will's mom in this segment? (inferencing). (e) What weekly wage does Will's grandmother receive as a cleaner? (factual). (f) What does Will's grandmother do with the money she makes as a cleaner? (factual). (g) What might Will learn about his grandmother and the nature of her life as a Sto: loh woman by her employment as a cleaner by the parish priest? (speculative).

Assorted questions for Dreamtime Segment 4: Working at the hopyard (168). (a) What family members appear simultaneously to Will in this segment? (factual). (b) How does the kinship term used in this segment (i.e., *Momma*) help Will to distinguish one grandmother from the other? (factual). (c) How old are Will's grandmothers in this segment? (speculative). (d) What is notable for Will about his grandmothers' positioning in the hopyard? (factual). (e) What unsettles Will about the way his grandmothers appear to him at night? (factual).

Assorted questions for Dreamtime Segment 5: Knowing (168). (a) What realization about the appearance of his grandmothers in the previous segment precipitates Will's encounter with his great grandfather in this new segment? (factual). (b) Which of Will's family members are the two women identified in this segment, wife and daughter? (factual). (c) What compels Will's great grandfather to speak to him first with his eyes open and then with his eyes closed? (speculative). (d) How does the bathroom stall cease to impede Will's dreamtime view of his great grandfather's face? (speculative). (e) From the perspective of Will's great grandfather, what is helpful for everyone to know about the dangers women face in their lives? (factual).

Recommended Resources
University of Florida, IFAS Extension. "How to Install Twines in a Hopyard." YouTube. https://edis.ifas.ufl.edu/publication/HS1418.
UW–Madison. "Farming Hops." YouTube. www.youtube.com/watch?v=oqPjmaAVLPM.

Will's Dreamtime Questions 9

Relevant chapter. 18

Contextualizing event. Will experiences dreamtime in the hospital during a visit from his grandfather.

Internet research and word meaning questions (a) What basic information about the movement of African American people during the Great Migration can be learned from trustworthy sources? (b) What does the buffalo bean plant look like (i.e., *Thermopsis Rhombifolia*, Golden Bean)? (c) What does the broom flower look like (i.e., Amphiachyris dracunculoides, Prairie Broomweed)? (d) What is pemmican? (e) How does the online *American Heritage Dictionary* define the word *slop*?

Dreamtime experience segments. Will's dreamtime experience in chapter 18 includes four dreamtime segments:

Dreamtime segment 1: Freedom on horseback
Dreamtime segment 2: Tethered people coming and going
Dreamtime segment 3: Herded women
Dreamtime segment 4: Leaping salmon

Dreamtime framing question: Segments 1–3 (190–92). How do the experiences of African American and Indigenous peoples past and present intersect in this dreamtime experience?

Assorted questions for Dreamtime Segment 1: Freedom on horseback (190–91). (a) What Indigenous person appears to Will at the start of this first dreamtime segment? (factual). (b) How many freedom seekers (i.e., slave runners) come running into view? (factual). (c) How has the Indigenous man prepared for his encounter with the three freedom seekers? (inferencing). (d) What does the Indigenous man teach the two men about traveling by horseback? (factual). (e) How does the Indigenous man use plants and darkness to keep everyone safe? (factual). (f) What purpose is served by the third horse? (speculative). (g) At what point do the four travelers part ways? (factual).

Assorted questions for Dreamtime Segment 2: Tethered people coming and going (191–92). (a) What landscape feature appears to Will as the dreamtime sky parts? (factual). (b) What is notable for Will about the first group of people who appear to him in this segment? (factual). (c) What is notable about the second group of people who appear to him? (factual). (d) Why is the identity and appearance of both groups of people indistinct? (speculative). (e) Why do some of the tethered people refuse to eat or drink, and how do others respond to their refusal? (inferencing, speculative, factual). (f) How many ships and how many tethered men appear to Will in this dreamtime segment? (factual).

Assorted questions for Dreamtime Segment 3: Herded women (192). (a) What women appear to Will in this third dreamtime segment? (speculative). (b) Where are the men who once shared their lives with these women? (speculative). (c) What group of people is herding these women north? (factual). (d) What future hardships do these women envision for themselves? (factual).

Assorted questions for Dreamtime Segment 4: Leaping salmon (193). (a) Whose sudden interruption and urgent need to speak about his own people, the Sto: loh, precipitate this last dreamtime segment? (factual). (b) Whose dreamtime activities capture Will's attention in the first half of this segment? (factual). (c) What activities does Will observe in the first half of the segment? (factual). (d) What does Will observe about his own activities in the second half of the segment? (factual). (e) How might Will use the meaning of this final dreamtime segment as a Sto: loh man? (speculative).

Recommended Resources

Kansas State University. "Broomweed." Kansas Wildflowers and Grasses. www .kswildflower.org/flower_details.php?flowerID=289.

Maureen Lee and Glen Lee. "Thermopsis Rhombifolia (Golden Bean)." Saskatchewan Wildflowers. www.saskwildflower.ca/nat_Thermopsis-rhombi folia.html.

U.S. Department of the Interior, National Park Service. "Underground Railroad: Language of Slavery." www.nps.gov/subjects/undergroundrailroad /language-of-slavery.htm.

Wikipedia. "Great Migration (African American)." https://en.wikipedia.org/w /index.php?title=Great_Migration_(African_American)&oldid=1166244962.

Wikipedia.   "Pemmican."   https://en.wikipedia.org/w/index.php?title
=Pemmican&oldid=1161102464.

Question Set 2: Group B Features

Traditional Wood Carving and Beadwork (Category 7), Will's Garden

Traditional Wood Carving Questions

Relevant chapters. 2, 3, 11

Contextualizing event. Thoughts about his father, a traditional Sto: loh wood
carver, pass through Will's mind as he works toward the completion of his first
beaded cape (chapters 2–3). Will learns details about his father's life as a wood
carver from his brother (chapter 11).

Video research question. What can be learned about Coast Salish (Sto: loh) and
other West Coast Indigenous wood carvers, wood carvings, and wood carving
workshops from trustworthy sources?

Factual questions about Will's father as a traditional Sto: loh wood carver. (a)
Where does Will's father produce wood carvings, and what carved wooden
objects does he produce? (15, 22–23). (b) What is notable for Will about the
appearance of his father's carved puffin? (22). (c) Where can this puffin be
seen? (22). (d) What series of carved wooden masks, produced by Will's father,
appears in his father's workshop? (22). (e) What is notable for Will about the
appearance of one of these masks? (22). (f) How much time does Will's father
generally spend in his workshop? (22, 26). (g) What large, carved, wooden
object is delivered to the house by truck midway through chapter 3? (26–27). (h)
What is notable for Will about the carved portion of this object? (27).

Speculative questions about the ornamentation of carved wooden objects (23).
(a) What is appealing for the women in Will's family about carved wooden
objects featuring the family crest? (b) Why might carved wooden objects
like bowls, spoons, and plates decorated with a family crest appeal to many
Sto: loh women?

Assorted questions about becoming a wood carver (108). (a) At what point
in his life did Will's father start carving objects out of wood? (inferencing).
(b) According to Will's oldest brother George, what motivated their father to
become a wood carver? (factual). (c) For how many years now has Will's father
been self-employed as wood carver? (inferencing). (d) What likely appeals to
Will's father about wood carving? (speculative).

Recommended Resources

Canadianindianart. "First Nations Art Work: Canadian Indian Art." YouTube. www.youtube.com/watch?v=dEsRzPlqZ_8.

Eric W. Thomson. "Canada's Coast Salish Tribes: A Culture of Wood Carving." YouTube. www.youtube.com/watch?v=LAEbLrNh7bk.

Jaguar Bird. "Hwunumetse: Grandfather Simon Charlie." YouTube. www.youtube.com/watch?v=303z6mwYPdk.

Phil Ives. "Herb Rice, Cowichan Coast Salish Native Pacific Northwest, Master Carver." YouTube. www.youtube.com/watch?v=9hZ6h0rqc4M.

Phil Ives. "Randy Goldsmith: Coast Salish Master Carver." YouTube. www.youtube.com/watch?v=mPZn0axQHx4.

Spirits of the West Coast Art Gallery. "Karver Everson: Northwest Coast Artist." YouTube. www.youtube.com/watch?v=te_ZBs2oFho.

Traditional Beadwork Questions 1: Beadwork Projects and Special Beading Relationships

Relevant chapter. 2

Contextualizing event. As Will and his cousin Sarah work on their individual beading projects, Will recalls the starting point of their special beading relationship.

Internet and video research questions. (a) What can be learned from images of beaded barrettes, bags, and vamps (i.e., moccasin tops) obtained from Google searches using the exact phrases "First Nations beaded barrettes," "First Nations beaded bags," and "First Nations beaded vamps"? (b) What recurring design elements are observable in these beaded items? (c) How do Indigenous people use a small plate or saucer when doing beadwork?

Assorted questions focusing on beadwork projects. (a) At whose house has Will's cousin Sarah come to do beadwork? (factual, 11, 15). (b) What specific items is Sarah decorating today with beads? (factual, 14). (c) What will Sarah do with her finished beaded items? (inferencing, 15).

Assorted questions focusing on Will and Sarah's special beading relationship. (a) At what age did Sarah and Will start beading together? (factual, 18). (b) What circumstances landed Will in the living room that day, sitting with his mother and aunt, cleaning and sorting beads? (summative, 18–20). (c) What amazed Will that day, watching Sarah, beading? (factual, inferencing, 20). (d) What special beading project was Sarah working on that day? (factual, 20). (e) How did Will and Sarah end up beading together that day? (factual, 20). (f) What motivated Will to do beadwork with Sarah from that point on? (inferencing, speculative, 20–21). (g) Why does Will use the analogy of a garden to describe the emerging artistic pattern on the beaded surface of a cloth? (speculative).

Recommended Resource
Angela Gonzalez. "Beading Slipper Tops." YouTube. www.youtube.com/watch
  ?v=awDgNnQJs0E.

Traditional Beadwork Questions 2: Selling Beaded Items

Relevant chapter. 3

Contextualizing event. Thoughts about the sale of his beaded items pass through
Will's mind as he works toward the completion of his first beaded cape.

Video research question. What can be learned about powwows from trustworthy sources?

Factual questions (23–24). (a) At what popular summertime events do Will and
Sarah sell the beaded items they produce during the year? (b) Which family
members accompany them to these events? (c) How do Will and Sarah split the
profits they make selling their beaded items? (d) How much money has Will
been able to save from selling his beaded items?

Recommended Resources
CBC News. "What's a Powwow?" YouTube. www.youtube.com/watch?v
  =EVkgqmpyDfg.
OsioyTV. "Powwow Education." YouTube. www.youtube.com/watch?v
  =w0Qq3HNrvuc.

Traditional Beadwork Questions 3: Will's Traditional Beadwork

Relevant chapter. 3

Contextualizing event. Will continues to bead through the evening and finishes
his beaded cape by midnight.

Internet research questions. (a) What can be learned about the design of beaded
flowers in terms of shape, number of petals, exterior lines, fill, inner parts, size,
and color from images obtained from a Google search using the exact phrase
"First Nations beaded flowers"? (b) What can be learned about the appearance
of beaded capes from images obtained in a Pinterest search using the exact
phrase "First Nations beaded capes"?

Factual questions (32–33). (a) What is somewhat unusual and a bit mystifying
for Will about his interest in beading and beadwork? (b) What beaded pattern
(i.e., a specific configuration of beads) comes easily to Will at age fifteen? (c)
What beaded item does Will complete at the end of chapter 3? (d) Why does
Will stop beading at midnight and turn in?

Inferencing question (33). What makes stitching beads harder on the body than quilting?

Traditional Beadwork Questions 4: Two New Projects and Beaded Gardens

Relevant chapter. 5

Contextualizing event. Will and Sarah continue to do beadwork together at Will's house.

Internet research questions. (a) What can be learned about the design of beaded roses and beaded rose barrettes from images obtained in a Google search using the exact phrase "Native American beaded rose"? (b) What is distinctively different about the appearance of wild and domestic roses?

Assorted questions focusing on two new projects. (a) What new beaded item does Will start working on in this chapter? (inferencing, 44, cf. 33). (b) What beaded item is Sarah working on at the start of the chapter? (inferencing, 44, cf. 51). (c) What is striking for Will about the emerging pattern in Sarah's new beading project? (factual, 44, 51). (d) Why would the beaded patterns taking shape in this chapter cause Will to experience dreamtime? (speculative, 47).

Assorted questions focusing on beaded gardens (51–52). (a) What type of rose does Will's mother grow on a trellis in the front yard? (factual). (b) What details in the beaded rose on Sarah's new barrette make Will think about the roses on his mother's trellis? (factual). (c) Why might one beaded rose on the front of a barrette appear to Will as a full-fledged garden? (speculative).

Traditional Beadwork Questions 5: Will's Newly Completed Cape

Relevant chapter. 6

Contextualizing event. Will regards his newly completed cape with wonder.

Factual questions (56–60). (a) On what part of his newly completed cape has Will stitched roses? (b) How many roses has he stitched on this new cape? (c) What is striking about the appearance of these roses (i.e., their size, color)? (d) How has Will achieved the overall effect of a rose garden like his mother's rose garden in the yard using beaded vines, stems, thorns, and buds? (d) What beaded background ornamentation appears on the cape? (e) How does Sarah respond to this cape? (f) How do Will's brothers respond to this cape? (g) What complementary beading projects do Will and Sarah agree to undertake next to address the mismatch between the beaded design of Will's newly completed cape and Sarah's newly completed barrette?

Traditional Beadwork Questions 6: Beading Gardeners and Garden Designs

Relevant chapter. 9

Contextualizing event. An unexpected design emerges on Will's new cape.

Assorted questions (90–93). (a) From Sarah's perspective as a skilled beader, what likely takes root in a beaded garden when a beader focuses on negative thoughts while beading? (inferencing). (b) What insights does Will gain from Sarah and his brothers about the history of beading among Cree and Sto: loh peoples and the prominence of flowers in traditional beading designs? (factual, inferencing). (c) What pleases and surprises Will about the emerging design on his new beaded cape, and how does he explain this emerging design? (factual, inferencing). (d) How does Sarah respond to the unexpected design on Will's new cape? (factual).

Traditional Beadwork Questions 7: Will's Rose Garden Cape

Relevant chapter. 10–11

Contextualizing event. Will is on hand when all the quilted blankets and other gifts for his Becoming Man Ceremony are set out on the floor and surveyed (chapters 10–11).

Assorted questions. (a) How do Will's family members including his mother, sister, aunts, and cousins each respond to Will's rose garden cape completed in chapter 6 but only shared with them now in chapter 10? (factual, inferencing, 96). (b) How has Will expressed his love for and gratitude to his mother in this one beaded cape? (inferencing, 96, 117, cf. 56–57). (c) What motivates Will to let his mother decide who will receive the cape as a gift? (factual, speculative, 117). (d) What might be revealed to Will's mother in a dream that will guide her decision about the ownership of the special rose garden cape? (speculative, 117).

Sto: loh Becoming Man Ceremony (Categories 4–6), Will's Garden

Pre-Ceremony Details Questions 1: A Special Prayer Time Event (Sacred Songs, Sacred Offerings, Prayer, and Expressing Gratitude)

Relevant chapter. 12

Contextualizing event. Will joins his parents in the yard for a special prayer time event on the day of his Becoming Man Ceremony.

Special prayer time event note. The special prayer time event held in Will's yard at sunrise includes a beginning, middle, and end and focuses largely on his father's prayer time actions, words, and offerings.

Factual questions focusing on prayer time initiation and attendance (119–20). (a) Which family members have initiated this special prayer time event that is already underway when Will emerges from the tent shortly before sunrise? (b) Which family members and friends join Will in the yard for this early morning prayer time event?

Factual prayer time questions focusing on Will's father (119–20). (a) How does Will's father begin and end his special prayer time event this morning? (b) Why is he grateful for the coming changes in his life? (c) Why is he grateful for his daughter Callie's son? (d) What personal thoughts about aging and death does he express in words while praying?

Speculative prayer time questions (119–20). (a) What spiritual meanings might the presence of water bring to a prayer time event? (b) What spiritual meanings might the presence of a crafted copper object, especially one holding water, bring to an outdoor prayer time event? (c) What is significant about Callie's presence at this special prayer time event? (d) Why is it important for Will's father to offer his last son Will to the world, as he likely offered his other two sons, in a formal sunrise ceremony attended by family members?

Pre-Ceremony Details Questions 2: Sacred Songs and Purification Practices

Relevant chapter. 12

Contextualizing event. Will further prepares for his upcoming Becoming Man Ceremony by purifying himself in a sweat lodge.

Factual purification event questions (120–22). (a) Which members of Will's immediate and extended families accompany him to the river and join him in the sweat lodge? (b) Which of these family members have come to the river but do not join Will in the sweat lodge? (c) What purification roles are performed by Will's uncle Eli, cousin George, and grandfather?

Speculative purification event questions (122). (a) What might cause a young Sto: loh man like Will or older Sto: loh men like his brother George or their father to laugh or cry during a purification event? (b) How does laughing and crying induce healing? (c) What personal problems can be resolved during a purification event? (d) What personal problems might Will have resolved in the sweat lodge this morning?

Will's Becoming Man Ceremony Questions

<u>Relevant chapter</u>. 12

<u>Contextualizing event</u>. Will attends his Becoming Man Ceremony at the Longhouse.

<u>Internet research and word meaning questions.</u> (a) How might the traditional Sto: loh skirt worn by Will's mother during his childhood have looked? (see Burnaby Museum resource guide cited below). (b) How does the online *Free Dictionary* by Farlex define the idiom "lighten (one's) load"?

<u>Ceremonial segments</u>. Will's Becoming Man Ceremony includes four main segments.

> *Ceremonial segment 1*: Will prepares to deliver his ceremonial speech.
> *Ceremonial segment 2*: Will delivers his ceremonial speech.
> *Ceremonial segment 3*: Will completes his ceremonial speech with gift-giving.
> *Ceremonial segment 4*: Will participates in a celebratory feast.

<u>Assorted questions for Ceremonial Segment 1: Will prepares to deliver his ceremonial speech (122–23)</u>. (a) What might a burning fire signify for participants in a Becoming Man Ceremony? (speculative). (b) What actions does Will perform before delivering his speech? (factual). (c) How does Will respond to his uncle Eli's quip about needing to speak before tending to gifts? (d) What explains the joyful atmosphere in the Longhouse this morning? (factual, inferencing).

Ceremonial Segments 2–3 notes (123–24). Will delivers his ceremonial speech in the second and third segments of his Becoming Man Ceremony. In the first part of his speech, he expresses his gratitude to key people in his life, women and men, for helping to shape his identity and character and for lightening his load. In the second part of his speech, Will shares his future plans as a Sto: loh man while his brothers distribute gifts on behalf of him and the family, gifts that include blankets, sheets, pillowcases, towels, and cans of salmon and jam (97, 115–16). The exploratory questions below focus on four family photographs shared by Will during the first part of his speech, his acknowledgement of his nephew William and Sto: loh men, details about Will's career plans, and the distribution of gifts.

<u>Ceremonial Segments 2–3 framing questions (123–24)</u>. (a) What does a young Sto: loh man like Will gain from expressing his gratitude to family and community members and sharing his future career plans publicly in a formal ceremony? (b) What do Will's family and community members gain from his ceremonial expressions of gratitude and the sharing of his future career plans?

<u>Assorted questions for Ceremonial Segment 2: First family photograph (123)</u>. (a) Which two family members are featured in Will's first family photograph? (factual). (b) What is each family member doing in the photograph? (factual,

inferencing). (c) When was the photograph taken? (inferencing). (d) What is significant for Will about the arms in the photograph? (factual). (e) In what ways was Will's mother invisible to him at this age, and in what ways was she continuously present to him? (inferencing, speculative). (f) What made it difficult for Will to see his mother at this age? (speculative). (g) Why does the long skirt worn by his mother during his childhood figure so prominently in his memories? (factual).

Assorted questions for Ceremonial Segment 2: Second family photograph (123–24). (a) Which two family members are featured in Will's second family photograph? (factual). (b) What is the age difference between Will and his sister? (inferencing). (c) When was this second family photograph taken? (inferencing). (d) In what ways did Will's sister help to raise him? (factual).

Assorted questions for Ceremonial Segment 2: Third family photograph (124). (a) Which two family members are featured in Will's third family photograph? (factual). (b) What is each family member doing in the photograph? (factual). (c) When was the photograph taken? (inferencing). (d) In what ways did Will's aunt help to raise him? (factual).

Assorted questions for Ceremonial Segment 2: Fourth family photograph (124). (a) Which two family members are featured in Will's fourth family photograph? (factual). (b) What is each family member doing in the photograph? (factual). (c) When was the photograph taken? (inferencing). (d) What conversations might Will's grandmother have had with him and others while supporting him as he slept on her lap? (speculative). (e) How might these conversations have shaped the development of Will's character? (factual, speculative).

Assorted questions for Ceremonial Segment 2: Will's acknowledgement of William (124). (a) What prompts Will to shift his attention away from the second family photograph and focus briefly on his nephew William after acknowledging his sister? (inferencing). (b) What important personal responsibility toward his nephew does Will publicly acknowledge? (factual).

Assorted questions for Ceremonial Segment 2: Will's gratitude to Sto: loh men (124–25). (a) How might the Sto: loh men in Will's life have lightened his load, growing up (i.e., helped to make things less difficult, upsetting, or overwhelming for him)? (speculative). (b) What do these same Sto: loh men need to do for Will before being finished with him? (speculative). (c) What does Will promise future generations of Sto: loh men? (factual).

Assorted questions for Ceremonial Segment 3: Will's career plans (125). (a) What field of study does Will plan to pursue at the university? (factual). (b) How does Will as a Sto: loh man plan to care for the land as past generations of Sto: loh men have done? (factual). (c) What might caring for the land as a Sto: loh man entail? (speculative). (d) Why would Will seek to expand his traditional knowledge about caring for the land before completing a program of study at a university? (speculative). (e) How does Will plan to advocate on behalf of the earth and the local environment? (factual, speculative).

Assorted questions for Ceremonial Segment 3: Gift-Giving (125). (a) Which family members distribute gifts on Will's behalf and on behalf of his family? (factual). (b) Why are no gifts given to Will during this segment of his Becoming Man Ceremony? (speculative). (c) Why might Sto: loh people like Will and his parents more highly value the giving of gifts to others during an important community event like a Becoming Man Ceremony than receiving gifts themselves? (speculative).

Assorted questions for Ceremonial Segment 4: Will participates in a celebratory feast (125–28). (a) Which family members and friends share a table with Will and eat with him during his celebratory feast? (factual). (b) How does Will plan to use his time and energy productively in the future? (factual). (c) What new Indigenous novel is Will made aware of during this segment? (factual). (d) How is Will reassured about his future by sitting next to Lei-Lani and spending time with her at this point in time? (factual, speculative). (e) Why is Will confident that his future relationship with a woman will work out well both for him and the woman? (factual).

Recommended Resource
Burnaby Village Museum. "Indigenous History in Burnaby Resource Guide." Burnaby, BC: City of Burnaby, 2019.

RAY'S WORLD IN *LITTLE VOICE*

Features Summary

The fictional world in the Indigenous novel *Little Voice* (Slipperjack 2001) is indigenized by thirty-two features in the categories of ancestry, religious beliefs and practices, cultural values, cultural traditions, and language use and stories. The full set of indigenizing features for this fourth contemporary realistic novel is shown in textbox 6.3. As shown in the table, no indigenizing features from Group D appear in the novel.

Exploratory Question Sets Focus

Two sets of exploratory questions are provided for the novel *Little Voice* (Slipperjack 2001). Question set 1 focuses exclusively on Group A features: ancestral lands and identity (Category 3). Question set 2 focuses

Textbox 6.3.
Indigenizing Features Summary for *Little Voice* (Slipperjack 2001)

Group A features: (3) <u>Ancestry</u>: ancestral lands, ancestral identity, ancestral beings

Group B features: (4) <u>Religious Beliefs and Practices</u>: beliefs about the Creator, praying and prayers, sacred offerings, medicine bags; (5) <u>Cultural Values</u>: expressing gratitude; (7) <u>Cultural Traditions</u>: traditional roles, large game hunting, snaring, trapping, fishing, water travel, snow travel, traditional houses, traditional shelters, traditional clothes, traditional clothing accessories, mats and baskets, wood carving, traditional implements, traditional weapons, traditional materials, traditional foods, traditional drinks, traditional medicines, food preparation

Group C features: (8) <u>Language Use and Stories</u>: ancestral language, stories about legendary individuals, mythical stories, personal stories

exclusively on Group features: water travel, traditional foods, and wood carving, (Category 7).

Supplementary Resources for Question Set 1: Ancestral Trees

Ancestral trees appear in many stories about the Ojibwe culture hero Nanabozho. The appearance of ancestral trees in traditional stories—their specific identification and roles—construe important cultural meanings. This is true for three traditional Ojibwe stories included by Jones (1917) and Densmore (1928) in their respective books about sacred Ojibwe storytelling and plant use. These stories, newly revised by the author, and a summative account of the uses of specific trees are provided below as supplementary resources that will help readers to understand the importance of trees to Indigenous people like the Ojibwe.

THREE TRADITIONAL STORIES
CONTAINING ANCESTRAL TREES

Nanabozho and the Moose-Skull

Again he was traveling around. And he met a man, a very handsome man with feathers on his head. Nanabozho said to the man, "My friend, where are you headed?"

"I'm just traveling around," said the man. "What about you? Where are you headed?"

"I'm traveling around too," said Nanabozho. Nanabozho looked hard at the man's bow. "That's a fine bow. Bring it here. Let me see how it pulls."

"No. Only I handle this bow," returned the man.

"Come on, my friend, one little pull," said Nanabozho. Finally the man gave in and surrendered the bow. Nanabozho pulled on the bow, testing it. "Yes, for sure, a very fine bow. Now give me an arrow," said Nanabozho coaxingly. The man held back for a bit then surrendered an arrow. Nanabozho loaded the bow, pulled the bowstring back, and shot the man dead.

But this in fact was not a man after all lying dead in front of him but rather a moose, and a fat one at that. Nanabozho was very pleased to have so much food. He skinned the moose, took some meat for a meal, put it in a pot, and cooked it for himself. He was just about to eat when he heard a sound. "*Cree-ee-ee-ee-eak. Cree-ee-ee-ee-eak*," went the sound. "You stop that right now," snapped Nanabozho.

But the creaking sound grew louder. Nanabozho got up from the ground and took a helping of fat tenderloin from his pot. "I can't eat with all this racket. Here, you eat too," said Nanabozho. He placed the helping of meat on the ground to stop the racket and would have gone straight back to his meal had he been able to move. But he was stuck fast in that spot, away from his meal, and couldn't get back.

Drawn by the smell of meat, various animals arrived—wolves, martens, fishers, foxes, and ravens; and only when all of the animals and meat were gone could Nanabozho move about freely again. He returned to his moose. Only bones were left, and the moose's skull.

Nanabozho stared at the skull hungrily. He noticed some mice by the skull, darting in and out of it, carrying food in their mouths. They were feeding on bits of leftover brain. "I could go for some of that," said Nanabozho desperately. He told the mice how he wished to be small like them. "I want to go inside that head like you," said Nanabozho.

"You're too big. We can't make all of you small," said the mice.

"Just my head needs to be small," said Nanabozho.

The mice agreed and made his head the same size as theirs. But they warned him: "Eat slowly and keep your head down."

Nanabozho flopped to the ground and thrust his head into the moose-skull. He was wildly hungry. He loaded his mouth with brains and threw back his head to swallow them quickly. But had he not been told to eat slowly and keep his head down? In a flash, Nanabozho's head was big again, and there he was standing helplessly among the mice with two heads, one lodged in the other.

Nanabozho kept on. He left that place with his head fully covered by that moose-skull. Who knew where he was going? The moose-skull blocked his view. He constantly bumped into things trying to make his way through the woods. He bumped into lots of trees walking along with that moose-skull covering his head—tamarack trees, birch trees, poplar trees. He asked each tree, "Who are you?"

And one of them in time replied, "A cedar tree."

"So I'm close to a lake," said Nanabozho.

Sure enough, his next few steps landed him in water. He was relieved, hot and tired from walking along with that heavy moose-skull stuck on his head. "Let me swim for a bit," said Nanabozho. He waded deeper in the lake and set off swimming.

Some people spotted him swimming. They were camped along the lake-shore. They called to each other excitedly: "Look, in the water there, a moose. Quick, grab your weapons." Then with their weapons in hand, they launched their canoes and came paddling towards him, aiming to kill him.

With remarkable speed, Nanabozho spun around in the water and headed back to the shallows and land. He swam doubly fast even with that large moose-skull weighing him down. The people paddled on, hot in pursuit. They were gaining on him, some with loaded bows.

Nanabozho's feet finally touched bottom. He plowed through the shallows with the strength of a bull moose, hoisted himself from the water, and fled for cover among the trees along the lakeshore. But not far from the water's edge, Nanabozho lost his footing, tripped, fell, and hit his head on a large rock.

The moose-skull cracked on impact, split in two, and fell away; and with that, Nanabozho, fully a man again, could see. He saw the people coming at him with loaded bows and darted into the woods.

That's all for now.

Nanabozho and the Birch Tree

One day, when Nanabozho was still a young man, he wanted to know about the largest fish in the lake. So he asked his grandmother what fish it was. His grandmother quickly replied, "Why do you ask? It's not good for you to know. There's a great fish that lives over by that rocky ledge. But that fish is very powerful and will harm you." Nanabozho asked his grandmother, "Could the fish be killed?" His grandmother replied, "No. He lives below the rocks and no one can get down there to kill him."

Nanabozho thought it over and decided that he would learn to fight and kill that dangerous fish. So he got some wood and began to make bows and arrows. He asked his grandmother if she knew whose feathers he could add to his arrows to make them effective. The old woman replied, "The only bird whose feathers would make your arrows effective is a bird that lives at the opening of the clouds in the sky. One would have to go up there to get those feathers."

Nanabozho gave it some thought: how he could get those feathers? At last he said to himself, "There's a high cliff by the lake. I'll go to that cliff and stay there for a while." Off he went. No sooner had he arrived at the cliff than he turned himself into a rabbit and stayed there, biding his time.

One day, from the highest point on the cliff, he spotted an eagle far up at the foot of the clouds. He called to the eagle, saying, "Eagle, come here. You should take me to play with your children. I'm very clever. I can teach your children many things." The eagle, a thunderbird, flew down to the cliff and saw the rabbit playing there cleverly by himself. The rabbit impressed him, so he collected him from the cliff and flew with him upward toward an opening in the sky.

When the thunderbird reached his nest he called to his children, saying, "Come see. I've brought you a playmate. He's very clever." His wife was there. She got very upset and scolded him. "You know very well that Nanabozho is around, and for all you know he could have taken the form of this rabbit." But the rabbit was much too quiet and meek to be that bothersome Nanabozho, so the thunderbirds let him stay in their nest and play with their children. And off they went hunting, leaving their children in his care.

Nanabozho played with the thunderbird children for several days while both thunderbird parents were away from the nest. Then he tired of playing with the children, changed himself back into a man, clubbed the children on their heads, stripped them of their feathers, tied his feathers in bundles, and jumped with them from the nest. His long fall to earth didn't hurt him in the least, being a spirit. It just made him sleepy.

Nanabozho hadn't much time to rest from his long fall to the earth. A great tumult directly overhead hastened him from sleep.

The thunderbirds had just returned from hunting, found their children dead, stripped of their feathers, looked around for the playmate, and realized that they had been tricked. And down they flew with vengeance, with clamorous voices and lightning flashing from their eyes.

Nanabozho leapt to his feet, grabbed his bundles of feathers, and fled. He gripped his feathers tightly, running with them awkwardly this way and that, trying to evade the thunderbirds and their deadly claws.

Then all at once, he spotted an old birch tree, a hollow one, lying on the ground, and just in the nick of time Nanabozho plunged inside.

The thunderbirds swooped round and landed on the ground near that old birch tree. They spoke to Nanabozho calmly about his good fortune, hiding from them in a birch tree. "We honor this one," said the thunderbirds reverently. "Birch trees are our children. They offer protection for all. We created them for that purpose." And off they flew, leaving Nanabozho safely hidden in that old birch tree.

When the thunderbirds were gone and all was quiet again, Nanabozho crawled out from his hiding place. He looked appreciatively at that old birch tree on the ground and marveled at the little markings on its bark that looked like little thunderbirds. Then he blessed the tree, saying, "As long as the world exists, birch trees will protect us. They will provide us with many things we need. We will store our food in its bark to preserve it. And we will honor this tree before taking its bark by offering tobacco to show our gratitude."

Nanabozho collected his bundles of feathers and went home. He fixed the little thunderbird feathers to his arrows and killed the great fish.

That's all for now.

Nanabozho and the Cedar Tree

Many generations ago, when Nanabozho had ceased to travel about, he settled down forever on an island in the east, in the land of the sunrise. The land of the sunrise signified life, and the land of the sunset in the west signified death. And while Nanabozho lived a settled life on this island in the east, a certain man, a grand medicine man, lost his daughter unexpectedly, his only daughter.

The man had loved his daughter very much and could not go on living without her. He told his friends that he wanted to travel to the land of the spirits and bring his daughter home to live with him again. He was told by his friends that only Nanabozho could help him. Only Nanabozho knew the way to the land of the spirits.

The man consulted with other grand medicine men like himself, and five of them agreed to accompany him on his quest to the land of the spirits. But first they had to find Nanabozho, who had to be somewhere. Nanabozho was a spirit, so he couldn't be dead. So the men visited the graves of their friends and called to their spirits, saying, "Can you help us to find Nanabozho?" And the spirits of their friends told them where to go.

The six men traveled east by boat on the Great Lake (now called Lake Superior) and found Nanabozho living on an island. Nanabozho was old now, too old to travel about. On his head was a beautiful cedar tree. Nanabozho wore that tree as an ornament, and surrounding him was a majestic display of its winding and intertwined roots.

So captivated was one of the men by Nanabozho's exalted appearance that he inquired of Nanabozho if could live like him forever. Nanabozho said, "No. You cannot live like me forever. You can only live for a certain number of years; unless I turned you into a stone like this one here beside me." On one side of Nanabozho was a great stone, smooth and round. "Yes," said the man. "Turn me into a stone." And it was done.

Now the other men spoke up. Five men were left. They explained their situation. Nanabozho agreed to help them. He gave each man a snake chain and instructed him to tie it securely around his waist. Then he warned the men, saying, "Wear these chains at all times. Don't remove them for any reason."

Then he charged the men not to stay longer than four days and nights in the land of the spirits. "You will not see a spirit during the day. They appear at night and dance in a long wigwam. Enter the wigwam quietly and sit there inside." Then to the dead girl's father, Nanabozho said, "Your daughter might be there. Watch for her to appear. You might see her dancing. Take a bag with you. Put her in the bag. Hold on to her tightly."

The five men did as they were told. They went to the land of the spirits, sat quietly in the long wigwam throughout the night, and watched the spirits dance. All went well for them that first night, but on the second night one of the men carelessly removed the chain from around his waist and instantly became a spirit, never to be seen again.

For the next two nights, the remaining men sat quietly in the wigwam, watching for the dead girl's spirit to appear; and late that fourth night, she appeared. Her head was covered with a blanket, but her father recognized her; and when she came within reach, he grabbed her—she struggled to get away—but with the help of his friends, he forced her into the bag, and held on to her tightly, as Nanabozho had instructed him to do.

The four grand medicine men left the land of the spirits and returned to the island where Nanabozho lived. They needed Nanabozho to tell them what to do next: how to restore the girl to a human form and get her home. Nanabozho instructed the men to begin their journey home. "But when you stop at night to rest, before making camp," said Nanabozho, "store the bag at a safe distance from your campsite, so your voices can't be heard, and make sure the bag is tightly closed. Do this every night until you get home."

The men did as they were told; and when they were safely back home, they built a sweat lodge, as Nanabozho had instructed them to do. "There must be no lamentations for your daughter nor outbursts of any kind," Nanabozho had advised the dead girl's father. "Build a new sweat lodge and place the bag with your daughter's spirit inside on a bed of fresh cedar boughs, then wait outside."

The dead girl's father did as he was told. He waited outside the new sweat lodge and finally his daughter called to him, saying, "Come and let me out." The man rushed into the sweat lodge to release his daughter from the bag; and she emerged from bag fully human, looking and sounding exactly as she did before she died. The man could hardly contain his joy, but he vividly recalled Nanabozho's instruction. He spoke to her quietly and simply welcomed her home.

That's all for now.

Important Uses of Ancestral Trees

Tamarack Trees
bark: used as a laxative, tonic, diuretic (i.e., to reduce fluid in the body), and alterative (i.e., to restore healthy body function)
leaves: used for burns
roots: used for boat building (stitching the edges of canoes) and weaving bags

Cedar Trees
bark: used for making shelters, storage bags, and splints
boughs: used for interior shelving, bedding, charcoal, and pain relief (mixed with dried bear's gall and worked into the skin at the temples
inner bark: used for dye (red, mahogany) and making mats
sprigs: used for rheumatism

Black Poplar Trees (Balsam Poplar)
buds: used as a sealant; used to clear the lungs of phlegm; used as an aromatic; and used for sprains or strained muscles (before the buds open)
root, bud, blossom: used for heart problems

White Poplar Trees (American Aspen)
sap: used for food
roots: used to stop excessive menstrual flow

Pine Trees
top branches (red pine): used for fish-drying frame construction
moss (white pine): used as food and for rheumatism (when ground)
inner bark (white pine): used for cuts (as pulp)
needles (red pine): used for making toy figures

Birch Trees

bark: used for house and boat building; used for making containers, winnowing trays, dishes, cones, spoons, stirring paddles, ladles, fans, splints, decorative patterns (i.e., transparencies), and toy figures; used for torches, tinder, burial wrapping, and stomach pain (black birch)

> **inner bark (white birch):** used for enemas and dye (red)
> **sap:** used for food

Book Sectioning

Part I: First Summers with Grandma, 1978–1979 (1–4)
Part II: First Full Summer with Grandma, 1980 (5–7)
Part III: Longest Visit with Grandma, 1981 (8–12)
Part IV: A Seagull Summer, 1982 (13)

Question Set 1: Groups A and C Features

Ancestry Lands, Identity, Language, Names, Naming (Categories 3 and 8), Little Voice

Ancestral Lands Questions: Trees

Relevant chapter. 3, 5, 10, 12, 13

Contextualizing event. While visiting her grandmother and traveling with her to various locations, Ray is struck by the presence of trees.

Internet research questions. (a) What can be learned from trustworthy sources about the indigenous species of tamarack, cedar, poplar (white, black), and pine trees (i.e., eastern white pine, jack pine, pitch pine, red pine) that grow in the Canadian province of Ontario? (b) What do these specific species of trees look like?

Supplementary resource questions 1: Three traditional stories containing ancestral trees. What meaning do ancestral trees contribute to traditional stories about the Ojibwe culture hero Nanabozho?

Supplementary resource questions 2: Important uses of ancestral trees. What traditional knowledge about the important uses of ancestral trees did Ojibwe men and women impart to Frances Densmore?

Assorted questions focusing on ancestral trees. (a) What species of tree does Ray spot on the sandy shoreline as she nears her grandmother's campsite by canoe in chapter 3, and how does the appearance of these trees capture her attention? (factual, inferencing, 39). (b) What two species of trees does Ray encounter on her solo travels by canoe in chapter 3? (factual, 48). (c) How does Ray use one species of tree to treat a wound and another to deal with mosquitoes? (factual, 48–49). (d) What species of tree grows near the train station in chapter 5, and how does the appearance of these trees capture Ray's attention? (factual, inferencing, 77). (e) What species of tree grows along the river in chapter 10, and how does the appearance of these trees capture Ray's attention? (factual, inferencing, 165). (f) From which species of tree, as noted by Ray in chapter 10, has the small clump of fragrant branches in Joshua's cabin been taken? (factual, 166). (g) What two species of trees does Ray spot in chapter 12, and how does the appearance of these trees capture her attention? (factual, 210). (h) What species of tree does Ray spot in chapter 13, and how does she use the information conveyed by these trees for snaring? (factual, inferencing, 243).

Recommended Resources
Government of Ontario, Ministry of Natural Resources. "The Tree Atlas: Northwest Region." www.ontario.ca/page/tree-atlas/ontario-northwest.
University of Guelph. "Trees." Aboretum. https://arboretum.uoguelph.ca/thingstosee/trees.

References
Densmore, Frances. *Uses of Plants by the Chippewa Indians*. Washington, DC: Bureau of American Ethnology, 1928.
Jones, William, and Truman Michelson. *Ojibwa Texts*. Leyden: Brill, 1917.

Ancestral Identity Questions

Relevant chapter. 1

Contextualizing event. Ray, her mother, and her siblings cook supper outside when they return from grocery shopping.

Background questions (1–6). (a) How did Ray's father die? (b) What financial impact did his death have on the family, and what emotional impact did his death have on Ray's mother? (c) Why does Ray feel such compassion for her mother while looking closely at her in the kitchen? (d) What sudden inspiration about supper infuses Ray's mother with life at the kitchen table? (e) What is restorative for Ray's mother, Ray, and Ray's siblings about cooking supper outdoors over a fire?

Factual questions (7–8). (a) How do Ray and her siblings respond to the ancestral stories shared with them by their mother after supper? (b) What familiar Ojibwe culture hero (i.e., ancient trickster) and group of ancestral beings come to life for Ray imaginatively in her mother's stories and fireside storytelling? (c) What is significant for Ray about her mother's ancestral stories? (d) What is significant for Ray's brother Billy about stories focusing on the Ojibwe culture hero (i.e., ancient trickster) Weesquachak?

Summative response questions (1–8). How does Ray's mother improve her spirits and bring hope to her children by sharing ancestral Ojibwe stories and legends around a fire?

Ancestral Language Questions 1: Language Identification

Relevant chapters. 1, 5, 7, 9, 11–13

Target pages: 11, 78, 81, 112, 119, 156, 208, 220, 230

Contextualizing event. At various times from 1979 to 1982, Ray identifies and thinks about the Ojibwe language, her ancestral language.

Inferencing questions. (a) What specific personal experiences prompt Ray to identify and think about her ancestral language? (b) What insights about herself or others does Ray gain, if any, by thinking about her ancestral language at various times?

Ancestral Language Questions 2: Conversations between Ray and Her Grandmother

Relevant chapters. 3, 5, 9–13

Contextualizing event. During their time together at her grandmother's cabin and while traveling about by foot or canoe, Ray and her grandmother increasingly speak to each other in Ojibwe.

Table 6.1 note. Locational information for relevant chapters about the conversations in Ojibwe between Ray and her grandmother are provided in table 6.1. Readers will locate specific conversations in each chapter using the information in the table and for each conversation will respond to the factual and summative questions provided below.

Factual questions for each conversation. (a) What year is identified at the start of the chapter (e.g., chapter 3, 1979)? (b) How old is Ray in the chapter (e.g., chapter 3, eleven years old)? (c) Where exactly are Ray and her grandmother physically located, and what physical activity are they engaged in when speaking to each other in Ojibwe (e.g., chapter 3, 41–42; beside their campsite fire, cooking)? (d) What is the focus of their conversation (e.g., chapter 3, 41–42) with a pregnant woman camping close to them)?

Table 6.1. Ray's Conversations with Her Grandmother in Ojibwe

Chapter	Pages	Year	Event
3	41–42, 53	1979	Ray's grandmother returns home briefly between visits, returns from delivering a baby, and cautions Ray about traveling about alone.
5	88, 93	1980	Ray and her grandmother rise early one morning and get ready for an outing. Ray and her grandmother return from their outing to find various things missing from the cabin, including money.
9	148–59	1981	Ray and her grandmother leave the cabin by canoe for an unknown and then known destination and camp out along the way.
10		1981	Ray and her grandmother's conversations are dominated by one topic.
11	180–81	1981	Ray and her grandmother share their thoughts about Joshua's new pet while traveling to an island to pick blueberries.
12	208–27	1981	Ray and her grandmother engage in various conversations at her grandmother's cabin during the fall, winter, and spring. Fall: 208–9, 209–11, 212; Winter: 216, 218–19; Spring. 222–24, 224–27.
13	235–36; 245–46	1982	Ray and her grandmother share their observations and thoughts about a baby seagull and Joshua.

Summative response questions for each conversation. (a) What is notable or significant for Ray about the physical activity she and her grandmother are engaged in during their conversation in Ojibwe? (b) What does Ray learn from her grandmother during their conversation in Ojibwe? (c) What does Ray learn about her grandmother from their conversation in Ojibwe?

Ancestral Language Questions 3: Cumulative Significance.

Relevant chapter. 13

Contextualizing event. Ray and her grandmother spend one more night camping before visiting Joshua at his cabin.

Background question (239). What answer does Ray receive unexpectedly from her mother to her long-standing question about living permanently with her grandmother? (also see chapter 8, 134).

Factual questions (241–42): (a) Where do Ray and her grandmother stop to spend the night on their way to Joshua's cabin in the second half of chapter 13? (b) What are Ray and her grandmother doing when False Teeth joins them by their campfire? (c) What is notable for Ray about her grandmother's voice that night? (d) What does Ray slowly begin to understand about the significance of her grandmother's comment about her hands and her mother's decision to let her live permanently with her grandmother?

Name Questions

Relevant chapter. 1

Contextualizing event. During her grandmother's visit in the summer of 1978, Ray and her grandmother have an important conversation about her name.

Background questions (9–13). (a) What unexpected circumstances have made it possible for Ray's grandmother to visit her, her mother, and her siblings at the end of the summer in 1978? (b) How many years have passed since her grandmother last came to visit, and what was her grandmother's purpose for visiting then? (c) What has Ray's grandmother learned from Ray's mother this summer about Ray's lingering grief for her late father?

Factual questions 1 (13). (a) By what name does Ray's grandmother address her? (b) What was challenging for her grandmother about the English name *Ray*, and what prompted her to call Ray *Naens* instead? (c) What does the word *naens* mean in her grandmother's first language, Ojibwe? (d) What newly concerns Ray's grandmother about the meaning of Ray's name?

Naming Questions

Relevant chapter. 1

Contextualizing event. Ray learns about the circumstances of her naming from Hitz and her mother one afternoon after school.

Background questions (17–18). (a) What prompts Hitz to stop and talk to Ray on the road? (b) Why does Ray and not her younger brother and sister recognize Hitz? (c) What does Ray recall about her (paternal) grandfather during her short conversation with Hitz on the road?

Summative questions (18–19). (a) What details does Ray learn about the circumstances of her naming from her brief conversation with Hitz on the road? (b) What additional details about her naming does Ray learn from her mother at home that afternoon?

Question Set 2: Group B Features

Water Travel (Category 7), Little Voice

Traveling by Canoe with Her Grandmother Questions 1: 1979

Relevant chapter. 3

Contextualizing event. Ray's grandmother collects her from the train station and travels with her by canoe to a campsite on a big lake with a river.

Internet, map, and video research questions. (a) What can be learned from trustworthy sources and maps about the geography of northern Ontario? (b) What is notable about the presence of rivers and lakes in northern Ontario? (c) What can be learned about railway services in northern Ontario? (d) What can be learned about the train route from Sudbury to Sioux Lookout? (e) What can be learned from informative videos about canoe travel in northern Ontario and the traditional ways Ojibwe people paddle canoes?

Factual questions (36–39). (a) Where is Ray seated in her grandmother's canoe? (b) What does Ray first observe about her surroundings while paddling her grandmother's canoe? (c) Where is her grandmother's regular campsite located? (d) Where does Ray's grandmother place a pinch of tobacco soon after entering the big lake with the river, and what is her reason for doing this? (e) What does Ray observe along the lakeshore that leads her to believe that she and her grandmother have reached their destination?

Recommended Resources
New World Encyclopedia. "Canadian Shield." www.newworldencyclopedia.org /p/index.php?title=Canadian_Shield&oldid=678554.
Ontario Parks. "Birchbark Canoe Build at Killbear Provincial Park." YouTube. www.youtube.com/watch?v=OHwSR-_n2fE&t=99s.
Railway Association of Canada. "Canadian Rail Atlas." https://rac.jmaponline .net/canadianrailatlas/.
Terra Incognita. "Wabakimi Provincial Park." YouTube. www.youtube.com /watch?v=VenJQuraa2M.
Travel by Water. "Solo Paddle Down the Mississipi [*sic*], Ontario, Canada." YouTube. www.youtube.com/watch?app=desktop&v=tnH2U8XCBt8.

Traveling by Canoe Alone Questions

Relevant chapter. 3

Contextualizing event. Ray takes her grandmother's canoe out on the lake while her grandmother is visiting people a short distance away.

Factual questions 1 (42–46). (a) What motivates Ray to take her grandmother's canoe out on the lake? (b) How does Ray manage to steer the canoe straight through the water traveling alone? (c) What paddling skill does Ray's grandmother possess that Ray does not? (d) How does Ray manage to leave the campsite in her grandmother's canoe without being noticed by her grandmother or people camped further along the lakeshore? (e) What alarming first discoveries does Ray make when she wakens from a peaceful nap in the canoe? (f) What does Ray observe about the stretch of river that immediately precedes the rapids, and what does she observe about the rapids themselves? (g) What causes Ray first to lose her paddle and then be thrown from the canoe? (h) What does Ray observe about the force of the current and the movement of her body as she passes through the rapids? (i) How does Ray manage to free herself from the current and get safely ashore?

Factual questions 2 (51–52). (a) Who helps Ray to locate her grandmother's missing canoe and paddle? (b) In what condition does Ray find her grandmother's canoe? (c) How does Ray get back to the big lake on the other side of the rapids? (d) How does Ray get back to her and grandmother's campsite on the shore of the big lake?

Traveling by Canoe with Her Grandmother Questions 2: Summer 1981

Relevant chapters. 9–10

Contextualizing event. Ray and her grandmother travel for two days by canoe to visit Joshua at his trapping cabin (chapters 9–10).

Internet research questions. (a) What can be learned from historical photographs about the traditional ways Ojibwe people seated themselves in canoes? (b) How can readers use these photographs to enhance their understandings about Ray's personal experiences traveling by canoe with her grandmother?

Factual questions 1 (150–54). (a) How in her grandmother's canoe do Ray and her grandmother each seat themselves while preparing to depart from her grandmother's cabin? (b) What specific route do Ray and her grandmother take in their canoe to the open lake? (c) Why does Ray's grandmother want them to spend the night by a big rock cliff close to the railroad tracks on their first day traveling? (d) What does Ray observe about her new surroundings on the large (long) lake when she and her grandmother are back in their canoe and paddling? (e) What adjustments do Ray and her grandmother make in terms of paddling when they spot a huge black cloud coming their way?

Factual questions 2 (161–62). (a) What route do Ray and her grandmother take by canoe the next morning to get within walking distance of a large patch of blueberries by the rock cliff, and where do they leave their canoe so they can travel part of the way by foot? (b) At what point in the day do Ray and her grandmother head back to their campsite by canoe?

Factual questions 3 (164–66). (a) What does Ray observe about her surroundings the next day when she and her grandmother are back in the canoe paddling slowly and softly toward Joshua's trapping cabin? (b) What notable observations does Ray make about the moose she spots on the lakeshore while paddling? (c) What does Ray observe about her new surroundings that afternoon while paddling along a river? (d) Why is Ray relieved when she and her grandmother leave the river and enter a lake? (e) At what point in the day do Ray and her grandmother round an island and reach the end of that lake? (f) Where is Joshua's cabin located, and what is notable for Ray about its location?

Recommended Resources

Canadian Museum of History. "Birchbark Canoe Is Invented." www .historymuseum.ca/blog/birchbark-canoe-is-invented/.

First People. "Canoe Pictures." www.firstpeople.us/FP-Html-Pictures/canoe -pictures-7.html.

Traveling by Canoe with Her Grandmother Questions 3: Summer 1981

Relevant chapter. 11

Contextualizing event. Ray and her grandmother travel by canoe to visit Joshua for several weeks at his cabin before heading back to her grandmother's cabin with unexpected stops along the way.

Word meaning and background questions. (a) How does the online *American Heritage Dictionary* define the word *purpose*? (b) How does the same dictionary define the word *determination*? (c) Why do Ray and her grandmother end their visit with Joshua early?

Assorted questions focusing on Ray's travels by canoe to an island close to Joshua's cabin (179–81). (a) What activity have Ray and her grandmother planned for themselves when they leave Joshua's cabin by canoe at the start of chapter 11? (factual). (b) What distracts Ray from paddling that morning? (factual). (c) What destination do Ray and her grandmother reach by canoe that morning? (factual). (d) From Ray's perspective, why do they paddle back to Joshua's cabin slowly? (factual). (e) From Ray's grandmother's perspective, why do they paddle back to Joshua's cabin slowly? (speculative).

Assorted questions focusing on Ray's travels by canoe back to her grandmother's cabin (182–84). (a) How might Ray and her grandmother appear to an observer paddling along the lake "quietly with a purpose"? (speculative). (b) What is likely relaxing, comforting, and restorative about paddling along a familiar lake like that? (speculative). (c) Why does Ray's grandmother abandon her original plan to return directly to her cabin after the last portage, where do they travel to instead, and for how long do they stay at this other location on her grandmother's lake? (factual). (d) What might Ray gain by memorizing the shoreline as she and her grandmother paddle home? (speculative).

Traveling by Canoe with Her Grandmother Questions 4: Summer 1982

Relevant chapter. 13

Contextualizing event. Ray spends the first part of her summer holiday traveling by canoe with her grandmother.

Assorted questions focusing on a notable island (234–36). (a) What is notable for Ray about an island she and her grandmother pass while traveling by canoe to a familiar campsite at the start of the new summer, and what compels Ray to hold her paddle still while approaching the island? (factual). (c) What compels Ray's grandmother to place her own paddle across her lap and share her thoughts with Ray softly? (inferencing, speculative). (d) What pros and cons guide Ray's decision about the orphaned baby seagull floating nearby? (factual). (e) What occupies Ray next as her grandmother paddles on alone and delivers them safely to their campsite? (speculative).

Assorted questions focusing on Ray's travels by canoe to visit Joshua (240–44). (a) How are Ray's two pets positioned in the canoe as Ray and her grandmother head off to visit Joshua at his cabin? (factual). (b) What compels Ray's pet seagull to maintain its specific position while Ray and her grandmother paddle along the lake? (inferencing). (c) What causes the seagull to change its position? (factual).

Traveling by Canoe with Her Grandmother Questions 5: Portage Routes

Relevant chapter. 3, 9

Contextualizing event. Ray and her grandmother travel back and forth between lakes by canoe and land routes during the summers of 1979 and 1981.

Word meaning and video research questions. (a) How does the online *Collins Dictionary* define the word *portage*? (b) What can be learned from informative videos about portaging in Ontario?

Assorted questions focusing on Ray's experience at age eleven traveling by canoe with portage routes (37–38). (a) How does Ray know that she and her grandmother have just paddled past the Mile One portage route? (inferencing). (b) By which portage route is the regular campsite of Ray's grandmother located? (factual). (c) What bodies of water lie beyond the Mile One portage route, how many portage routes must be crossed to reach these bodies of water, and where does the rail line run in proximity? (factual). (d) What motivates Ray's grandmother to take this first portage route rather than maintaining a course to her regular campsite? (speculative). (e) What does Ray quickly observe about the portage route that lies between the skinny lake and big lake with a river, and how many trips does it take Ray and her grandmother to transport their canoe and things to the other side of the portage route? (factual). (f)

What pleases both Ray and her grandmother about Ray's first experience crossing a portage route? (inferencing).

Factual questions focusing on Ray's experience at age thirteen traveling by canoe on portage routes (148–54). (a) What equipment and supplies does Ray identify in the first four pages of chapter 9 that she and her grandmother will take with them on their upcoming travels by canoe (to visit Joshua)? (b) How many trips does it take Ray and her grandmother to transport their canoe and things to the other side of the first portage route, what problem does Ray encounter delivering the canoe with her grandmother, and how do Ray and her grandmother respond to this problem? (c) What does Ray quickly observe about the next portage route? (d) What is challenging for Ray about transporting the canoe to the other side of this new route? (e) What weakens the effectiveness of the mosquito repellent Ray has applied to herself?

Recommended Resource
Covering Water. "Ontario Canoe Camping Trip." YouTube. www.youtube.com/watch?v=w5yMPBg1_OQ.

Traditional Meals and Wood Carving (Category 7), Little Voice

Traditional Meal Questions: Traditional Foods

Relevant chapters. 3, 5, 9–13

Table 6.2 note. Locational information for relevant chapters about the traditional Ojibwe foods that are an integral part of the daily meals shared by Ray and her grandmother are provided in table 6.2. Readers will locate specific meals and foods in each chapter using the information in the table and for each meal respond to the factual questions below.

Factual questions. (a) What traditional Ojibwe foods are an integral part of the daily meals shared by Ray and her grandmother? (b) What identified traditional

Table 6.2. References for Traditional Ojibwe Meals in *Little Voice* (Slipperjack 2001)

Chapter	Reference Pages
3	39–41
5	78, 81, 83, 88, 92
9	144, 155, 162
10	163, 173, 175
11	182–83, 185, 196, 203, 205
12	221, 212, 226
13	234, 238, 243

Ojibwe foods will be an integral part of a future meal shared by Ray and her grandmother? (c) What daily meal is most often absent for Ray and her grandmother at her grandmother's cabin or at their various campsites?

Wood Carving Questions

Relevant chapters. 10–12

Contextualizing event. Ray carves special wooden objects for important people in her life.

Internet research question. How are canes and walking sticks similar and different?

Assorted questions focusing on Ray's first carved wooden object: 1981. (a) Where is Ray when she carves her first wooden object, how old is she, what object does she carve, and what surprises her about the object? (factual, 173–74). (b) Why does Ray give the object to Hitz as a gift? (inferencing, see chapter 6, 102). (c) What does Ray tell Hitz about the object, and how does Hitz respond to Ray's gift? (factual, 195).

Assorted questions focusing on Ray's second carved wooden object: 1981. (a) What event in early September prompts Ray and her grandmother to talk about walking canes? (factual, 207–9). (b) For an old, traditional Ojibwe woman like Ray's grandmother who has spent most of her life in a remote Ojibwe community in northern Ontario, what differences would she likely discern between a cane, a walking stick, and a walking cane, and why is her use of the term *walking cane* appropriate? (speculative, 209). (c) What challenging personal situations identified by her grandmother would be less challenging for her if she could travel about with a walking cane? (factual, 209). (d) What surprises Ray about her grandmother's response to Ray's offhand offer to carve a walking cane for her? (inferencing, 209–10). (e) What species of tree does Ray's grandmother identify as a perfect tree for a walking cane, and what event in the lifespan of that tree has made the tree perfect for a walking cane? (factual, 210). (f) How long does it take Ray to carve the new walking cane for her grandmother, what is special about its handle, what recent experience surely inspired Ray to carve the handle this way, and what thoughts about the special carved figure on the handle does her grandmother share with her? (factual, 210–12). (g) What does this newly carved object reveal about Ray from her grandmother's perspective? (factual, 212).

Chapter 7

Fantasy Worlds (Past, Present, Future)

CHAPTER OVERVIEW AND TARGET QUESTIONS

This chapter focuses on fictional worlds in two fantasy novels, the mythical novel *The Curse of the Shaman* (Kusugak 2006) and the dystopian novel *The Marrow Thieves* (Dimaline 2017). The first novel recounts the experiences of an Inuit man named Wolverine who struggles from childhood to early adulthood to overcome a curse that was placed on him as a newborn by a volatile Inuit shaman. The second novel recounts the experiences of a sixteen-year-old Metis boy named Frenchie as he and a small group of Indigenous people travel north in Ontario seeking freedom from a self-serving and autocratic national government.

The two novels are suited for exploratory studies of indigenized worlds in grades 5–10 and 7–10 respectively. For this chapter, readers will seek to answer the following target questions.

What basic story details for each novel are conveyed through the publisher summaries?

Which indigenizing feature is specifically defined, and how is it defined?

Which specific indigenizing features appear in each novel?

How is each novel subdivided for an exploratory study?

What sets of questions and recommended resources can be used to explore the indigenizing features shown in textbox 7.1?

What supplementary resources are uniquely provided for an exploratory study of indigenizing features in the second novel?

Which specific questions and recommended resources can teachers and students use in grades 5–10 and 7–10 to gain insights about two Indigenous young people, Wolverine and Frenchie, their families, and their communities?

Textbox 7.1.
Targeted Indigenizing Features in *The Curse of the Shaman* (Kusugak 2006) and *The Marrow Thieves* (Dimaline 2017)

Group A features: ancestral lands
Group B features: snow travel, water travel, boat building, boat repair, supernatural powers, traditional knowledge of local wildlife, large-game hunting, whaling, house and shelter building, a spring festival with traditional games, songs, and a wedding ceremony
Group C features: stories about legendary individuals, widely circulated stories of contemporary renown, personal stories
Group D features: material appropriation, forced relocation from homeland, forced separation of children from parents, subjugation, elders, councils

TWO FANTASY WORLDS

Selected Novels: Bibliographic Information and Individual Summaries

Kusugak, Michael. 2006. *The Curse of the Shaman* Toronto: HarperTrophyCanada. Paperback. 158 pages. Twenty-three chapters. Includes an afterword. Illustrated. Fantasy fiction (literary legend). Grades 6–10 novel. Not leveled.

Story details from back cover. Sometimes even shamans get cranky. That was baby Wolverine's misfortune—to be cursed by an out-of-sorts shaman frustrated by his own baby daughter's incessant crying. Not only has shaman Paaliaq forbidden the future marriage of Wolverine to Breath, Paaliaq's beautiful but teary baby girl, he has cursed Wolverine, banishing him when he becomes a young man. And even when a contrite Paaliaq later revokes the curse, the shaman's even crankier magic animal will not. Now Wolverine finds himself stranded on a barren island, locked in a life-or-death struggle to return to his home, his family and a very special young girl.

Dimaline, Cherie 2017. *The Marrow Thieves.* Toronto: DCB. Paperback. 231 pages. Twenty-seven chapters. Not illustrated. Fantasy fiction. Grades 8–12 novel. Guided Reading Level not available. Lexile Measure 810L.

Story details from back cover. Just when you think you have nothing left to lose, they come for your dreams. In a world nearly destroyed by global warming, the Indigenous people of North America are being hunted for their bone marrow, which carries the key to recovering something the rest of the population has lost: the ability to dream. Frenchie and his companions, struggling to survive, don't yet know that one of them holds the secret to defeating the marrow thieves.

The Curse of the Shaman: Key Fictional World Details

Specific Indigenous Groups and Individuals
Inuit, Wolverine (birth to marrying age)
Fantasy Settings
Mythical time, northwest coast of Hudson Bay, Nunavut

The Marrow Thieves: Key Fictional World Details

Specific Indigenous Groups and Individuals
Metis, Frenchie (age 16)
Fantasy Settings
2050, Great Lakes northern region

WOLVERINE'S WORLD IN *THE CURSE OF THE SHAMAN*

Features Summary

The fictional world in the Indigenous novel *The Curse of the Shaman* (Kusugak 2006) is indigenized by forty-two features in the categories of time, ancestry, religious beliefs and practices, cultural values, cultural events, cultural traditions, language use and stories, family life and kinship, subjugation, and restoration. The full set of indigenizing features for this fantasy novel is shown in textbox 7.2.

Exploratory Question Sets Focus

Three sets of exploratory questions are provided for the fantasy novel *The Curse of the Shaman* (Kusugak 2006). Question set 1 focuses on Group A–B features: ancestral lands (Category 3); snow travel, water travel, boat building,

Textbox 7.2.
Indigenizing Features Summary for *The Curse of the Shaman*
(Kusugak 2006)

> **Group A features:** (1) Time: seasonal habitation cycles; (3)
> Ancestry: ancestral lands
> **Group B features:** (4) Religious Beliefs and Practices: supernatural
> powers; (5) Cultural Values: valuing sharing and peaceful relations
> with neighboring nations; (6) Cultural Events: stationary games,
> toss-and-catch games, traditional songs and singing, spring festi-
> val, Inuit wedding ceremony; (7) Cultural Traditions: traditional
> knowledge about local wildlife, traditional roles, large-game hunt-
> ing, rabbit hunting, bird hunting, fishing, whaling, water travel,
> snow travel, traditional houses, house and shelter building, boat
> building and repair, tanning, traditional clothes, traditional cloth-
> ing accessories, traditional weapons, traditional materials, tradi-
> tional foods, food preparation, food storage
> **Group C features:** (8) Language Use and Stories: ancestral lan-
> guage, names and naming, stories about legendary individuals,
> mythical stories, personal stories, widely circulated stories of con-
> temporary renown (9) Family Life and Kinship: extended family
> households, sibling care, childbirth, childhood play, respecting
> one's in-laws
> **Group D features:** (10) Subjugation: subjugation; (12)
> Restoration: restoration

boat repair (Category 7); supernatural powers (Category 4); and traditional
knowledge of local wildlife, large game hunting, whaling (Category 7).

Question set 2 focuses on more Group B features: house and shelter building (Category 7); and a spring festival with traditional games, songs, and a
wedding ceremony (Category 6). Question set 3 focuses on Group C features: stories about legendary individuals and widely circulated stories of
contemporary renown (Category 8).

Book Sectioning

Part I: Wolverine Enters the World (1–8)
Part II: Wolverine Grows toward Manhood (9–16)
Part III: Breaking the Curse (17–21)
Part IV: Marrying Breath (22–23)

Question Set 1: Group A–B Features

Ancestral Lands, Travel, Boat Building and Repair (Categories 3, 7), The Curse of the Shaman

Ancestral Lands Questions 1: Islands, Inlets (Bays), and Points of Land

Relevant chapters. 1, 9, 10, 17, 20

Contextualizing event. While standing outside his igloo one evening looking at the sky, The-man-with-no-eyebrows decides to move his new family south (chapter 1). Wolverine travels close to his mother's birthplace by dog team to meet his grandparents for the first time (chapter 9). Wolverine hugs his grandmother before she and his grandfather depart for the big island beyond the strait (chapter 10). Now fourteen years old, Wolverine accompanies his father whale hunting near Marble Island (chapter 17). He camps on Marble Island with his father but is prevented from leaving the island by Paaliaq's curse (chapter 20).

Factual questions. (a) What ancestral islands are identified in chapters 1, 17, and 20 (4, 7, 109, 127)? (b) What ancestral inlets are named in chapters 4 and 11 (15, 57)? (c) What ancestral points-of-land are identified in chapters 1, 9, and 10 (4, 37, 50)?

Inferencing question. What motivated Inuit people to name each island, inlet, and point-of-land as they did?

Research questions. (a) Where is Marble Island situated? (b) What is distinctive about Marble Island? (c) What whales frequent the waters surrounding Marble Island? (d) What wildlife is abundant on the island?

Ancestral Lands Questions 2: Lakes and Rivers

Relevant chapters. 13, 16, 21

Contextualizing event. Now nine, Wolverine spends lots of time with Breath at their usual summering place and eventually helps his father and Paaliaq to build kayaks (chapter 13). Just south of their summering place, Paaliaq and Auk's daughter Breath helps her mother to make clothes out of seal and caribou skins (chapter 16). Wolverine finally manages to leave Marble Island with his kayak (chapter 21).

Factual questions. (a) What ancestral lakes are identified in chapters 13 and 16? (75, 101). (b) What ancestral river is named in chapter 21 (135)?

Inferencing question. What motivated Inuit people to name these lakes and river as they did?

Snow Travel Questions

Relevant chapters. 3, 4, 9

Contextualizing event. Paaliaq encounters a huge polar bear while hunting seals on the sea ice with his sled and dog team (chapter 3). In early spring, The-man-with-no-eyebrows travels south by dog sled to several locations with his new family (chapters 4, 9).

Book, video, and Internet research questions. (a) How did Inuit people travel long distances on the snow and ice before snowmobiles? (b) What did traditional Inuit dog sleds look like? (c) What breed of dogs did Inuit people typically use as sled dogs? (d) What is distinctive about traditional Inuit snow goggles? (e) Why do Inuit travelers make and wear such goggles while traveling by dog sled?

Factual questions. (a) What device does The-man-with-no-eyebrows use to hold his dogs' line to the sled? (12). (b) What challenge does The-man-with-no-eyebrows face traveling by dog team during the day in early spring? (15). (c) How does The-man-with-no-eyebrows address this challenge? (15). (d) What knowledge about lead dogs did The-man-with-no-eyebrows acquire from his father? (15–16). (e) How does Can't-see typically help her husband and the dogs to keep the sled moving through wet snow? (16). (f) Why today, while traveling south by dog team in the long afternoon, does The-man-with-no-eyebrows insist that his wife stay on the sled? (16). (g) Under what circumstances does The-man-with-no-eyebrows equip his dogs with bootees? (16). (h) What protection do bootees offer sled dogs? (17). (i) How do sled dogs typically respond to wearing bootees? (17). (j) Where on his father's dog sled is young Wolverine positioned, relative to his parents, as his family travels south of Tikirarjuaq ("Long-forefinger" in English)? (37–38). (k) What is distinctive about Wolverine's position on the dog sled? (38). (l) How does Wolverine pass the time while traveling with his parents by dog sled? (38). (m) How does The-man-with-no-eyebrows use a sealskin whip while traveling south by dog sled? (38). (n) What prompts The-man-with-no-eyebrows to leave the sled at certain times, run beside his dogs, then return to the sled and be seated? (38–39).

Recommended Resources

Alexander, Cherry, and Bryan Alexander. *Flashback History: Inuit*. New York: PowerKids Press, 2010.

Awa, Solomon, and Andrew Breithaupt. Igluvigaliurniq Qamusiurnirlu. How to Build an Iglu & a Qamutiik. Iqaluit, Nunavut: Inhabit Media, 2013.

Burch, Ernest S., and Werner Forman. *The Eskimos*. Norman: University of Oklahoma Press, 1988.

Casey, Brigid, and Wendy Haugh. *Sled Dogs*. New York: Dodd Mead, 1983.

Corriveau, Danielle. The Inuit of Canada. Minneapolis, MN: Lerner Publications, 2022.

Gleason, Carrie. *Nunavut*. Toronto: Scholastic Canada, 2009.

Ipellie, Alootook, and David MacDonald. The Inuit Thought of It: Amazing Arctic Innovations. Toronto: Annick Press, 2007.
Lajiness, Katie. *Inuit*. Minneapolis, MN: Big Buddy Books, 2017.
MacDonald, John. Inuit Wayfinding. Iqaluit, Nunavut: Nunavummi, 2022.
Montcombroux, Geneviève. *The Canadian Inuit Dog: Canada's Heritage.* Second edition. Inwood, MB: Whippoorwill Press, 2002.
Olson, Barbara, and Megan Kyak-Monteith. *Inuit Tools of the Western Arctic.* Iqaluit, Nunavut: Nunavummi, 2020.
Siska, Heather Smith, and Ian Bateson. *People of the Ice: How the Inuit Lived.* Buffalo, NY: Firefly Books, 1995.
Yacowitz, Caryn. *Inuit Indians*. Chicago: Capstone, 2016.

Water Travel Questions

Relevant chapters. 12, 17, 20, 21, 22

Contextualizing event. One summer, at age seven, Wolverine hears the legendary story of young Kiviuq, a boy himself at the time, who travels by kayak for many days alone on the open sea (chapter 12). Wolverine and his father travel to Marble Island to hunt whales (chapter 17). Wolverine winters alone on Marble Island (chapter 20). The following spring Wolverine secures himself in his kayak and starts for home (chapter 21). Assisted by his father, Wolverine arrives home safely at Fish River (chapter 22).

Video research questions. (a) How did Inuit people in the past propel their kayaks through the water? (b) How did Inuit people in the past perform kayak rolls? (c) What benefit did Inuit people in the past derive from rolling their kayaks?

Factual questions. (a) What stopped Kiviuq from sinking to the bottom of the sea like the majority of boys who took to the sea in their kayaks in pursuit of the little boy in a sealskin suit? (69–70). (b) How did Kiviuq manage to travel such a great distance on the sea with his kayak? (70). (c) Where does Wolverine build his own kayak for the first time? (107). (d) How long does Wolverine practice paddling his first kayak before becoming proficient at it? (107). (e) Why does The-man-with-no-eyebrows refuse to take Little-loved-one hunting with them to Marble Island? (107). (f) What ancestral islands do Wolverine and his father pass in their kayaks before striking out on the open sea to Marble Island? (109). (g) How long does it take Wolverine and his father to reach Marble Island from In-there? (109). (h) What kayaking skills displayed by the legendary Kiviuq does Wolverine speak about to his faithful companion Ukpigjuaq on Marble Island? (130). (i) How does Wolverine's mastery of kayak rolling help him to battle the forces that seek to prevent him from leaving Marble Island? (134–35). (j) What prevents The-man-with-no-eyebrows from traveling to Marble Island to help his son to get home safely? (136). (k) What makes Wolverine's companion Ukpigjuaq happy while looking down on him in his kayak in stormy waters? (136). (l) What assistance is The-man-with-no-eyebrows able to offer his son

when the sea is calm again that brings him safely home to Fish River? (141).
(m) What is the focus of Wolverine's dream when he is back at Fish River and
sleeping in his parents' tent? (141).

Inferencing questions. (a) How did the majority of boys in the legendary story of
Kiviuq display their inexperience as kayakers? (69). (b) Why did it make good
sense for Wolverine to practice paddling his first kayak around the islands in
their summering place? (107). (c) Why is Wolverine so determined to continue
rolling his kayak despite his many failures and near drowning? (131–32).

Recommended Resources
Alaska Film Archives—UAF. "Kayak Roll and Gut Parkas." YouTube. www
    .youtube.com/watch?v=RuCbJ_tsVhQ.
PeriscopeFilm. "Eskimo Life & Walrus Hunt." YouTube. www.youtube.com/
    watch?v=mq1jiR1bXM8.

Boat Building and Repair Questions

Relevant chapters. 13, 20

Contextualizing event. At age nine, while summering at In-there with his family,
Wolverine helps his and Breath's parents build kayaks (chapter 13). Wolverine
repairs his kayak before paddling out to deep water to practice kayak rolling
(chapter 20).

Video research question. How did Inuit people in the past make kayaks mainly
from driftwood and sealskins?

Factual questions. (a) How is wood obtained by The-man-with-no-eyebrows
and Paaliaq to build new kayak frames at their summering place? (75, 82). (b)
What dangers might the two men encounter in their pursuit of wood for new
kayaks? (76). (c) How precisely do the men use the wood they obtain? (83). (d)
What specific kayak-building tasks are undertaken by the two men's wives and
children? (83). (e) What specific kayak-building tasks are undertaken by the
two men? (83). (f) What specific repairs does Wolverine make to his kayak on
Marble Island? (131).

Recommended Resource
Alaska Extreme. "Tuktu 2: The Big Kayak (How to Build a Kayak Out of
    Driftwood)." Youtube. www.youtube.com/watch?v=tKbwNdes0SY.

Supernatural Powers (Category 4), The Curse of the Shaman

The Shaman's Power Questions 1

Relevant chapter. 2

Contextualizing event. Paaliaq becomes irritated by his daughter's crying.

Word meaning and research questions. (a) How does the online *American Heritage Dictionary* define the word *shaman*. (b) What additional information about shamans is provided on the Wikipedia and *Britannica* websites?

Factual questions (10–11). (a) Why should shamans like Paaliaq know the cause of such ordinary life events as a babies crying? (b) What qualifies Paaliaq as a good shaman? (c) What personal shortcoming is Paaliaq known to possess? (d) What shamanic powers (i.e., special gifts) does Paaliaq put to use to help people? (e) What two objects identify Paaliaq as a shaman?

The Shaman's Articulated Curse Questions

Relevant chapter. 5

Contextualizing event. Three days after the birth of his first child, The-man-with-no-eyebrows makes his way to Paaliaq's igloo to present his newborn son.

Factual questions (22–25). (a) Why does Paaliaq get angry when Can't-see holds his new baby Breath? (b) How does The-man-with-no-eyebrows fuel Paaliaq's anger while his wife is cuddling Breath? (c) What causes an enraged Paaliaq to reject The-man-with-no-eyebrows's offer of an arranged marriage between their newly born children? (d) What curse does Paaliaq place on The-man-with-no-eyebrows's newborn son? (e) Why does Paaliaq let the curse stand rather than retracting it?

The Shaman's Actualized Curse Questions 1

Relevant chapter. 7

Contextualizing event. Shortly after his newborn son is cursed by Paaliaq at Bit-of Sand, The-man-with-no-eyebrows is filled with dread and anger at his sighting of a siksik near Paaliaq's igloo.

Background question. What information about the siksik (i.e., Mr. Siksik) and his relationship with Paaliaq is provided in chapter 6?

Factual questions (29–31). (a) What species of animal is a siksik? (b) Why is The-man-with-no-eyebrows surprised to see a siksik outside Paaliaq's igloo in this chapter? (c) Why does the sighting of a siksik concurrent with Paaliaq's curse fill The-man-with-no-eyebrows with dread?

The Shaman's Actualized Curse Questions 2

Relevant chapters. 17, 18

Contextualizing event. Strange goings-on prevent Wolverine from returning home with his father after a successful day of hunting in the waters by Marble Island (chapter 17). Paaliaq seeks answers about the strange goings-on near Marble Island as reported to him by The-man-with-no-eyebrows by entering a shamanic trance and conjuring up his tuurngaq (chapter 18).

Factual questions. (a) What strange goings-on in the waters by Marble Island impel The-man-with-no-eyebrows to return to the mainland alone temporarily? (110–13). (b) At what point does The-man-with-no-eyebrows realize that Paaliaq's curse, articulated in chapter 5, is now preventing Wolverine from coming home? (114–16).

The Shaman's Broken Curse Questions

Relevant chapter. 21

Contextualizing event. While Wolverine endeavors to paddle home on a stormy sea, his faithful friend Ukpigjuaq flies this way and that way looking for food, a lemming or ground squirrel, to satisfy Wolverine's hunger.

Background questions. (a) Why did Mr. Siksik keep the curse on Wolverine when Paaliaq expressly renounced it in chapter 15? (99). (b) What limitations in his shamanic powers did Paaliaq admit with respect to his curse on Wolverine when he first came out of his trance? (116). (c) How did The-man-with-no-eyebrows respond to this admission? (116–17). (d) What course of action did Paaliaq agree to take to remove the curse? (117–18). (e) How did Mr. Siksik respond to Paaliaq's proposed course of action? (118).

Factual question (139–40). How are the conditions at sea, as experienced by Wolverine aboard his kayak, immediately impacted by the demise of Mr. Siksik?

The Shaman's Power Questions 2

Relevant chapter. 23

Contextualizing event. Now back on the mainland, Wolverine asks his father about the curse that trapped him on Marble Island.

Factual questions (144). (a) What information about Paaliaq's shamanic powers does Wolverine learn from his father when he awakens from his long sleep? (b)

According to The-man-with-no-eyebrows, how does Paaliaq plan to restore his shamanic powers?

Traditional Wildlife Knowledge, Hunting, Whaling (Category 7), The Curse of the Shaman

Traditional Knowledge about Local Wildlife Questions

<u>Relevant chapters</u>. 11, 16

<u>Contextualizing event</u>. At age seven, Wolverine learns about caribou while hunting with his father (chapter 11). At age fourteen, Breath watches the huge herds of caribou as they pass by her springtime camp (chapter 16).

<u>Video Research question</u>. What knowledge about caribou in the Canadian Arctic can be gained from viewing informative videos?

<u>Factual questions</u>. (a) What knowledge about caribou does seven-year-old Wolverine acquire from his father? (58–59). (b) What does Wolverine observe first hand about male caribou while hunting with his father? (58). (c) What observations does fourteen-year-old Breath make about fall caribou at the start of chapter 16? (101–2). (d) What observations does Breath make about spring caribou later in chapter 16 as they pass by her springtime camp in great numbers? (104). (e) What new knowledge about caribou does Breath acquire from her mother when Breath asks her mother about the destination of the spring caribou? (104–5).

<u>Recommended Resource</u>
Danny. "Caribau [*sic*] Migration." Youtube. www.youtube.com/watch?v =r6jcqCm5C1Q.

Large Game Hunting Questions 1

<u>Relevant chapters</u>. 9, 11

<u>Contextualizing statement</u>. The meat obtained from large land and sea mammals by Inuit men brings health and security to Inuit families like Wolverine's.

<u>Factual question</u>. What large game animals identified in chapters 9 and 11 are routinely hunted for food by The-man-with-no-eyebrows, Paaliaq, Wolverine, and other Inuit men, young and old? (40, 58).

Large Game Hunting Questions 2

<u>Relevant chapters</u>. 9–10

Contextualizing events. Wolverine listens attentively to his father's recount of his recent adventures hunting seals on ice floes (chapter 9). The-man-with-no-eyebrows hunts seals with his dogs (chapter 10).

Word meaning, book, Internet, and video research questions. (a) How does the online *American Heritage Dictionary* define the word *eiderdown* and its constituent parts *eider* and *down*. (b) What does one eiderdown feather look like? (c) How is eiderdown used by Inuit hunters to locate seals?

Factual questions. (a) What details about his recent capture of a seal does The-man-with-no-eyebrows share with his family members? (42–43). (b) What is Wolverine's summative response to these details? (43). (c) What changing ice conditions, reported at the start of chapter 10, is The-man-with-no-eyebrows familiar with as an experienced Inuit hunter? (45). (d) How does The-man-with-no-eyebrows use his sled dogs when traveling on new ice? (46). (e) What specific information about seals is typically provided by The-man-with-no-eyebrows's two best sniffing dogs? (47–48). (f) How is a small strand of white eiderdown used by Inuit hunters like The-man-with-no-eyebrows to hunt seals? (49).

Recommended Resource
Documentary Educational Resources. "At the Spring Sea Ice Camp (2)." YouTube. www.youtube.com/watch?v=FeAKVGKSAxQ.

Whaling Questions

Relevant chapters. 14, 17

Contextualizing events. Inuit men can often be seen whaling at In-there (chapter 14). Wolverine and his father set out by kayak to hunt whales by Marble Island (chapter 17).

Factual questions. (a) What species of whale is routinely caught at In-there by Inuit hunters? (86). (b) What species of whale do Inuit men like The-man-with-no-eyebrows set off to hunt by Marble Island? (106). (c) What hunting preparations does Wolverine make before heading to Marble Island with his father? (107–8).

Inferencing question. Why are wary whales difficult to hunt? (110).

Question Set 2: More Group B Features

House and Shelter Building (Category 7), The Curse of the Shaman

House Building Questions: A Family Igloo

Relevant chapter. 8

Contextualizing event. The-man-with-no-eyebrows builds an igloo for his family near Paaliaq's family igloo.

Video Research questions. What knowledge about family igloo building in the Canadian Arctic can be gained from viewing informative videos?

Factual questions. (a) What two tools does The-man-with-no-eyebrows use to build an igloo for his family? (32). (b) What qualities does The-man-with-no-eyebrows look for in the snow he will use to build an igloo? (32). (c) What is the purpose of the circle The-man-with-no-eyebrows draws in the snow with a stick? (32). (d) What factors did The-man-with-no-eyebrows consider when drawing a circle of a specific size? (33). (e) What assistance does Paaliaq offer The-man-with-no-eyebrows as he trims his cut blocks and taps them into place? (33). (f) What task do The-man-with-no-eyebrows and Paaliaq do together when the last block of snow has been dropped into place on the roof? (35). (g) How long does it take The-man-with-no-eyebrows to build an igloo for his family? (35).

Recommended Resource
National Film Board of Canada. "How to Build an Igloo." YouTube. www .youtube.com/watch?v=K3pd-wxNEKQ.

Shelter Building Questions: A Festival Igloo

Relevant chapter. 32

Contextualizing event. The whole community at Bit-of-sand helps to construct a giant festival igloo.

Video Research question. What knowledge about communal igloo building in the Canadian Arctic can be gained from viewing informative videos?

Factual question (147–48). How do the men, women, and children at Bit-of-sand use an assembly-line approach and specialized tasks to erect a festival igloo that includes a main igloo and smaller connecting ones?

Recommended Resource
Alaska Extreme. "Tuktu-4—The Snow Palace (How to Build a REAL Inuit Igloo)." YouTube. www.youtube.com/watch?v=BWKfJQpZtaM&t=554s.

A Traditional Spring Festival and Wedding Ceremony (Category 6),
The Curse of the Shaman

Spring Festival Questions

Relevant chapter. 23

Contextualizing event. Many Inuit families gather at Bit-of-sand at the end of a
very good winter and decide to celebrate their good fortune by holding a festival.

Factual questions. (a) What conditions reported at the start of the chapter make
this gathering of Inuit families at Bit-of-sand a perfect time for a festival?
(146–47). (b) Who announces the festival? (147). (c) How do the people employ
two long sleds and a strong rope in their festival preparations? (148). (d) What
indoor activities do people first engage in when the festival igloo is complete?
(149). (e) What festival activities are held that first night when Wolverine and
Breath, now husband and wife, retire to a connecting igloo to spend some time
together? (151–52).

Inferencing question. Why does it make sense for spring festival participants
like Paaliaq to refer to the festival as a party? (147–48).

Traditional Inuit Wedding Ceremony Questions

Relevant chapter. 23

Contextualizing event. As the spring festival gets underway in the festival igloo,
Paaliaq makes an important public announcement.

Factual questions. (a) What public admission does Paaliaq make at the start
of the festival before honoring his word and offering his daughter Breath to
Wolverine in marriage? (149). (b) What wedding gift does Paaliaq give his new
son-in-law? (150). (c) What wedding gift does The-man-with-no-eyebrows give
his son? (150). (d) What simple words do Breath and Wolverine exchange that
seal their marriage? (150). (e) What gifts does Can't-see give her son and new
daughter-in-law at the end of the festival? (153).

Traditional Songs and Singing Questions

Relevant chapters. 9, 22, 23

Contextualizing events. A childhood song recounts Wolverine's personal experiences staying back with his mother while visiting his grandparents for the first
time (chapter 9). Now home on the mainland and sleeping in his parents' tent,
Wolverine recalls a song from his childhood (chapter 22). After the wedding

feast in honor of Wolverine and Breath, people gather around a drum and chant a traditional song (chapter 23).

Inferencing questions. (a) How specifically do the song lyrics at the start of chapter 9 reflect Wolverine's experiences later in the chapter when he visits his grandparents for the first time? (40–44). (b) How is the recalled song that appears in chapter 22 meaningful for both Wolverine and his sister Little-loved-one? (142–43). (c) What makes the song chanted in the festival igloo in chapter 23 appropriate both as a wedding and spring festival song? (151–52).

Traditional Games Questions

Relevant chapters. 9, 23

Contextualizing events. Wolverine plays games with children for the first time while visiting his grandparents south of Tikirarjuaq (chapter 9). Games of strength and a game of soccer are played during the spring festival (chapter 23).

Factual questions. (a) How specifically are the games of tag and toss-and-catch played by the Inuit children Wolverine encounters south of Tikirarjuaq? (41). (b) How does Wolverine respond to the new experiences of laughing, teasing, and taunting while playing games with other children? (41). (c) For what amount of time do games occupy Wolverine and his new playmates? (41). (d) What games of strength are played during the spring festival? (152). (e) What do these games entail? (152–53). (f) What is special and perhaps unusual about the soccer game played during the spring festival? (153).

Question Set 3: Group C Features

Stories (Category 8), The Curse of the Shaman

Stories about Legendary Individuals Questions: Kiviuq

Relevant chapter. 12

Contextualizing event. Breath's grandmother gathers her seven-year-old granddaughter Breath and two other young children in her tent, including seven-year-old Wolverine, and tells them a story about the greatest man who has ever lived—Kiviuq.

Internet research questions. (a) What does a red-necked phalarope look like (*saurraq* in Inuktitut)? (b) What is distinctive about the feeding behavior of these birds?

Background question (62–63). What specific information about the legendary Inuit man Kiviuq does Breath's grandmother share with her listeners before beginning her story?

Factual story questions 1: The little orphan boy swims out to sea (63–69). (a) Why is the orphan boy considered naughty? (63). (b) What motivates the village boys to bully him? (64). (c) What circumstances force the grandmother to address the orphan boy's problem differently with the mean village boys? (64). (d) How does the grandmother prepare the orphan boy for his next encounter with the village boys? (65–67). (e) What prompts the village boys to go after the orphan boy in kayaks? (67). (f) What action does the orphan boy take to stop the village boys from pursuing him further out to sea? (68–69).

Factual story questions 2: Kiviuq keeps afloat on stormy waters (69–70). (a) How does young Kiviuq manage to survive in the same stormy waters that claim the lives of so many village boys? (b) Where does Kiviuq find himself when the sea is calm again?

Factual story questions 3: Kiviuq reaches land (70–73). (a) How does the saurraq feather attached to Kiviuq's coat help him to find land in the middle of the ocean? (b) How many times does Kiviuq set off in the direction of land before finally reaching land with his kayak?

Widely Circulated Stories of Contemporary Renown Questions: Paaliaq

Relevant chapter. 3

Contextualizing event. Paaliaq's remarkable encounter with a polar bear in the past earns him respect as an Inuit hunter and shaman.

Factual story questions (12–14). (a) How do sled dogs help Inuit hunters in their pursuit of polar bears? (b) What exactly do Paaliaq's sled dogs do to help him to kill the huge polar bear he encounters one day on the sea ice? (c) What problem does Paaliaq soon encounter with his spear? (d) What action does Paaliaq take to solve this problem? (e) What makes Paaliaq's actions and this particular encounter with a polar bear worth circulating? (f) How is the story of Paaliaq's encounter with a polar bear circulated far and wide?

FRENCHIE'S WORLD IN *THE MARROW THIEVES*

Features Summary

The fictional world in the Indigenous novel *The Marrow Thieves* (Dimaline 2017) is indigenized by twenty-nine features in the categories of ancestry, religious beliefs and practices, cultural events, cultural traditions, language use and stories, divestments and subjugation, and leadership. The full set of indigenizing features for this second fantasy novel is shown in textbox 7.3.

Exploratory Question Sets Focus

Two sets of exploratory questions are provided for the fantasy novel *The Marrow Thieves* (Dimaline 2017). Question set 1 focuses on Group D

Textbox 7.3.
Indigenizing Features Summary for *The Marrow Thieves* (Dimaline 2017)

Group A features: (3) Ancestry: ancestral identity, ancestral scents
Group B features: (4) Religious Beliefs and Practices: sacred songs, sacred drums and drumming, purification practices; (6) Cultural Events: round dance, traditional songs and singing; (7) Cultural Traditions: traditional roles, large-game hunting, rabbit hunting, trapping, tracking, traditional houses, traditional shelters, traditional clothes, traditional weapons, traditional materials, traditional foods
Group C features: (8) Language Use and Stories: ancestral language, names and naming, personal stories, Indigenous writing
Group D features: (10) Divestments and Subjugation: material appropriation, forced relocation from homeland, forced separation of children from parents, subjugation, brutality; (11) Leadership: councils, elders

---

features: material appropriation, forced relocation from homeland, forced separation of children from parents, subjugation (Category 10); and elders and councils (Category 11). Question set 2 focuses exclusively on the Group C feature of personal stories (Category 8).

Three personal stories are explored in the second set of questions. These stories convey the personal experiences of a young Indigenous man, Frenchie (age fifteen, chapter 1), a young Indigenous woman (Wab, age eighteen, chapter 8), and an older Indigenous man of an unknown age (Miig, chapter 11). The three personal stories unfold in a three- or four-part structure and are similarly identified as coming-to stories.

Defined Feature

A question set for *The Marrow Thieves* (Dimaline 2017) focuses in part on the Category 10 indigenizing feature of subjugation. The terms *subjugation* and *subjugate* are defined below.

subjugation: a state of forced submission to control by others

subjugate: to bring under control especially by military force; to make subordinate to the will of others

Book Sectioning

Part I: Miig's Camp (1–4)
Part II: On the Move (5–6)
Part III: The Four Winds Resort (7–9)
Part IV: On the Move (10–18)
Part V: The Council Camp (19–24)
Part VI: On the Move (25–26)

Question Set 1: Group D Features

Destruction (Category 10), The Marrow Thieves

Material Appropriation Questions 1

Relevant chapter. 2

Contextualizing event. Miig teaches Frenchie and other members of his camp about the relationship between Indigenous bone marrow and dreaming.

Internet research questions. (a) What is bone marrow? (b) How is marrow stored in human bones? (c) What functions of bone marrow in humans have scientists identified? (d) What is the relationship between bone marrow and spongy bone?

Factual question: (18–19). According to Miig, what is the relationship between human dreams, bone marrow, and DNA?

Material Appropriation Questions 2

Relevant chapter. 3

Contextualizing event. Miig shares the first part of his story with Frenchie, a newcomer to his camp.

Map research questions. (a) How abundant is fresh water in the expansive tract of land between Hudson Bay and the Great Lakes within the borders of present-day Ontario? (b) For which Indigenous peoples was this expansive tract of land ancestral? (c) Which Indigenous communities are located in this region today?

Factual questions (24–25). According to Miig, what precipitated the Water Wars, how did these wars impact Indigenous peoples (esp. Anishinaabe peoples), and how did the wars end?

Inferencing question (24–25). What qualifies the removal and depletion of fresh water resources on Indigenous ancestral lands as material appropriation?

Material Appropriation Questions 3

Relevant chapter. 9

Contextualizing event. Miig shares the second part of his story with RiRi and others.

Factual questions (87–90). According to Miig, (a) what circumstances caused people to stop dreaming, and (b) what solution was devised by the governors and others to make people dream again?

Inferencing question. What qualifies the extraction of bone marrow from Indigenous young people by employees of new residential schools as material appropriation?

Forced Relocation from Homeland Questions

Relevant chapter. 3

Contextualizing event. In the first part of his story, Miig shares details about the Water Wars and the effect of these wars on Anishinaabe people north of the Great Lakes.

Factual question (24–26). According to Miig, how did the Water Wars force Anishinaabe people to relocate from their homeland?

Inferencing question (23). How does the opening sentence in Miig's story relate to the indigenizing feature of forced relocation from homeland?

Forced Separation of Children from Parents Questions

Relevant chapters. 1–3, 9

Contextualizing events. Over time Frenchie expands his knowledge about the forced separation of Indigenous children like himself from their parents.

Book research questions. *Canadian experience.* (a) What was the purpose of the residential school system in Canada? (b) Where were residential schools located? (c) How many students attended these schools each year? (d) How many months in a year did students typically spend at these schools? (e) What was the curricular focus at these schools? (f) What impact did these residential schools have on students? *American experience.* (g) What was distinctive about the residential school system and residential schools in the United States? (h) What impact did residential schools in the United States have on Indigenous students?
Factual questions. (a) What information about the old and new residential school systems for Indigenous peoples does Miig share with the council in chapter 1? (5). (b) What details about residential school life and its impact on Indigenous peoples does Miig include in his story, parts 1–2, in chapters 3 and 9? (23, 89).

Inferencing question (16, 20–21). Which school-age members of Miig's self-identified family experienced forced separation from their parents?

Comparison question. How are the situations and experiences of the school-age members of Miig's family as described in chapters 1–3 and 9 similar to and different from the situation and experiences of many residential school survivors?

Recommended Resources
Cohen, Robert Z. *Canada's First Nations and Cultural Genocide.* New York: Rosen Publishing, 2017.
Florence, Melanie. *Residential Schools: The Devastating Impact on Canada's Indigenous Peoples and the Truth and Reconciliation Commission's Findings and Calls for Action.* Second edition. Toronto: James Lorimer & Company, 2021.
Haig-Brown, Celia. *Resistance and Renewal: Surviving the Indian Residential School.* Vancouver, BC: Tillacum Library, 1988.
Hudak, Heather C. *Residential Schools.* Collingwood, ON: Coast2Coast2Coast, 2019.
Jordan-Fenton, Christy, and Margaret-Olemaun Pokiak-Fenton. *Fatty Legs: A True Story.* Toronto: Annick Press, 2010. www.deslibris.ca/ID/453138.
Stout, Mary. *Native American Boarding Schools.* Santa Barbara, CA: Greenwood Press, 2012.

Subjugation Questions 1

Relevant chapter. 1

Contextualizing event. Frenchie avoids being captured by the Recruiters.

Factual questions. (a) What details about Recruiters come to mind while Frenchie lies low in a tree house a few hours away from Southern Metropolitan City (present-day Toronto)? (2). How does Frenchie describe the Recruiters who capture his brother Mitch in the tree house? (4).

Subjugation Questions 2

Relevant chapters. 17, 20, 24

Contextualizing event. Minerva is captured and held captive by the Recruiters.

Factual questions. (a) What series of events in chapter 17 results in Minerva's capture by the Recruiters? (145–46). (b) What details about Minerva's captivity at the residential school in the Espanola settlement does Frenchie learn from a council member in chapter 20? (171–174). (c) What action does Frenchie take to free Minerva from her captivity at the school? (202–11). (d) What is the outcome of Frenchie's efforts to free Minerva from captivity? (211). (e) What impact does this outcome have on Frenchie? (211).

Leadership (Category 11), The Marrow Thieves

Elders Questions

Relevant chapter. 2

Contextualizing event. One night by the fire, Frenchie observes Miig and his family members closely.

Word meaning questions (20). (a) How does the *American Heritage Dictionary* define the word *elder* as a noun. (b) Which definition most aptly fits the usage of the word *elder* in TMT?

Factual questions (19–20). (a) Whom does Frenchie identify as elders in Miig's family? (b) What observations does Frenchie make about the elders in Miig's family?

Inferencing question (20). Why is the word *elders* capitalized in chapter 2?

Speculative question. What responsibilities likely fall on the elders in Miig's family?

Councils Questions

Relevant chapters. 1, 5, 19–20

Contextualizing event. Frenchie recalls the last days of the council to which his father belonged then encounters his father and members of a new council in a remote location surrounded by rock walls.

Factual questions. (a) What unexpected situation prevented Frenchie's father from attending his last council meeting in their home city? (7). (b) What cultural groups are represented in the reconstituted council to which Frenchie's father belongs in chapter 19? (169). (c) How many members belong to this new council in chapter 19? (169).

Speculative questions. (a) What population of people did Frenchie's father and other members of the original council identified in chapter 1 likely represent? (5, 7, 43, 168). (b) What did these original council members likely aim to achieve in their last-ditch effort to talk to the governors in the capital? (7). (c) What likely happened to these original council members when they arrived in the capital? (43). (d) What shared set of circumstances and needs likely motivated Frenchie's father and others to form a new council in a secure location? (169).

Question Set 2: Group C Features

Personal Stories (Category 8), The Marrow Thieves

Frenchie's Personal Story Questions

Relevant chapter. 1

Contextualizing event. After separating from his brother Mitch, Frenchie travels alone by foot for an unknown number of days, closes his eyes one night, and wakens days later in a stranger's small camp somewhere in the woods.

Story structure and content. Frenchie's personal coming-to story unfolds in four parts and largely consists of his present-time observations and thoughts about his flight north and personal recollections of recent events in his life.

Assorted Part 1 questions: In the tree house with Mitch. (a) Where are Frenchie's parents? (factual, 1–2). (b) What makes this particular tree house an ideal place for Frenchie and his brother to stay temporarily while traveling north? (inferencing, 2). (c) Why does Frenchie's brother direct him to leave the interior of the tree house and climb onto the roof alone? (inferencing, 2–3). (d) What details about his brother's capture by the Recruiters does Frenchie witness firsthand? (factual, 4).

Factual Part 2 questions: Alone at the tree house. (a) What thought first crosses Frenchie's mind when the Recruiters leave with his brother? (4). (b) How does Frenchie counter this thought? (4). (c) What details does Frenchie recall about his stay at and departure from the New Road Allowance? (5–6).

Assorted Part 3 questions: The first few days of traveling. (a) Why does Frenchie travel without sleeping that first night? (speculative, 7). (b) How does Frenchie react during and after his encounter with a pack of feral guinea pigs? (factual, 8). (c) Why does a northeast route strike Frenchie as the best route through the woods? (inferencing, 9). (d) How does Frenchie satisfy his hunger while traveling north? (factual, 10). (e) What details does Frenchie recall from his last conversation with his mother? (factual, 11). (f) How are Frenchie's thoughts about his mother connected to his thoughts about the friendship center near his last home? (factual, 13). (g) How does the rain impact Frenchie while he is traveling north? (factual, 12–14).

Assorted Part 4 questions: Regaining consciousness. (a) How might Frenchie feel, now conscious, opening one eye and seeing a man who looks like his father? (speculative, 15). (b) How might Frenchie feel, looking around with both eyes open now, and his physical needs met, observing native people like himself? (speculative, 16). (c) What immediate connection does Frenchie make when the unknown man identifies himself as Miigwans? (factual, 16). (d) Which words, spoken directly by Miigwans to Frenchie with a firelit face, cause Frenchie to break down? (inferencing, 16). (e) Why is Frenchie embarrassed by his breakdown? (speculative, 17). (f) Why is Frenchie's embarrassment about his breakdown short lived? (factual, 17).

Summative response questions, Parts 1–4. (a) Why is Frenchie's personal story appropriately identified as a coming-to story? (b) Why do Frenchie's family members figure so prominently in his coming-to story?

Wab's Personal Story Questions

Relevant chapter. 8

Contextualizing event. Frenchie listens attentively to Wab as she shares her coming-to story with him and other members of Miig's family.

Background questions. (a) What does Frenchie note to himself about Wab in his first encounter with her in chapter 1? (21). (b) What does Frenchie note to himself about Wab in his more substantive encounter with her in the manager's office of the Four Winds Resort in chapter 7? (76–78).

Story structure and content. Wab's personal coming-to story unfolds in three parts and focuses primarily on a childhood event that left her traumatized and disfigured.

Factual Part 1 questions: Inner city life eight years ago. (a) How does Wab describe the quality of life in an inner city like Toronto when she and her mother lived in an apartment? (80). (b) What circumstances compelled Wab and her mother to abandon their apartment and live in a dumpster? (80–81). (c) What firsthand experiences with the Recruiters did Wab have at age ten? (81).

Assorted Part 2 questions: Life as a runner. (a) What motivated Wab to become a runner? (factual, 32). (b) What did Wab's job as a runner entail? (factual, 32). (c) What made Wab a successful runner? (inferencing, 82). (d) How long did Wab work as a runner? (factual, 82).

Factual Part 3 questions: Capture and assault. (a) What details does Wab recall about a bogus delivery she was hired to make as an eleven-year-old runner? (82–85). (b) What details does Wab report to Frenchie and the others about being repeatedly assaulted by different men for a period of two days while forcibly confined in an old freezer? (85). (c) What support did Wab receive from her mother or family friends when she returned to the dumpster after her traumatic assaults? (85).

Summative response questions, Parts 1–3. (a) Why is Wab's personal story appropriately identified as a coming-to story? (b) Why does childhood trauma figure so prominently in her coming-to story?

Miig's Personal Story Questions

Relevant chapter. 11

Contextualizing event. Frenchie listens compassionately to Miig as he shares his coming-to story with him and other members of Miig's family.

Background questions. (a) What new information does Frenchie learn about Miig in the last five paragraphs of chapter 10? (factual, 99). (b) Why does Frenchie suddenly go silent at the end of chapter 10 and allow Miig to talk about his personal experiences with the Recruiters? (inferencing, 99).

Story structure and content. Miig's personal coming-to story unfolds in four parts and focuses on his and his husband's startling capture by the Recruiters.

Factual Part 1 questions: The cottage. (a) What information does Frenchie learn about Miig's cottage at the start of chapter 11? (100). (b) What prompted Miig and his husband Isaac to stay at their cottage during the winter? (100).

(c) How long did Miig expect to stay at their cottage without anyone troubling them? (100). (e) How long in fact did he and Isaac live at the cottage trouble free? (100).

Assorted Part 2 questions: First trouble. (a) Why did Miig and Isaac arm themselves with a rifle before setting off to investigate the commotion they heard near their cottage one night? (inferencing, 101). (b) Why did they hesitate before approaching the three strangers spotted in a clearing near their tool shed? (inferencing, 101–2). (c) Why did Miig limit the length of time the three strangers could stay with him and Isaac in their cottage? (speculative, 101–2). (d) For Miig, what was mysterious, strange, and possibly alarming about their guests? (inferencing, 102–3).

Inferencing Part 3 questions: Second trouble. (a) Why did their youngest guest urge Miig to run? (104–5). (b) Why did all three guests barricade themselves in the spare room? (105).

Factual Part 4 questions: Failed plans. (a) What was Miig's getaway plan? (105). (b) Why did Miig insist that he and his husband should get away while they could? (106–7). (c) Why did Miig's getaway plan fail? (107). (d) What action would Miig have taken with his shotgun had it been handy? (107).

Summative response questions, Parts 1–4. (a) Why is Miig's personal story appropriately identified as a coming-to story? (b) What prompted Miig's regretful statement at the start of chapter 11 about him and Isaac not being as careful as they should have been? (c) Why does regret, kindness, trust, and contrasting perspectives figure so prominently in Miig's coming-to story?

Index

Abenaki captives, 81
Abenaki people, 73–82
Abenaki village, 38, 75
Aboriginal Peoples Television
    Network, 143
acknowledgement, 122
acting calmly, humbly, and
    honorably, 55
Adventures of Tom Sawyer, 20, 47
African American people, 132
after-reading actions, 16
Akiwenzie-Damm, Kateri, 26
albino wildlife, 112
ancestral beings, 9, 55, 73, 79, 122–
    23, 151
ancestral environments, 26
ancestral identity, 27, 55, 73, 83, 100,
    102, 116, 122
ancestral islands, 167
ancestral lakes, 165
ancestral lands, 11, 12, 26–27, 36, 55,
    66, 73, 83, 100, 122, 143, 163–
    64, 179
ancestral language, 84, 152
ancestral points-of-land, 165
ancestral symbols, 73, 83, 100, 122
ancestral trees (uses of), 149
ancestral village, 75

ancestry, 54, 73, 83, 99, 108, 121, 142,
    163, 177
Anishinaabe people, 45, 179
arranged marriages, 84, 122

Barkerville, 128
baskets, 122
Battle of Greasy Grass, 100
beaded bags, 7, 11, 39, 55–56, 127,
    135, 149
beaded barrettes, 7, 135, 137
beaded cape, 134, 136, 138
beaded roses, 7, 137
beaded vamps, 7, 135
beading, 5–8, 127–28, 135–38
beadwork, 5–8, 11, 13, 121–22, 135–37
Bear Girl, 3, 63–64
bear spirit, 61
bear woman, 61
beliefs about the creator, 55, 73, 122
berry picking, 120
binder, 130
Birchbark House series, 3–4, 11, 44,
    51–52, 54–55, 57
Birchbark House, 3–4, 11, 44, 51–55, 57
bird hunting, 55, 164
Black Hills, 101
Black River, 80
blanket making, 55

blankets, 55, 138, 140
boat building and repair, 12, 73, 164
bone marrow, 64, 163, 178–79
Bridge to Terabithia, 20
British Territories, 72
broom flower, 132
Bruchac, Joseph, 42
brutality, 11–12, 72, 77, 84
buffalo bean plant, 132
building coherence, 16
bullying, 120

Canadian Arctic, 173
canes, 160
Canyon De Chelly, 70, 84
captivity, 29, 70, 79, 82, 93, 181
Carrie, 98–99, 108–17
carved wooden objects, 134
celebratory dance, 103
ceremonial capes, 6
Chateauguay, 115
Cheam Mountain, 123
Cheyenne, 102
chiefs, 122
childbirth, 164
childhood play, 55, 164
childhood trauma, 184
Choctaw wedding ceremony, 32
clamming, 122
clan membership, 122
clarifying, 16
close reading, 16, 41
closeness to cousins, 11, 100
Coast Salish (see also Sto: loh), 134
colonization, 27
coming of age, 6
coming of age speech, 125
coming-to stories, 182–85
commercial literature study, 20, 23
copper object, 139
core academic skills, 14–15
corn harvest, 32
corn pollen, 88
cosmic coherence, 31, 99
councils, 177

courtship, 122, 129, 131
Cree, 5, 138, 144
critical thinking, 24
cross-curricular learning, 22
Crown Point, 72
cultural anthropology, 25, 27–28
cultural competence, 14
cultural curiosity, 14
cultural events, 28, 55, 73, 99, 121,
    163, 177
cultural pride, 34, 99, 108
cultural recovery, 26
cultural studies, 25, 27
cultural traditions, 28, 55, 73, 83, 108,
    142, 177
cultural values, 28, 55, 73, 83, 99, 108,
    121, 142, 163
Curse of the Shaman, 162–76
Custer State Park, 100

Danny Blackgoat, 83–96
Danny Blackgoat (novels) series, 11–12,
    46, 69, 70, 72, 83–84
daycare center, 130
defense of homes and homelands, 34
defense of sovereignty, 34
denigration, 27, 83–84, 108, 121–22
Densmore, Frances, 38
diabetes, 11, 109, 113–14
diabetic shock, 113
dialog journal, 5
Dimaline, Cherie, 43
disdain, 11–12, 72, 84, 94–95
disease, 27, 54–55, 66, 67, 73, 108
divestments, 55–56, 83, 99, 121, 177
dog sled, 166
Dorval, 115
dream elements, 110
dreamtime, 6, 11–13, 39, 55, 109,
    121–33, 137
Driving Hawk Sneve, Virginia, 43
drying rack, 62
during-reading actions, 16

eagle stories, 122

eiderdown feather, 172
elders, 55, 73, 122, 177, 181–82
embroidery work, 73
English language arts, 13, 15–16
epidemic, 67
Erdrich, Louise, 44
ethnographic methods, 28
ethnography, 27
evil being stories, 33
execution site, 87
expressing gratitude, 9, 121–22
extended family households, 55, 164
extending kinship to strangers, 73

family campsite, 65
family life, 28, 54–55, 83, 99, 108, 121, 163
family stories, 55, 122
fancy dance, 122
feast, 3, 52–53, 62, 140, 142
fictional world individual, 29
fictional world, 29
fishing, 44, 55, 120, 122, 164
floral designs, 6–7
food preparation, 55, 73, 122, 164
food storage, 55, 164
forced relocation from homeland, 9, 13, 27, 55–56, 73, 177, 180
forced relocation, 66
forced removal from homeland, 84
forced separation of children from parents, 12, 122, 177
forced sterilization, 34
formulating, 16
Fort Carillion, 82
Fort Davis, 70, 72, 84–86, 89–90, 94, 96
Fort Sumner, 72
framed reading, 25
framework tools, 30
Frenchie, 163, 177–85

game of silence, 31
Game of Silence, 4, 44, 52, 54
games of strength, 175
Gluskabe, 74

grandparents, 38–39, 44, 65, 75, 126, 128, 165, 175
grass dance, 42, 103
grazing land, 88
Great Lakes, 179
Great Migration, 132

Halkomelem language, 125
harassment, 34
harvest, thunder, and moon dances, 31
Hells Gate, 127
hemorrhagic smallpox, 67
herding, 11, 83–84, 87–88, 133
holy man, 107
homophobia, 120
honoring the dead, 55
hoop dance, 11, 100, 102, 104
hop harvesting, 130
hopyard, 129
house and shelter building, 55, 164
Hudson Bay, 179

igloo, 165, 169–70, 173–75
indigenized world, 12
indigenizing features, 8–15, 19, 24–25, 27, 30, 34–35, 39, 42, 51, 56, 69, 72–73, 83, 97, 99, 108–9, 119, 121–22, 142, 161, 163, 177
Indigenous communities, 179
Indigenous education, 15
Indigenous knowledge, 26
Indigenous novel, 12
Indigenous Novels, Indigenized Worlds, 30
Indigenous people(s), 12
Indigenous people(s), 3, 9, 11–13, 15, 17, 25–27, 29, 35, 38, 59, 67, 75, 104, 112–13, 133, 135, 143, 161, 163, 179–80,
Indigenous person, 12
Indigenous perspectives, 3, 19
Indigenous studies, 13–16, 25–26
Indigenous writing, 26, 122
infant travel, 32
interdependence, 27

Inuktitut, 176
Inuit people, 163–76
Inuit snow goggles, 166
Inuit wedding ceremony, 164
Island of the Golden-Breasted
    Woodpecker, 52, 66–67

jingle dance, 103
Johnny Tremain, 20, 47
Julie of the Wolves, 20, 47

Kahnawake, 97
Kanehsatake, 114
kayak(s), 44, 58, 165, 167–68, 170, 172,
    176, 203, 205–6, 208, 210, 214
kinship relations, 27
kinship with local animals, 9, 73, 84
Kit Carson, 92
Kiviuq, 167, 168, 175, 176
Kiwakwe, 76
Kusugak, Michael, 44

Lake Memphremagog, 78
Lake of the Woods, 3
Lakota calendar, 98
Lakota cosmology, 101
Lakota moons, 102
Lakota names, 102
Lakota naming ceremony, 105–6
Lakota paradigm, 107
Lakota ribbon dresses, 105
Lakota (Sioux) people, 98–108
Lakota way, 98, 102
Lori, 98–108
Lana's Lakota Moons, 98–108
large game animals, 172
large game hunting, 12, 55, 164
linguistics, 25, 28–29
literature circle, 10, 20, 21, 24
literature study unit, 10, 20, 41
Little Voice, 120–21, 142–60
longhouse, 43, 140

Makoons, 44, 63–64
maple festival, 32

Maracle, Lee, 5, 6, 11, 13, 45, 119
Marble Island, 165, 167–68, 170–72
Marrow Thieves, 163, 177–85
material appropriation, 12, 36, 73, 84,
    177, 179
material deprivation, 11, 72, 84
mats, 122, 149
meaningful dialog, 24
medicinal plants, 60
Mohawk people, 108–17
Mohawk War Society, 114
Mount Rushmore, 101
mythical stories, 73, 122, 164

names and naming, 55, 73, 164
naming feast, 61
Nanabozho and the Birch Tree, 145
Nanabozho and the Cedar Tree, 147
Nanabozho and the Moose-Skull, 144
Nanabozho, 38, 62–63, 143–50
narrative studies, 25, 29
narrative, 29
National Film Board of Canada, 114
Native American writers, 26
Navajo campsites, 90
Navajo historian, 91
Navajo Long Walk, 70, 92
Navajo prisoner(s), 36, 70, 85, 92–95
Navajo sheep herders, 87
net making, 32
Newbery Medal, 20
non-Indigenous governing systems, 26
northern Ontario, 155
notable events, 11, 73–74, 83, 100, 122
notable people, 9
notable places, 83

Ojibwe language, 3, 152
Ojibwe people, 55–67, 120–21, 142–60
Ojibwe spirit, 4
Oka Crisis, 98, 114, 116
old paddling song, 79
Omakayas, 3–5, 55–67
organizational scheme, 12
ornamentation, 138

outdoor fire-making, 55
Owens, Louis, 26

Paaliaq's curse, 165, 170
Pacific National Exhibition, 124
pemmican, 40, 132
personal growth, 17
personal stories, 12, 56, 122, 164, 177–78
phalarope, 176
photographs, 141
plant harvesting, 32, 55
Porcupine Year, 3–5, 53–67
portage, 40, 64, 80, 157–59
postcolonial perspective, 27
powwow, 103
prayer, 36–37, 86, 88–92, 106, 109, 129, 139
praying, 55, 83–84, 91, 121–22, 139
presaging dreams, 109
prescience, 12, 73, 83, 109
proficient reading actions, 25
purification practices, 11, 56, 83, 121–22
purposeful reading, 3, 14–15

question development, 23–24
question prompts, 35
question refinement, 24
quillwork, 122

rabbit hunting, 55, 164
Rankin Inlet, 11
Ray, 120–21, 142–60
reading for understanding, 16
reading workshop, 20–21, 24
real-time dreams, 109–11
reconfiguring, 16
reconstruction, 26
recorded dreams, 109
recovery, 9, 27, 37, 55, 72–73, 82–84, 99
religious beliefs and practices, 55, 73, 83, 122, 164
rereading, 25

residential school survivors, 180
residential school system, 180
residential schools, 45, 179–80
respecting one's in-laws, 164
respecting others, 55
restoration, 11, 27, 55, 73–74, 82, 99, 108–9, 163–64
Revelstoke, 127
roadblocks, 114
Rogers's Rangers, 77
rose garden, 8, 137–38
runner, 184

sacred drumming, 11, 40, 73, 103, 109–10, 113, 122
sacred drums, 73, 109, 122
sacred objects, 122
sacred offerings, 55, 83, 121–22
sacred songs, 55, 121
Saxso, 73–82
seal and caribou skins, 165
seasonal activity cycle, 56
seasonal habitation cycles, 9, 164
self-discovery, 26
shaman, 161–62, 169, 176
shamanic powers, 171
shamanic trance, 170
sibling avoidance, 55
sibling care, 164
siksik, 169–70
Sioux Lookout, 155
Sioux Nation, 101
six language arts, 22, 24
slavers, 86
Slipperjack-Farrell, Ruby, 45
slop, 132
smallpox, 11, 37, 55–56, 66–67, 73
snaring, 151
snow snakes, 31
snow travel, 12, 55, 163–64
soccer, 175
social studies, 13–17, 22, 25, 186
societies, 34, 99
Socratic circle, 10, 20, 23, 24
Socratic seminar, 20

South Dakota, 97
sovereignty, 9
spirit bundle(s), 4, 5, 13, 55–56, 58–59
spirit guide, 11, 112
spiritual lesson, 127
spiritual travel, 73, 83
spring festival, 164, 174–75
springtime camp, 171
Spussum, 127
St. Francis River, 80
St. Francis, 72
stationary games, 122, 164
stealth, 72–74, 83
stick and ball games, 31
Sto: loh Becoming Man Ceremony,
    6, 11, 13, 121–22, 125, 138–39,
    140, 142
Sto: loh Nation, 119
Sto: loh people, 121–42
Sto: loh Sunrise Ceremony, 127
stories about animal tricksters, 73, 122
stories about culture heroes, 9, 11, 55,
    73, 74
stories about legendary individuals, 11,
    13, 55–56, 164
stories about the creator, 73
storytelling (art of), 122
storytelling time, 55
strawberry festival, 32
subjugation, 12, 72–73, 163–64, 177–78
Sudbury, 155
summarizing, 5, 16
sunrise, 88–91, 127, 139, 147
supernatural powers, 12, 164
sustained focus, 10, 17, 24
sustained study, 24
sweat lodge, 56, 59–61, 139–40, 148–49
Systemic-functional linguistics, 28

tag (the game), 175
tanning (hides), 164
tattooing, 73
thematic unit, 10, 20, 22, 24
Tingle, Tim, 45
titular acronyms, 9

tobacco, 147, 155
Toronto, 181
toss and catch games, 31
toy making, 33, 108
tracking, 11, 73–74, 81, 83
traditional Abenaki canoe, 78
traditional clothes, 73, 164
traditional clothing accessories, 55,
    73, 122
traditional dancers, 31, 98, 100
traditional drinks, 55, 73, 106
traditional foods, 11, 39, 51, 55–56, 62,
    73, 106, 122, 143, 159–60, 164
traditional houses, 55, 73, 83, 164
traditional implements, 55
traditional knowledge about local
    wildlife, 55, 164
traditional materials, 60, 73, 122, 164
traditional medicines, 11, 56, 73
traditional novel study, 10, 20, 24
traditional roles, 55, 83, 164
traditional shelters, 55, 73, 122
traditional song, 175
traditional Sto: loh skirt, 140
traditional weapons, 145, 164
transdisciplinary approach, 17
transformative understandings, 9, 17,
    28, 30
trapping, 55, 156–57
tribal history, 83, 99, 121
trickster (beings), 151–52
Turners Fall Massacre, 75
Turners Falls, 76
tuurnngaq, 170
types of exploratory questions, 35–41

valuing dreams, 55–56, 83, 109
valuing sharing and peaceful relations
    with neighboring nations, 164
Vancouver, 125
Village Below the Falls, 38, 75, 76, 77
vision, 109

walking sticks, 160

water travel, 11, 55, 73, 74, 79, 143, 163, 164
way of seeing, 28
wedding feast, 175
Weesquachak, 152
Western paradigm, 107
whaling, 164, 172
Where I Belong, 98–99, 108–17
white captors, 69
white eagle, 112
White, Tara, 46

widely circulated stories, 12, 164
wiindigoo moon, 61
wild rice harvesting, 55, 57
Will, 120–42
Will's Garden, 5–8, 120–42
winter gathering dance, 67
Winter People, 73–82
Wolverine, 162–76
wood carving, 11, 73–74, 121–22, 134–35, 143

About the Author

Don K. Philpot is a teacher, teacher educator, and writer. He is a co-author of the critically acclaimed, bilingual, children's picture book *The Move, kā-āciwīkicik*, selected as a finalist in the category of Illustrated Book for Young People in the prestigious Governor's General Literary Awards 2022 competition in Canada. He is the author of the book *Indigenous Novels, Indigenized Worlds* (2023) and three books in the Reading Actively Series published by Rowman & Littlefield including *Collaborative Explorations of Character Experience* (2021); *Reading Actively in Middle Grade Science* (2020); and *Reading Actively in Middle Grade Social Studies* (2019). He is the author of the ground-breaking book *Character Focalization in Children's Novels* and numerous works of conventional and experimental fiction for children and adults including *Assignments*; *The Moons of Goose Island*; *Numbering*; *The Victorian House*; and *Formations and Lines*.

Dr. Philpot received his doctoral degree in language and literacy education from the University of British Columbia in Vancouver and specializes in the areas of reading pedagogy, children's literature, children's literature stylistics, and disciplinary literacy. He has been actively involved in K–8 education for four decades and is currently a member of the Literacy Faculty at Shippensburg University where he teaches courses on reading comprehension, content area literacy, children's literature, reading instruction for English language learners, and most recently American Sign Language.

www.ingramcontent.com/pod-product-compliance
Lightning Source LLC
Chambersburg PA
CBHW020812060726
47498CB00017B/2765